WICKED WISTERIA

Wisteria Witches Mysteries

BOOK #2

ANGELA PEPPER

CHAPTER 1

THREE GENERATIONS OF redheaded witches walked into an ice cream parlor.

We ordered our treats and took a seat by the window, only to be distracted by the sound of a young woman at the table next to us sighing loudly. What was her problem? Who can be depressed inside a place with so much ice cream? She was sitting at a small table by herself, reading a hardcover book. Her heavy sighs only grew louder as she flipped through the pages.

Being a librarian, I feel personally responsible whenever someone is unhappy with a book. I finally turned around, smiled sweetly, and asked, "Is that book getting you down?"

She jerked her head up and stared at me with big brown eyes. She was petite, mid-twenties, and pretty, with dark eyelashes and black hair falling in loose waves around a perfectly round face. She wore a black men's fedora with a tropical-print tunic and a short skirt. She looked artsy and fun, like someone I might hang out with despite our age difference.

Hipster Chick glanced around the cafe in surprise. "Are you talking to me?"

"Yes. I couldn't help but notice you seem disappointed with your book."

"You could say that."

"I happen to know of a place where you can get some other, less disappointing books."

She wrinkled her nose. "I'm sort of on a budget right now."

"I know a place where the books are free."

"You mean the library? That's where I got this." She tilted up the hardcover in her hands. There was a Wisteria Public Library stamp along the top edge of the pages. One of ours! Now I felt twice as responsible for her unhappiness.

"You don't have to finish every book you start," I said.

"I know, but this book was supposed to be good enough to take my mind off my troubles." Hipster Chick scowled and tucked her long, dark bangs behind one ear. "But there's so much missing."

I looked at the book. It was a rock-star memoir, a popular one from a big publisher.

"They probably left out the juicy bits," I said. "Authorized biographies rarely tell everything."

"But the book is literally incomplete." She slammed the book shut in disgust and tossed it on the table. She didn't notice it landing dangerously close to a patch of spilled coffee on the table. But I noticed.

I used my witch powers to grab a napkin from a nearby table, float it over, and soak up the coffee spill before it could stain the book.

My aunt, Zinnia Riddle, must have noticed me using levitation in public. She kicked me in the shin under our table. As my mentor witch, she was teaching me the ins and outs of magic. She wanted me to do boring drills and basic spells for practice, but not in public. Despite all the magic coursing through the town, its existence was still a secret to most people.

Across the table, my daughter, Zoey Riddle, looked mortified—not about me using levitation in public, but because I was talking to a stranger. Being sixteen, she was easily mortified. And being a recent transplant to the small town, she wasn't used to the friendly way strangers talked to each other. When we'd first arrived, she had been suspicious of the too-perfect town. She had a theory that the local townspeople were robots, like in *Westworld*, or even hired actors for a secret *Truman Show* style prank. No such luck. It turned out the town of Wisteria was just brimming with magic, thanks to the local witches, shifters, and other supernaturals. All of that magic had the pleasant side effect of making people happy, healthy, and unable to gain weight despite the many bakeries and eateries. The ice cream parlor we were currently seated in was only one of a dozen ice-cream-themed eateries.

Hipster Chick grabbed her large purse and dug around for her phone, which was buzzing when she pulled it out. Her purse was an expensive designer bag, yet her phone had a crack on the screen and was held together with tape. She answered the call tersely. "Now what, Dad?"

I wondered if she was a terrible person, or if her father deserved such treatment. Some fathers did, but even so, it never reflected well on the child to be so rude.

She rolled her eyes. "What do you mean, it needs more power? Can't you plug it into the stove socket?" She pushed her chair back and got to her feet with an exasperated sigh. "I don't care what you have to plug it into, just do whatever it takes. I need that money." She paused, listening, then pleaded in a syrupy tone, "Please, Daddy? For me?"

I turned back to my table, giving her back her privacy. I asked my aunt and my daughter, "What did I miss?"

Zoey answered, "Auntie Z was telling me how you used to say the funniest things when you were little. You called scissors *snizzers*."

"And she did it on purpose," Zinnia said to Zoey. "Even as a toddler, Zara knew very well how to say scissors, and refrigerator, and hamburger. But it made her mother's eyes bug out when she said *freezerator* and *hangaburger*, so that's why she did it."

Zoey laughed, and the two of them compared more notes about me. I tried to pay attention, but I couldn't stop listening to Hipster Chick pulling emotional blackmail on her father. She was quite good at manipulation.

After a few minutes of her talking about some sort of machine, she huffed loudly, grabbed her purse, and stomped out of the ice cream parlor. In her haste, she left behind the library book. It was a good thing I hadn't yet learned any hexes, or I might have cast a mild one on her. The nerve of some people who treat any public space as a library return slot!

I grabbed the book, planning to bring it with me to work on Monday.

As soon as I put the book on our table, the conversation stopped. My daughter grabbed it and riffled through the pages. After a minute, she said, "I wonder where the good stuff starts."

Zinnia whispered something in Witch Tongue, then proclaimed, "Page seventeen."

Zoey and I exchanged a surprised look before staring at the elder witch.

"You naughty girl," I teased.

She blushed. "If you must know, I cast a page-finding spell when Zoey was riffling the pages. It's one of our basic bread and butter spells, which you both would know all about if you'd been doing your homework."

Zoey flipped to page seventeen in the rock-star memoir. "There's nothing here," she said.

Zinnia replied, "If page seventeen's not to your liking, try fifty-one." She cleared her throat delicately. "If you like that sort of thing."

Zoey lifted the book and leaned in to stare closely. "That's odd. I think there's something wrong with this book."

I held out my hand. "Let the librarian have a look."

She handed the book over. A mild static shock discharged as I took it into my hands, and the sound in the restaurant changed. The clatter of customers' spoons in glass bowls of ice cream sundaes receded. The whoosh of an employee steaming milk for a cappuccino became a far-away hiss. The volume of the jazz music on the sound system dropped down to distant plinking.

Magic! It sure has a way of grabbing your attention and blotting out everything else.

What are you trying to tell me, book? I opened it to a random page. My breath caught in my throat. I saw the strangest thing I've ever seen inside a book.

Now, having worked in libraries for a number of years while working my way up to librarian, I've seen a lot of strange things inside books. I've seen flip-art cartoons in the margins, hand-scrawled comments that are more entertaining than the book itself, and even a slice of bacon used as a bookmark. But I'd never seen anything like this.

Before my very eyes, letters on the page were disappearing. Not all of them at once, but a word from one sentence and then a short phrase from the next paragraph.

Suddenly, a shadow passed over me. Someone yanked the book from my hands.

Hipster Chick was back. She must have remembered the book and returned for it. She gave me a dirty look and said, "This book belongs to the library!" And then she was gone again.

Zoey looked at me, then at my aunt, and giggled. Imitating Hipster Chick, she said, "This book belongs to the library!"

My aunt gave me an amused look. "No good deed goes unpunished."

"Did you see what was happening with the pages?" I asked. "The ink was erasing itself."

Zoey said, "There were some blank spots. Isn't that just a misprint?"

"I know what a misprint is," I said. "This was something else."

Zoey leaned in. "Magic?" She leaned back again just as quickly. She was caught between showing her excitement about magic and keeping her cool teen detachment. She was also still dealing with the fear that something was wrong with her own witch powers. She'd turned sixteen, the age most witches—at least the ones who aren't me—get their powers. It had been over a month since her birthday, but her ability to execute spells hadn't kicked in yet.

"Hang on," Zinnia said. She mouthed something in Witch Tongue, accompanied by quick hand gestures. "Done. The sound dampening spell is in place now. We have our privacy, as long as you don't get too boisterous."

"The words were magically disappearing right in front of me," I said. "That's why Hipster Chick said the book was missing stuff. Because it was."

Zoey's hazel eyes widened. "Do you think that book could be an ancient, magical codex with prophecies and powerful spells?"

"It's a trashy rock-star memoir that released last October," I said. "Being the resident expert on library books, it's my professional opinion that it was just a regular hardcover."

Zoey shrugged. "It's still interesting." She asked my aunt, "Does stuff like this happen around here all the time?"

Zinnia was slow to answer, tilting her head from side to side thoughtfully. "Not typically." She folded her hands together on the table. "It is best for a witch to stay out of matters that aren't one's business."

I reached into my pocket and dug around. "What if this disappearing ink thing *is* our business?" I grabbed the card I'd picked up earlier that afternoon and laid it on the table. I flipped it over to show the other Riddles that it was blank on both sides. "The ink came off this card, too."

Zinnia picked up the card and examined it closely. "I can see the impressions of lettering on one side." She narrowed her eyes and tilted the card. "The Gingerbread House of Baking?"

"That is what the card said," I paused for drama, "before it mysteriously went blank on our way here."

Zoey eyed me with suspicion. "Did you do this? Mom, don't mess around."

I held my hands up. "Zoey, I appreciate your belief in my abilities, but this is way above my level. You saw what I did to the orange juice this morning."

She smirked. "At least you got some extra practice using the sponge to clean the kitchen ceiling."

Zinnia didn't ask what happened to the orange juice. She kept looking at the card.

"Aunt Zinnia?" I asked. "Do you think these two things are connected?"

"Perhaps." She set the card on the counter and tapped it twice. "Regardless of any connection, it's not our business."

"But what if something big is going on? When I picked up that card at the bakery this afternoon, I noticed some other peculiarities."

Zoey interjected, "That's why your breath smelled like vanilla! You got pastries, and you didn't bring any for us."

"It was just one little donut." I waved for her to shush, and then I relayed to my aunt the other curious things I'd witnessed that afternoon. There'd been Griebel Gorman, the appliance repair shop owner, who'd run away from me before disappearing in an alley. And then I'd heard the owners of the bakery talking about how they might be giving birth to a "monster." The woman was already in labor, so they left the bakery to get into a van, which was when I noticed something usual with the woman's hair. Her blond curls seemed to have a life of their own. And then, on top of all that, they drove away in the opposite direction of the hospital.

When I finished relating the anecdotes, Zinnia stared at me with a horrified expression. "Zara, none of those things are any of your business," she said. "If you go around chasing people, and listening in on conversations, there will be no end to the trouble you'll bring down upon yourself." She blinked. "And your family."

I opened my mouth to defend myself but there was no defense. I *had* been chasing people, and eavesdropping. A hot wave of embarrassment washed over me, making my skin prickle. Just because I was a witch, that didn't mean I had permission to be a busybody. I closed my mouth.

My aunt abruptly pushed her chair back and stood.

"Lovely to see you both," she said through a tight smile. "I really must be going." She gave Zoey an affectionate squeeze on her shoulder. "Be patient and keep up your studies." She turned to me and lifted her chin. "Would it do any good for me to beg you to stay clear of business that isn't yours?"

"Probably not," I said.

She snapped the blank business card off the table, tucked it into her purse, and left without another word.

CHAPTER 2

HOURS LATER THAT Saturday, I was still thinking about the strange, self-erasing book.

I went to my kitchen, where I do my best thinking while puttering around.

Using my telekinetic powers, I pulled out a cutting board, several lemons, and a sharp knife. The old Zara Riddle—the one who didn't have witch powers—would have sliced the lemon in the Riddle family tradition, with both hands on the knife handle, safely away from the blade. Both my daughter and I suffer from a specific food prep phobia. We will run from the room if a character on a TV show starts slicing something on screen. But now that I didn't have to hold the knife at all, I had moved beyond chop-smashing helpless fruits and vegetables. I could do amazing things, such as create those thin little matchstick-sized carrot sticks that you find inside egg rolls.

And, thanks to having been host to a friendly ghost who loved fancy food and entertaining, I even knew what the vegetable sticks were called. From thickest to thinnest, they are called *batonnet,allumette, julienne,* and *fine julienne.* Cubes also have their own special names, but I won't go there right now. I've proved my point, which is this: being a witch is awesome.

My mind puzzled over the day's disappearing ink while I sliced lemons with both of my hands safely in my pockets.

Zinnia had told me not to get involved in things that were none of my business. She'd have been better off using reverse psychology. If she'd instead put me onto the Case of the Missing Words, I might not be thinking about it at all right now. I could have been working on my basic spells, such as the cantaloupe ripeness spell. But telling me *not to* think about something? It was like telling a kid not to stick their finger in a bowl of frosting.

I finished slicing the lemons and visited the back yard for some fresh mint. I didn't know half of what was planted out there in the jungle, but I was pretty sure I had mint, or possibly catnip. Either way, it was going into my iced tea.

When I came back inside, the doorbell was ringing.

Zoey, who was upstairs in her bedroom, yelled, "Doorbell!"

I yelled back, "Doorbell!"

"Doorbell!" she cried.

I replied, "Doorbell."

She thumped her way down the stairs as we exchanged a few more cries of "doorbell!"

I heard her open the front door and politely greet our guest.

A minute later, Chet Moore entered my kitchen, looking flummoxed. "If it's Zoey's job to answer the door, why do you both yell about it? Doesn't that defeat the purpose of having it be her responsibility?"

I used magic to pick up the pitcher of iced tea, and put my hands on my hips. "Whatever happened to saying hello before launching into a critique of someone's parenting skills?"

He didn't laugh. After a brief stare-off, he finally said, "Hello."

I bowed formally. "And a very cordial hello to you too, my good neighbor." I used my magic to pull two glasses from the cupboard. Other than my family, Chet was the only other person who knew about my abilities. I loved that I could be myself around him. "Would you care for some iced tea with fresh mint, or possibly catnip?"

He stared at the pitcher, which was floating midair, pouring tea into one glass and then the other.

While he was captivated by the levitating pitcher, I studied him, trying to memorize his features. If he wasn't looking at me, stirring up feelings, I could actually see more than his gorgeous green eyes. I noted the angles of his long face, high cheekbones, and hollowed-out cheeks that gave him a hungry look. His hair was nearly black, brightening to a rich, mahogany brown when the light from the window caught it. His eyebrows were thick and dark, and his long forehead contained two and a half wrinkles—two and a half because the lowest wrinkle line stopped halfway across his forehead, as though it was afraid of his right eyebrow. He was older than me, but he had zero gray hairs to show for it. Lucky guy. And yet he didn't have the air of someone who believed in his own good luck.

There was an aura of discomfort all around my neighbor. He'd hidden it with his wit and charm when we'd first met, but now that I'd known him for more than a month, I was through the first layer of the onion. Was this the real Chet Moore? A single father who could never relax, never let his guard down? His apparent discomfort usually disappeared when he smiled, but his smiles had been in short supply lately. I hadn't seen one since the day we pretended to be newlyweds to catch a killer. Had I done something wrong and scared him off? Too much gooey talk while we were playing pretend? Had he invited me for dinner that night so he could break the news that he had no interest in being more than friends?

I'd finished pouring the iced tea, but he continued to stare at the floating glasses.

I asked, "Is everything okay?"

"What do you mean?"

"You've been staring at that iced tea like you've never seen magic before. Do you want a glass or not?"

"Sure," he said gruffly.

"Chet, have I done something to offend you?"

"What do you mean? You were the one who got offended when I asked about your daughter and all the yelling about the doorbell."

"I wasn't offended." I gently floated the pitcher and glasses down to the counter, only spilling a few drops. I was getting more control.

"Oh." He frowned at the spilled drops. "My question about the doorbell was just a question. That's how normal people are supposed to communicate. Ask questions and listen."

"I don't know about *normal*, but I can answer your question," I said. "Zoey was raised in apartments, where we constantly got in trouble for yelling, or singing, or generally enjoying life more than our neighbors thought a poor single-mother family should. So we had to be careful to keep our voices down. And we always had an intercom or a buzzer, not a doorbell. Doorbells, and front doors, and porches were exotic things that sitcom families on television had. So, you'll have to forgive us if having both a doorbell and the freedom to yell about it has gone to our heads."

Chet quirked an eyebrow and gave me a prickly look. If he'd been a porcupine, he would have been bristling with barbed quills. Could he turn into a porcupine, or just a wolf? I had no idea.

"Fair enough," he said. "It really was just a question."

"I can do questions, too. For example, why does your wild-child son hang from your clothesline like it's a jungle gym? Is he part monkey?"

He blinked twice. "Corvin?"

"Yes, I'm talking about Corvin. Unless you have another hyperactive ten-year-old boy living with you."

Chet stared at me.

"Your son," I said, holding my hand four feet off the floor. "He's about this tall, has black hair, huge eyes, and enjoys terrorizing people. Yesterday, he climbed up on a stepladder outside my kitchen window and stood there, creepily staring at me through the herb garden for heaven knows how long. I went to harvest some chives, and he started screaming bloody blue murder, accusing me of trying to poke out his eyeballs to use them in a potion. He called me a witch."

"That's unacceptable," Chet said, his forehead furrowing.

"Well, he wasn't wrong," I said. "I *am* a witch."

"The boy needs to learn about respect. It's my fault for being too lenient with him." He smacked his hands together in a gesture that suggested corporal punishment.

I was surprised to see this new side of Chet, this sternly authoritative side.

Chet gave me a curt nod. "I'll see that he's punished."

"Kids will be kids," I said, trying to lighten the mood. "He's probably curious. Who wouldn't want to spy on the family of redheaded witches living next door? When Zoey was his age, she was so curious about our neighbors that she started a plant-watering service in our apartment building just so she could spend more time inside other people's apartments."

I smiled at the memory of her lugging around heavy watering jugs while dressed in her official watering clothes. She'd worn too-big overalls, and covered her hair with the red-and-white handkerchief she got from the building's superintendent. He was a gruff yet kind man who'd made her an official staff name tag, just like the one worn by his elderly mother, who vacuumed the threadbare carpets in the hallways. Thanks to his endorsement, Zoey's watering service was a hit. Half the residents of the building gave her their spare keys. The other half continued to complain about our noises and blame us for everything that went wrong in the building, but that was their loss.

I told Chet about this, and all he had to say was, "You let your ten-year-old daughter go into other people's apartments by herself?"

"Of course she went by herself. She didn't want to split her two dollars per hour with me." I took a sip of my iced tea. Too much lemon.

"Only two bucks an hour," he said. "They were taking advantage of her."

"Oh, it was never about the money." I lowered my voice, sensitive to the fact she might be listening from her room upstairs. "She wanted to see how other people lived, to see how we compared."

"I can imagine Zoey doing that. She's an inquisitive child."

"I told her it was too late for us to become normal, but she was so earnest. She thought if we stopped keeping wool sweaters in the oven, and started making more casseroles, we could be just like everyone else. She even got a recipe from Mrs. Hutchins, for tuna-noodle casserole."

"And how did that work out?"

"We got to know the local firefighters. And my poor sweaters were never the same." I fluttered one hand in front of my chest. "The buttons on my favorite cardigan melted."

Chet studied me, his eyes locking on mine. Once again, all I could see were his hypnotic green eyes. I was under his spell. Was he experiencing the same thing? Was he even half as charmed as I wanted him to be? From what I could see, he showed no signs of being amused by what I considered to be a delightful family anecdote. Most people loved the story about my melted sweaters, and how my daughter and I had shared tuna-noodle casserole with a bunch of firefighters.

Finally, he said, "You and I have very different parenting styles, Zara."

"How so?"

"You could say I prefer a more traditional approach to fathering."

The word *fathering* sent my imagination on a tangent. "How does that work, anyway?"

He gave me a funny look. "Raising kids? You have to employ both negative and positive reinforcement."

"No, I was wondering, how does parenting work as a wolf shifter? Do the females give birth in wolf form? Can they still shift between human and animal if there's a baby inside them? And what about the actual mating?"

Chet didn't move a muscle. He seemed to have stopped breathing. Oops. Asking about shifter mating habits might have crossed the line. Wow, were my dating small-talk skills rusty!

I decided to quickly distract him with a whole new line of questioning. "Can you turn into a porcupine?"

Judging by the look on his face, my questions were about as welcome as flatulent sounds in a packed sauna.

I laughed it off. "Never mind my silly curiosity. Are you ready for dinner?"

He grimaced and cleared his throat. "Dinner would be good. There are a few things I'd like to discuss." He grabbed his iced tea and tossed it back like a tequila shot. As he set the empty glass down, he made a choking sound. "Too much lemon," he gasped. "And why so much catnip?"

I kept a poker face. The green stuff hadn't been mint after all. I really had a lot to learn about gardening. "Next time, I'll make it without the catnip."

He coughed a few times. "I'll recover," he said hoarsely. "Let's go."

I glanced around the kitchen. "Hang on while I... act like a stereotypical female getting ready to leave the house. In other words, give me a minute to find my purse."

He crossed his arms and tapped his foot impatiently, acting like a stereotypical male. I hoped he was joking around, or it was going to be a long night. I ransacked the kitchen looking for my bag. When a physical search didn't work, I gave one of my new spells a try. First, I called an image of my purse to mind. Pink. Leather. Brass buckle on the strap. With the image in mind, I whispered the summoning incantation and started the gesture, twirling my right hand as though reeling in a fishing line.

No purse. I tried again. Still no purse. Had Zinnia taught me a useless spell, or was I just hopeless? Chet continued to tap his foot. I turned my back to him and tried again. I felt a happy twinge inside my chest as the magic snapped together. But still no purse. Had someone stolen it?

Chet asked, "Is there an animal trapped inside your refrigerator? Something's thumping around inside there."

I opened the fridge door, and there it was. My purse! It obediently hopped out of the fridge and hitched itself onto my shoulder.

"Ready to go," I said cheerfully.

"Why was your purse in the fridge?"

I gave him an innocent look. "Well, it's not exactly safe in the oven, is it?"

"It's not?"

"Chet, were you not paying any attention at all to my charming anecdote about the burned sweaters and the tuna-noodle casserole?"

"I guess not." He looked down and shuffled his feet. "I'm a bit rusty at this sort of thing."

"You and me both, mister. Let's go get some food. I'm excited about eating something that doesn't come out of a square box."

He nodded in agreement, and we walked toward the front door. He paused by the hall table where Zoey and I had been tossing the mail.

He pointed to the stack of unopened envelopes. "That's a lot of bills."

"Don't look directly at them. I repeat, do not make eye contact." I grabbed Chet's arm and steered him toward the door. "Come on. All that mail will be waiting right here when I get home."

He dragged his feet. "It's a big stack. Is that a water bill at the bottom?"

"Chet, don't worry. I'm on top of it!"

I kept my voice light and bright, but deep down I had a bad feeling. Well, two bad feelings. First, he was right about the stack of unpaid bills being in need of some adult supervision. Second, our date—if it even was a date—was off to a rocky start. If this was how it started, with us bickering over parenting styles and unpaid bills, how was it going to end? Physical combat?

CHAPTER 3

CHET DROVE US to the restaurant, since I didn't have a vehicle and it wasn't within walking distance.

The interior of Chet's vehicle was spotless, and still had that new-car smell. Chet took good care of his things, unlike me. I had to sell my old car to help finance the move to Wisteria, and it took several price reductions for the right buyer to see past the all the dents, not to mention the upholstery's ever-present Cheetos odor.

Chet's vehicle was refined, sensible, and grown-up, just like him. Was that what I wanted in a man? They say opposites attract. Chet was guarded with his emotions, but that could make him a good complement for me, a person who constantly makes inappropriate comments to cover the fact she doesn't quite understand how to act like a regular adult.

We arrived at the restaurant, Grazie, which featured authentic cuisine from... which European country? Go ahead and guess. If you said Italy, you're right.

The word *grazie* means *thanks* in Italian, and you can embellish your grazie with other words to make pleasing phrases such as *grazie di cuore*, which means *thank you from the bottom of my heart*. If you want to lay it on thick, you can say *grazie infinite* for *infinite thanks*.

That helpful lesson on the Italian language came courtesy of the informative text written on the back of the

Grazie menus. I had a lot of time to read the menu because as soon as we arrived at the restaurant, Chet's phone rang, and he disappeared to take an important call. All I caught was that it was someone named Carl, or maybe Arnie, on the phone.

Alone at the table, I checked out my surroundings. I had never been inside Grazie before. It was so pretty that I felt guilty for being there without my daughter, who loved anything castle-like or decorated with stones. One time I drove for hours to take her to a water park, and she barely touched the slides. She preferred to hang out inside the subterranean part of the building, which was a dungeon-like grotto where they served ice cream and ran the gift shop. With some prodding, Zoey eventually took a reluctant ride down the water slide. She quickly met some other kids her age, but after an hour I found her back in the stone-lined underground room, examining the lichen on the damp rocks.

Grazie didn't have lichen on its stone walls because the rocks were the fake, manufactured kind. When I searched for patterns, I spotted matching twin stones, taken from the same mold.

There was an older gentleman with thick glasses seated at a nearby table. He noticed me looking at the stonework and asked, "Are you visiting in town for long?" His wife, who had equally thick glasses, gave me a sweet smile.

"Actually, I live here now," I answered.

"Good for you," he said. "You like the rustic look of those walls?"

"I like old things."

"Hah!" He looked delighted. "If you like old things, you should pay a visit to Castle Wyvern, up the coast."

"Castle Wyvern? Sounds like a tourist trap," I said.

"No, miss. It's the real deal, a genuine castle."

"I'll put it on my list," I said. "My daughter loves anything with a dungeon."

"How about you?"

"I enjoy historical sites."

He grinned. "The older you get, the more you like being around anything that's older than you!"

His wife chuckled and swatted him on the arm. "Leave the nice girl alone, you old turnip."

Their waiter arrived with armloads of food, and the couple turned their attention to their dinner. The food smelled amazing. *What a great place.* The tables were decked out with cute checkerboard tablecloths, and topped with miniature bottles of olive oil and balsamic vinegar. My mouth watered. Our waiter, bless his heart, brought me a basket of warm rolls and a plate.

"*Grazie infinite,*" I told him, and I meant it. The heady fragrance of garlic and asiago cheese had my mouth watering.

The waiter excused his reach as he picked up the two bottles on the table. He poured golden oil and inky balsamic vinegar onto a large plate. "This is for dipping the bread," he said. "Unless you'd prefer butter?"

I tore a chunk off the crispy roll and dabbed it on the plate. "When in Rome," I said with a smile.

The waiter glanced at the empty chair across from me before angling his body away from it, giving my absent date the cold shoulder. He told me about the restaurant's wine list. I hesitated. If Chet was as "traditional" in dating as he was at parenting, I'd be stepping on his toes if I ordered a bottle for both of us. He'd probably make some vague comment about me playing from a different handbook. I snorted at the imagined conversation. Who was he to question my parenting style? My daughter was a model citizen compared to Corvin, who was barely house-trained.

"I'll wait for my date," I told the waiter. Then I took out my frustration on the bread.

When the waiter returned ten minutes later with a second basket of steaming bread, he gave me a pitying look. "Shall we revisit the wine list?"

"It can't hurt. Plus I need something to slow down my inhalation of bread. What would you recommend?"

"Perhaps a very small glass of the house red?"

"Oh, don't bother uncorking for a very small glass. I'll have a regular adult-sized glass, please and *grazie*."

He grinned. "Adult-sized. I like your style."

He returned with my wine, and we exchanged pleasantries again. My date was going well. My date with the waiter, that was. If only he wasn't a tall, skinny boy of perhaps nineteen.

I was on my second glass of wine and third basket of bread rolls when Chet finally returned with a brief, "Sorry about that."

"Work issues? Monsters climbing out of the ocean and attacking the town, Godzilla style?"

Chet frowned. "What makes you say that?"

I leaned in. "Am I right? Is it sea monsters?"

"Of course not." He glanced around. "I should have reserved one of the private rooms. We can't have much of a conversation here."

"Sure, we can. My aunt taught me a handy sound barrier spell."

He shook his head. "It's too soon, anyway. We can have this talk another time."

"Now I'm dying to know what it is you won't tell me." I twirled my finger. "Turn your head so you're not staring at me when I try this spell. You make me nervous."

He frowned, but he did turn his head and look away, pretending to admire the fake stone walls.

I murmured the incantation in Witch Tongue while interweaving my fingers the same way I'd seen Zinnia perform the spell earlier that day.

My first attempt didn't do much except fizzle. Casting a new spell could feel like trying to light a wet match. It wouldn't work, but then you'd generate enough heat to spark a reaction. I tried the incantation again, a little louder. Chet tilted his head and watched me out of the corner of his eye. I tried it a third time, this time with a hilariously bad Italian accent, for no reason whatsoever. What would you know? The accent did the trick. The spell lit up, and the sound barrier bubble formed around us. It was a brief visual flash that only I could see.

"We have our privacy now," I said proudly.

Chet looked skeptical.

I turned toward the elderly couple at the other table. "Hey, tell me more about old things!" Neither of them reacted.

"Not bad," Chet said.

I pointed at Chet's phone, which was on the table face down. "Now you can tell me what's going on. If it's not sea monsters, what is it? Big problems at head office for the X-Files?"

"I keep telling you, we're not part of the X-Files, mainly because they're fictional." He peered into the empty wicker basket and frowned at the crumbs. "Enough about me," he said. "I understand you were at the police station this morning for a follow-up on the Vander Zalm case."

"Yes, and I think it went well. I suggested that Detective Bentley should worry less about our investigative methods and worry more about why his own department hadn't brought in Dorothy Tibbits for murder. He totally bought it."

Chet nodded slowly. His eyes kept flicking around the room, ticking with movement every second, like a clock.

"And how is Detective Bentley? He's new in town, and he doesn't know the ropes."

"That pussycat?" I batted my eyelashes. "He was enthralled by my many charms."

Chet cupped his forehead with his hand. "Zara, please tell me you did not cast one of your spells on the town's new detective."

"Of course I didn't. But so what if I had? Isn't the whole point of being a witch that you get to use your powers?"

Chet winced. "Don't say that word in public."

"Witch? I'll say what I want. We're inside an impervious shroud of privacy."

"Impervious? Is that what you think?" He locked his eyes on mine, then he removed a seemingly normal pen from his pocket. He pressed the button to extend the nib. It clicked, just like a regular pen. With the click, the spell around us popped. The restaurant noise flooded in.

"Hey!" I reached across our table, grasping for his magic-busting pen.

He yanked it out of reach and tucked it away with a sly smile.

"No fair," I said. "You saw how hard I worked on that spell. It took me forever, and you poofed it away with one little click."

"I certainly did," he said proudly.

"Good for you. Now, what is that pen thing, and how do I get one?"

"It's a multi-pulse click generator, and you *don't* get one." He narrowed his eyes. "In fact, I shouldn't have even let you see it."

"Tease."

He glanced down at his menu. "How's Zoey fitting in at her new high school?"

"Zoey? Great. Her teachers love her."

"How are her grades?"

"Pointy," I said. "Because the letter A is pointy."

"She'll have plenty of options in life."

I agreed, and I went on to brag about my daughter's academic skills. While we talked about Zoey, I split my attention just enough to take another shot at the sound-muffling spell. This time, the spell worked on the second try. The bubble formed with a gentle shimmer, muting the restaurant noises while making our conversation more intimate.

Chet couldn't see the shimmer, but he was able to hear the sound change. He shook his head at me, but he didn't pull out his fancy pen.

"So much for a regular conversation," he said.

"Regular is boring," I said. "We're not regular people, so we don't *have* to be boring. Now, about the whole shifting thing. I'm sorry I asked you about mating, but you can't blame me for being curious. You don't have to tell me every gory detail, but come on. Give a girl *something*."

Through gritted teeth, he reluctantly said, "Shifters conduct all important business in human form."

"Okay, then. Now we're getting somewhere. What about leisure time? For example, do you ever shift and go frolicking on the beach just to feel the sand on your wolf toes? Maybe during a full moon?"

He seemed even more irritated than when I'd asked about sex. "Zara, we don't pervert the laws of thermodynamics and the natural order of the universe for mere amusement."

I held my hands up. "Yikes. Who said anything about perverting the laws of thermo-what-cha-ma-call-its?"

He reached into his jacket pocket and clicked the pen gadget without pulling it out. My spell popped. The surrounding noise returned with a flourish of musical guitar strums. A guitarist had taken to the restaurant's small stage to supply live music. The guitarist leaned in close to his microphone and sang. Loudly and off-key.

I cast the sound-dampening spell a third time, with little effort. Practice *was* making me better. Aunt Zinnia did know best.

Chet sighed as he reached into his pocket yet again. "You're going to make me wear out the charge." He examined the pen and frowned. "Only one click left. I should save it for something important."

"Why not leave my spell up and enjoy watching that singer without having to hear him?"

Chet put the pen away slowly. "I can try to enjoy myself, but I don't trust magic."

"What do you mean you don't *trust* magic? I would think that transforming into a big hairy wolf would make someone a believer."

"Not all magic is good, or even reliable."

I leaned in. "This is exactly the sort of thing I need to learn more about. Tell me about a time that magic was unreliable for you."

"Just one time?" He smirked.

I was so happy to see the hint of a smile that I beamed back at him. "Yeah. Tell me a story."

"Not yet." Chet looked down at his menu. "They make the most amazing seafood fettuccine here. Do you like seafood?"

"Seafood? If I see food, I eat it. So, yes."

"Great," he said, without any acknowledgment of my joke. Not that a pun deserves any encouragement, but still. *Tough crowd.*

The waiter arrived. I disarmed the spell, and we ordered dinner, with both of us getting the seafood fettuccine. Our meals arrived, and we began to eat. The nice older couple at the next table finished their meal and waved goodbye.

Seated on our other side was a young couple who appeared to be on a first date. The girl was eating slowly, cutting her breaded chicken into tiny cubes. The boy kept asking her if everything was okay, in between clearing his throat nervously. I watched as they shyly made eye contact, freezing in place until one of them blushed and looked away. I didn't have a crystal ball (not yet, anyway), but I could see some awkward kissing in their immediate future.

I looked across my table at my own date. At least he looked happier now that he was stuffing pasta into his face.

Had I misjudged Chet's interest in me, or had something changed? One week earlier we had been holding hands and making goo goo eyes at each other. Granted, it had been an act, but Chet had gazed into my eyes with sincere, heart-felt adoration. It was the exact same look he was now giving his fettuccine.

"You really are loading up those carbs," I said. "I guess the magic takes a lot out of you, too."

He kept eating. When the pasta was gone, Chet called for our waiter. "Two orders of tiramisu," he said.

The waiter looked at my barely-touched dinner and gave me a sympathetic look. "Would you like to take that home?"

"Yes, please." He took the plate away. I reached for my wine and tossed back the last sip.

Dessert arrived, and Chet promptly inhaled his portion.

Finally, I asked, "Are you in a rush to get somewhere?"

"As a matter of fact, I do have to be somewhere tonight," Chet said. "For work."

"What about that thing you wanted to talk to me about?" I made a dome shape with my hands. "We're inside my personal cone of silence. Now talk."

"I, uh, just wanted to thank you for being a good neighbor. That's all."

I leaned back and nodded. "This work emergency you're dealing with, does it have anything to do with the Taubs giving birth to a monster right now?"

His eyes widened. He quickly composed himself. "What do you know about that?"

"A witch has her ways. What are they having?"

"Chloe gave birth to a healthy baby boy."

"No tentacles?"

His eyes bulged again. "Why would you say such a thing?"

"Maybe I'm the monster." I reached for my dessert fork and took a bite of the tiramisu. It was so heavenly, I moaned.

"That's enough talk about monsters," he said. "Chloe and her family have been through a lot recently, so naturally their anxieties were high, but everything worked out."

"What's her power?"

"You wouldn't believe me if I told you."

"Gorgon," I said.

His jaw dropped.

I pointed my fork at him. "You need to work on your poker face. I was only fishing, and you gave it up."

"How did you know? Did a spirit communicate with you?"

"Not that I know of," I said, and I explained how I'd chased Griebel Gorman down an alley earlier that day, only to overhear the Taubs' private conversation, then see her hair undulating suspiciously.

"Stay away from Gorman. He looks harmless, but he's not."

"What is he, anyway? A forest sprite? An ugly pixie? A troll?"

Chet licked his lips and eyed my tiramisu. "Need some help with that?"

I pushed the plate to halfway between us. "You can have the rest if you tell me what Gorman is."

He pushed the plate back to me. "I'm not authorized to disclose that information."

"How about disappearing ink? What can you tell me about that?"

"Ink?" He blinked and raised his eyebrows. "I honestly don't know anything about that."

"Zinnia said it's probably nothing, and I should mind my own business."

"Good advice. She's a wise woman."

"Yup." I took a few big bites, finishing the dessert. "Now tell me about this favor you want."

He pulled his head back in surprise. "Who said anything about a favor?"

I tilted my head to the side. "Chet, I didn't fall off the apple tree yesterday. You want something."

He looked down and rearranged his utensils for a moment before finally asking, "Has your aunt taught you anything about spirit walkers? Astral projection?"

"You mean my spirit leaving my body? No, we haven't covered that one yet."

"I meant..." He coughed to clear his throat. "Well, some of us are trying to locate a spirit that might be traveling around."

"And there it is. You do need a favor. You want me to use my spirit charms to nab you a ghost."

"Not exactly. A ghost is the spirit of a dead person. This person is still alive. Technically."

"I'm listening."

He coughed again. "That's all I've got. If you or someone in your family happens to come across something like that, promise you'll let me know?"

"What's this wandering spirit like? Boy or girl? Big or small? Old or young?"

He looked into my eyes. "You'll know when the time is right."

"I'll know?"

"Yes. And when it happens, I hope you can find it in your heart to forgive me... for not telling you more."

CHAPTER 4

MY DATE DROPPED me off at home before zooming away on his secret mission. I walked into my house, went straight to the kitchen, grabbed a fork, and started eating the leftover fettuccine. I paused to stare into the waxed paper box. The noodles were swirling around as though trying to spell something. It was my magic, spilling out because my emotions were in turmoil. I stabbed the noodles with my fork until they were quite dead, and resumed eating. And to think, earlier that evening, I'd been looking forward to eating a meal that *didn't* come from a box.

I got comfortable at the kitchen island. I tossed something on the counter where I could get a better look at it. To the untrained eyes, it was nothing more than a regular retractable ballpoint pen.

Silly Chet had been so eager to give me the bum's rush out of his vehicle, he hadn't noticed me pick pocketing his multi-pulse click generator.

* * *

I awoke on Sunday morning to silence. Too much silence. Something was wrong with either my ears or the world. Was it a spell? Ear wax? A spell that increased the production of ear wax? Who would even think of such a thing?

I checked my ears with my pinkie fingers. Everything felt normal enough. More importantly, I heard the rustling of my quilts and sheets. A spring in the mattress groaned. My ears were working fine.

The only thing wrong with me was a dull ache in the center of my chest. Heartburn. Caused by my late-night eating binge, which was in turn caused by the other kind of heartburn—the kind you feel when your date dumps you off at your front door without so much as a fist bump, let alone a romantic sunset kiss on the porch.

But I wasn't going to mope around about it. My priorities in life were looking after my daughter, then myself, then my career, etcetera, with dating far down the list, somewhere in the vicinity of shoe shopping. Fun but frivolous.

I rolled over to check the time. My old alarm clock, which had received a few magical tosses recently, was sitting right where it had been the previous night. The screen was dark.

Power outage.

That explained the eerie silence. My portable air purifier wasn't making its pleasant white noise. The refrigerator downstairs wasn't humming.

Was the power outage related to my possession of Chet's clicky pen? I hadn't clicked it the night before, not even once. He'd mentioned a limited number of charges, and I didn't want to waste them. I pulled open the bedside table drawer. The clicky pen was right where I'd left it.

I got up, dressed, and went to wake Zoey.

"We've got a huge problem," I said.

She pulled her pillow over her head. "Can't we go a whole week without having a huge problem?"

"It's a non-magical problem. The power's out. I don't know if it's just the block or the whole town."

She sat up and gave me a sleepy look. "Were you sleep-toasting again?" She leaned forward to look deeply into my eyes. "Ms. Vander Zalm? Are you back?"

"It's just me. I'm not possessed, I swear." I looked up at the ceiling and shook my head. "This is my life now," I muttered. "I have to constantly reassure my daughter that I'm not possessed."

Zoey yawned. Just another normal day in the Riddle household.

I nodded toward her bedroom door. "Come downstairs and help me find something wooden that you're not too attached to. I'll make a fire in the back yard, and we can roast some frozen waffles over an open flame for breakfast. Plus marshmallows."

"Color me intrigued." Zoey slid out of her bed, her pajama bottoms wrinkling up to her knees. She yawned again, stretched as she walked toward her window, and pulled back the curtains.

Directly across from her window was the Moore residence, and the window for Corvin's bedroom. There he was, with his round face leaning in close to his window, his nose nearly touching the glass. His expression was utterly blank, like an appliance with the power unplugged. He saw Zoey, and his eyes lit up. As though he'd been waiting for her to wake up.

Zoey lifted her wooden window open with a groan. A fragrant spring breeze came in as she waved. "Good morning, Corvin!"

His round, pale face split with a huge, gap-toothed grin that bordered on maniacal. He waved back frantically and wordlessly.

"That kid is not right," I whispered to Zoey.

"He grows on you," she said.

"Like black mold."

She leaned down to the open window and called to Corvin across the gap. "Any word on when the power's coming back on?"

Instead of answering, he backed away from the window and disappeared from sight, which didn't surprise me at all. With Corvin, I'd learned to expect the unexpected.

The light inside his bedroom flicked off and on repeatedly.

"It's Morse Code," Zoey said excitedly.

I patted her on the shoulders. "Not so fast, Detective Overthinker. He's got light, which means he's got power, which means maybe I should have opened those orange envelopes from the Wisteria Electric Company."

Zoey looked at me, then rolled her eyes so hard that her disdain afflicted her entire body, and she had to collapse back onto her bed limply, wailing, "Moooooooooooom," which, incidentally, is my second-least favorite rendition of my title. My absolute least favorite rendition is the whining "mo-ho-hooo-whaaa-whaaa-herk-herk-whaa-whaa-whaaaaaa!" Luckily for me, Zoey never sang that tune, but I've heard it often enough in shopping malls, and it turns my blood to ice every time.

I looked over to see Corvin's big eyes staring back at me. I wondered if he ever wailed for his absent mother. Had the boy even known his mother long enough to throw temper tantrums in crowded malls? Chet wouldn't tolerate tantrums. Not for a minute.

As I wondered about the kid's past, he slowly shook his head. Could he read minds?

He smiled again. Knowingly.

Well, maybe it was for the best that my romance with Corvin's father was dead on arrival. I could still help the weird kid plenty, but just as a neighbor, and without having to explain his behavior to teachers.

I waved at Corvin and smiled. Then I slowly backed away from the window, still waving. Corvin and all his creepiness could be wondered about any time. I had to get the electricity running again, or else learn how to make cold-brew coffee, and the latter did not appeal to me at all.

* * *

Zoey and I got through our Sunday without power, and rejoiced at dinner time when the lights and buzzing appliances finally came back on.

My suspicion that the outage might have something to do with the unopened orange envelopes turned out to be correct.

Yay, me!

* * *

On Monday at work, I told my pink-haired coworker about my problems with the hard-bottomed, by-the-rules billing administrator at the Wisteria Electric Company.

Frank Wonder responded to my anguished tale with equal parts sympathy and sarcasm.

"That must have been very difficult for you," he said in a mock-soothing tone. "How dare those jerks at the electric company demand money in exchange for services?"

I glanced up from the book-return bin to shoot him a look, crossing my eyes and sticking out my tongue.

"Careful you're not making that face when a clock chimes, or it'll get stuck that way."

Innocently, I asked, "Is that what happened to you?"

"Ha ha." Frank ruffled his pink hair and screwed his face up into a grotesque mask. "The Spirits of the Deep do not take your mocking lightly!"

I quaked with mock horror.

Satisfied, he walked away to go help a library patron with a stack of *House of Hallows* paperbacks.

I sorted through the returned books while listening with amusement to Frank's conversation with the patron. They argued for twenty minutes over whether the popular fantasy series would ever be finished. The author was notoriously slow about delivering manuscripts to his publisher, and dying hadn't helped speed things up at all. The irony was that the constant complaining by fans was part of the reason for the series' success. Kvetching about the slow author was a favorite pastime for book lovers on the internet. Two people arguing often attracted a third onlooker who became curious enough to start reading the series, only to be left without a conclusion and turn into a complainer as well. And so *House of Hallows* spread. Plus they were great books.

After an hour of lifting stacks of books, my arms felt like overcooked spaghetti. Monday morning's returns are the heaviest because we're closed most Sundays. Ordinarily, we'd have one of the library's entry level workers do this task.

FYI, the title for the library's entry level position is *page*, not to be confused with the pages of a book. Back in medieval times, a youth being trained for knighthood would also be called a page. I always liked that explanation, and how it implied that becoming a librarian was similar to becoming a knight.

That Monday morning I wasn't patient enough to wait for one of our pages to come in for their shift. I was hoping to find a specific book. Ziggity! There it was, at the bottom, cheekily hiding under a coffee table book about knitting.

I checked around me to make sure nobody was watching, and then flipped through the rock star memoir. The pages looked normal. There were no blocks of text missing. The disappearing ink must have returned since Saturday, when I'd last seen the book at the ice cream parlor. I flipped through the pages once more, and then again, slowly.

Frank, who'd crept up behind me, said, "The good stuff starts on page fifty-one."

I slammed the book shut guiltily. "I wasn't reading this filth."

Frank raised his eyebrows, which were probably as gray as any fifty-five-year-old's, but had been dyed pink to match his hair. "Sure you weren't," he said, flashing his super-bright, nearly blue teeth.

"I was just flipping through because I thought I saw one of those stop-motion cartoons in the margins, but it I was mistaken."

He gave me a skeptical look. "Zara Riddle, you've got a guilty conscience about something. I wonder about you sometimes. How's it going with your beau?"

I sighed. "We are officially crossing Chet's name off the Beau List. His beau days are over. That beau is a no-go. A no-beau."

Frank shrugged one shoulder. "True love takes time. When you get older and wiser, like me, you'll learn to be more patient. Did he at least take you somewhere expensive on Saturday?"

"He took me to Grazie."

"That sounds romantic. Their stone walls are about as genuine as my sister's cleavage and her diamond earrings, but they do have good lighting. What happened? Did you ask too many questions about the boy's mother? Talk about your old flames?"

"Not at all. I was on my best behavior." I added, "By which I mean best behavior *for Zara Riddle*. I'm not the most conservative conversationalist."

"No kidding."

"I swear my intentions were pure. I just wanted to get to know him as a person, and not just a handsome face." I couldn't tell Frank I'd been too inquisitive about intimate shifter business. Frank didn't know about shifters, let alone that I was a witch. But I did go on to explain how Chet had taken a phone call, been evasive, and then given me a smooch-free sendoff.

Frank looked pensive. "I wonder, what is that silly boy thinking? You're a confident, professional woman who's a real kick in the pants. I don't want to inflate your head too much, but your presence has certainly livened things up around here. If Chet can't see what a catch you are, he's a fool."

I smiled my thanks. "You're too sweet."

"Sweeter than sweet tea, gorgeous." He winked. "I'm sure your date wasn't entirely bad."

"Oh, it was. The man might be a pasta-sexual." I described Chet's apparent bliss over his plate of fettuccine "There was so much slurping. It sounded like a bad teen make-out party."

"At least you know the way to his heart. Cook him up one of your fabulous gourmet dinners, like you did at that party you threw."

He was referring to my dinner party where I'd cooked multiple courses, assisted by the ghost of Winona Vander Zalm.

"I suppose I could whip him up something involving bacon. Guys do love bacon."

"Make spaghetti carbonara," Frank said. "One plate, two forks."

I pouted theatrically. "I probably couldn't tear his attention away from the noodles."

"You sound frustrated." Frank pointed to the memoir in my hands. "This explains why you're indulging in hedonism this morning."

"Nothing beats a trashy beach read."

"Flip forward to the hotel suite action on page two-twenty-one." His expression turned serious. "If you do try that one at home, I recommend a safety harness. You can pick up the equipment you need at any mountain-climbing store." He batted his eyelashes. "Or so I hear."

"Frank Wonder, you are my personal hero."

"I never get tired of hearing that." He backed away. In a regular speaking voice, which registered as loud within the quiet library, he said, "I'll leave you to your important librarian research, Ms. Riddle." Then he cupped his hand around his mouth and whisper-yelled, "Page one hundred is also good."

I checked the pages Frank recommended. The words were all there. Oh, boy, were they all there. After some reading that made my cheeks flush, I flipped through the book a few more times. Why had the book been erasing itself on Saturday? I couldn't have imagined it. Hipster Chick had also been frustrated, so she must have experienced the missing text as well.

I closed the book and scanned it into the computer. The patron who had last checked it out was named Margaret Mills. That struck me as unusual. Hipster Chick didn't look like someone who'd be named Margaret. It was a perfectly lovely name, but the name Margaret peaked in popularity in the '20s, and had been on a gradual decline ever since.

What did this new information mean? Why would ink disappear and then return again? I wished my aunt hadn't confiscated the bakery's business card.

The air conditioning kicked on with a vengeance, making me shiver. I grabbed the heavy cardigan from the back of my chair and pulled it on over my light cardigan. Librarian secret: there's no such thing as too many cardigans.

Frank rolled by with the book cart. "Nice look," he said. "You really can't have too many cardigans."

"So true." I rubbed my arms. "Darn air conditioner."

"The air conditioner's not on."

"Then why's it so chilly?"

He leaned in and studied my face. "Your lips are blue. Are you feeling okay?"

"Just cold." I pushed the chair back and stood. "I'd better get the ol' blood circulating." I shivered. "Are you sure the air conditioning is off?"

"Very sure." His eyes sparkled. "If you're feeling cold spots, maybe it's a ghost!"

I looked around warily. Maybe it was the ghost that Chet's mysterious crew was in search of.

CHAPTER 5

BY MIDDAY, I had stopped checking over my shoulder for ghosts. The cold spots weren't bothering me—not since I'd donned a third cardigan. Plus I had a brand-new mission.

My recent misadventures with the Wisteria Electric Company had highlighted a lack of literacy on my part. Not book literacy but *financial* literacy. This was not a new problem. For most of my adult life, my idea of an "investment strategy" had been to buy brand-name cereal boxes that I refilled with cheaper fare from the bulk bins.

I'd never worried too much about money before, trusting that I would always find a way to support my family. And I did support us—albeit not in a way anyone would describe as luxurious. But everything was different now. The stakes were higher. Now that I had my house, my beloved three-story Gothic Victorian with the triple lancet windows, I had something to lose. The power shutoff was a wake-up call. I had to get on top of my finances.

My new job paid a good wage, and I did have the funds to pay all my bills, but I'd made the mistake of mixing up the water bill with the electric bill. I'd never lived somewhere with metered water before, so when I paid the Department of Water, I thought the bill included my electricity. Why not combine the two? Wouldn't it make more sense to send a single employee out to check two meters at the same time instead of sending two different people? The clerk I spoke to at the Wisteria Electric Company did not appreciate my suggestions about how the town could reduce expenses. She just wanted my credit card number, and the chance to chastise me for not opening their orange envelopes.

In order to avoid such unpleasantness in the future, I would need to improve my financial literacy. Luckily for me, I knew of a place where all the collective wisdom of the modern world was available, for free. No, I don't mean Wikipedia, though it is a close second.

I visited the personal finance section of the library on a personal mission. In case you're ever in such a need yourself, the books are under: Social Sciences > Economics > Finance > Not set > Miscellany And Personal Finance > Personal Finance. The Dewey Decimal call number is 332.024.

As I browsed the titles, I sensed someone enter the aisle behind me. The person was moving quietly, their footfalls soundless, but their presence was given away by the subtle change in the aisle's acoustics. I assumed it was Frank sneaking up on me. I tensed my body and prepared to twist around suddenly and scare him before he scared me. Maybe he would shriek, setting off a chain reaction of dropped books and startled cries throughout the library. The pranks that Frank and I got up to were exactly the sort of thing librarians aren't supposed to do, which made it even more fun.

He drew closer and closer. I pretended to be fascinated by the nonfiction books on the shelf before me. The newer ones had fun, catchy titles that made household budgeting sound like a wild new hobby. All of them claimed to be "the only money book you need." A book with a snazzy purple spine caught my eye. The blurb on the front declared it, "the most personal guide to personal finance ever written!" How personal could this guide be? Did they have a chapter about sending your brilliant child off to an expensive college that you couldn't afford? I cast the page-finding spell Zinnia had taught me. It was a subtle spell I could cast in the presence of regular people, so I didn't worry about whoever was behind me seeing anything magical. I riffled the pages, and the book magically stuck open on a chapter. *Should you send your brilliant kid to an Ivy League college that you can't afford?* I smiled. *Nicely played, book.*

Frank still hadn't made his move behind me. The back of my neck itched with anticipation. I selected an armload of books, and commented out loud for Frank's benefit, "I hope there aren't any ghosts sneaking up on me who might scare me into screaming and dropping all these books."

He didn't respond. Was I imagining things? I whipped around and found myself facing a man who was not Frank. Not unless Frank had suddenly gone semitransparent. Like Frank, this man was mid-fifties and of average height and build. Unlike Frank, he had normal gray hair, and was as see-through as a foggy pane of glass.

Ghost!

I'd never faced a ghost before. I'd felt the presence of one, and even been possessed, but I'd never seen one. What does one say to a ghost?

My librarian instincts kicked in. "Sir, can I help you with something?"

The semitransparent man looked down at the books in my arms, and then back up at my face.

"Sir? Are you looking for a specific type of book?"

He shook his head. *No.*

"Are you lost?"

No response.

"Do you know you're dead?"

His eyes widened in surprise. He recovered and laughed silently. He mouthed what looked like, *I'm not dead.*

"If you're not dead, then you must be that spirit walker my friend is looking for."

He tilted his head in confusion.

"By spirit walker, I mean someone who's doing astral projection. I'm no expert, but the gist of it is that some people believe they can leave their bodies and go floating around. Sometimes people claim it happened to them during surgery. They go in to get their gallbladder removed, then they wake up and tell their family about things that they couldn't have seen or heard because they were unconscious on the operating table."

He nodded in recognition.

"So, you've heard of astral projection, and you know what it is?"

Another nod.

"And is that what you're doing right now?"

He laughed silently. Did that mean yes, or no?

"How did you do it? Did you drink a special tea made with magical herbs? Was transcendental meditation involved? Or mushrooms? Is your body in suspended animation somewhere?"

He shook his head and waved his hands, as if to say I was on the wrong track entirely.

"Fine. If you're not spirit walking, then answer this. Where is your body?"

He patted himself and looked at me like I was the ding-dong. His ghostly body must have felt real enough to him, with his ghostly hands.

"Sir, I'm sorry to break the news, but you are currently floating around without your body. Don't panic."

He looked anything but panicked.

"You're basically a ghost."

Still no panic.

"Stay right here, and I'll call my friend. Some people are looking for you. They work for a special organization that deals with stuff like this."

The man's eyes suddenly widened, this time in fear. He held his finger up to his lips, then mouthed, *you can't tell anyone what I'm doing. It's a secret.*

"Well, it won't be a secret for long, if you keep spirit walking around town, all semitransparent."

Another confused look.

"Have you seen yourself? Go to a mirror."

He frowned and shook his head, as though I was the crazy one.

"Do you even know you're in a library?"

He looked at the books in my arms, up at the shelves surrounding us, and back into my eyes. The expression on his face brightened. He pointed at the books and then at me, a question being implied.

"Yes, these are for me," I said. "Personal finance books. I'm not keen on cooking over an open fire in my back yard, so I'm attempting to educate myself in the mysterious ways of money." I waved a hand. "There was a whole thing with the Wisteria Electric Company."

Smiling, he pointed to his chest. Then he thumped his chest proudly with both hands.

"You're some sort of expert on money?"

He nodded and made a pinching gesture with both hands.

"Great! You need help, and I need help. We can both help each other." As soon as the words were out of my mouth, I regretted the offer. What was I getting myself into? My sense of smell hadn't returned to normal since the sleep-toasting electrocutions.

But the semitransparent man had heard my offer, and it was too late for take-backsies.

His foggy form wavered, and then—there's really no delicate way to put this—he turned into a wisp of smoke and disappeared up my nostril. My left nostril.

Immediately, I could feel him inside my head, banging around like a hungry houseguest looking for the cereal bowls.

Great. I'm possessed. Again.

CHAPTER 6

I WOKE UP on a bean bag chair in the Grumpy Corner.

The Grumpy Corner was not some cleverly named coffee shop populated with tattooed hipsters. It was a comfortable spot inside the library's staff lounge where we hardworking librarians, assistants, and pages could give ourselves a time-out as needed. Being preternaturally perky in personality, I'd never had to take a nap in the Grumpy Corner before, but there I was, with stray Styrofoam beads stuck to my face.

How had I gotten there? The last thing I remembered was standing in a book aisle, holding an armful of financial literacy books, and offering to help a semitransparent man. Then he had turned into a wisp of smoke and swirled up into his own personal Grumpy Corner, which was somewhere inside my skull.

I made a fist and rapped tentatively on the top of my head. "Hello? Are you still in there?"

No response came.

I couldn't detect anyone else rattling around up there, but ghosts could be flaky. My previous tenant had come and gone as she'd pleased, helping me cook complicated recipes when it suited her.

My aunt declared—or should I say *diagnosed*—me as being Spirit Charmed. Every witch has a specialty, and that was mine.

I knocked on my skull again, this time on the back of my head. "Are you comfortable, sir?"

"Not really," answered a man's voice. Except it wasn't the ghost. It was Frank, who I hadn't noticed sitting at the staff lunch table, eating his midafternoon snack of teddy-bear shaped graham crackers.

I stared at him as I tried to get my bearings. "What's going on?"

"You asked if I was comfortable," he said. "Then I said 'not really,' because these vintage corduroy trousers keep riding up." He leaned to the side on his chair and wiggled his cords down.

"Vintage clothes never fit right," I said. "People had different proportions back in the day. And they were shorter."

"Not me. These vintage cords have been aging in my own storage locker, so the only person I can blame is myself." He looked down at the teddy-bear shaped cookie in his hand. "Or maybe I should blame these cookies. Over the last thirty years, I must have gained at least two and a half pounds." He shook his head. "Disgraceful."

"You've only gained two and a half pounds over thirty years? They should get you to a lab and study your DNA."

He laughed. "Who? Mad scientists?"

"Something like that. How can you be so fit when you eat cookies every day?"

He shrugged. "There must be something about this town. Haven't you noticed there's something strange about Wisteria? The sky is a deeper blue, the grass is greener, and everyone here is so healthy."

I nodded in agreement. "We live in a magical town where all the children are above average."

He narrowed his eyes. "What do you mean, magical?"

I shrugged. "Just joking around." I wished I could tell him about my powers, but it wouldn't be safe. History hasn't been kind to witches. Other people haven't been kind, either. Back in the olden days, they didn't burn witches just because they'd run out of dry firewood.

I heaved myself up from the bean bag chair and walked over to the sink to get a glass of water. "How long was I asleep? I have zero memory of coming in here to lie down."

Frank snorted. "If I were you, I'd claim amnesia, too."

"Have I been misbehaving?" I played it off as a joke, but I did wonder what I'd done while possessed.

"You were so mean to that patron," Frank said. "The poor old gal just wanted a book about the best designer shopping destinations in the world, and you gave her a lecture about social responsibility and saving for her future."

"I did?"

"She was practically in tears when I took over and shooed you in here for a timeout."

"Sounds like I had..." *Don't say a ghost possession moment.* "A low blood sugar moment. Was she really upset? Now I feel terrible." I gasped. "I'm still on my probationary period. Is Kathy going to fire me?"

"Don't worry. I covered for you. I told her it was your *lady time*." He made a gagging face.

"Frank, that's inappropriate."

"I'm inappropriate?" He arched one pink eyebrow. "Is it appropriate for a certain woman who recently had her electricity cut off to lecture other people about money?"

"That wasn't me. It was..." *A ghost.* "Low blood sugar."

He pushed his remaining cookies across the table and nodded for me to join him.

* * *

Five minutes later, the head librarian, Kathy Carmichael, came in breathing heavily. Her forehead was shiny, and one of her medium-brown curls was stuck to the sweat. Her round glasses were sliding down her narrow, sharp nose.

Frank and I exchanged a look.

Kathy breathed heavily whenever we got a new batch of crafting books in, or when she was irate about the library's budget being threatened.

I asked her, "Everything okay, boss?" I hoped her hyperventilating wasn't about something I'd done while possessed. I suspected the ghost in my head—Mr. Finance Wizard, for lack of an actual name—might have been talking to her with my mouth. How would I explain that, let alone prevent it from happening again?

Kathy took a big breath as she pushed her glasses up her owlish nose. "Just when you think you've seen every trick in the book, there's a new one."

Frank clapped his hands. "Did some genius invent a whole new type of craft?"

"No."

Frank slumped his posture. "More budget cuts?"

"This is bad, but not that bad." She laid three hardcovers on the table next to Frank. "Some vandal has been ruining our materials. At first I thought it was just one book, but now two more vandalized titles have come to my attention."

Frank looked down at the books with interest. He carefully wiped the cookie crumbs off his fingers before leafing through the top book. I watched quietly from my chair. I had a strong premonition he'd find erased pages, but I didn't want to tip my hand.

"What am I looking for? These blank spots?" He looked up at her. "Someone must have gotten overzealous about removing pencil marks."

"I've already tested the pages in the repair alcove," Kathy said. "I tried all the cleaners we use, from Mötsenböcker's LIFT OFF, to Absorene's vulcanized natural rubber, and even the stinky stuff. None of them lifted the ink. This wasn't done by one of us."

Frank rotated the book to give me a glimpse of a page missing half its words. I nodded like someone who was seeing such a thing for the first time.

"These might be misprints," he said. "This happens at the printer whenever something falls on the page between the paper and the ink."

"Not in this case," Kathy said, still breathing heavily. "This isn't one isolated patch. The vandalism runs throughout the books, and it goes line by line, straight across. Whoever did this was very deliberate."

Frank scratched his head. "It could have been shredded paper, caught on a gust of wind at the printing house. My money is still on the misprint."

"But no two of those books came from the same printing house. This was deliberate vandalism."

Frank looked skeptical. "Can you even call this vandalism? They haven't drawn or scribbled anything in here. It's just been erased."

Kathy said, "It's either vandalism or censorship. Who would do such a thing?" She softly hooted, "Whooo?"

I decided that this was the point in which a normal non-witch librarian who didn't already know about the disappearing ink might join the conversation.

"Censorship?" I asked. "What makes you say that, Kathy? Is there a specific type of content that's being erased?"

She threw her hands in the air.

"Not that I can figure out," Frank answered for her. "And I'm a wizard at word puzzles."

I reached for one of the books and took a closer look. Unlike the hardcover at the ice cream parlor, the ink didn't lift away before my eyes. Part of me was disappointed. I checked the front cover for clues. It was a nonfiction title about deck building with local materials. *How random.* And the passages that had been erased were seemingly random as well.

Kathy finally got her breathing under control. "Who would censor a book about deck building?"

Frank stuck one finger in the air. "Ah-ah! I've detected a pattern." He put the books in a row and pointed at each in turn. "Deck building with *local materials*. Arts and crafts with *regular household objects*. And the third one is an artsy coffee table book about *found notes*. Do you see the connection?"

Kathy pushed her glasses up her nose again but said nothing.

I wagered a guess. "The common theme is recycling?"

"Exactly," Frank said. "Two points for Zara." He tossed me two of his graham cookies. He tossed some to Kathy, but the teddies bounced off her cardigan and hit the floor. She didn't even seem to notice. Wow. Kathy really was upset if she'd gone cookieblind.

I asked Frank, "Now what? Do we start an investigation? Look for someone who has an ax to grind about recycling, or coffee table books written by bloggers?"

He laughed. "You're funny, Zara. What we do is we order replacements for these books, write off the damaged ones, and hope our troublemaker loses interest."

"But don't you think it's strange?"

He raised his pink eyebrows at me. "Stranger things have happened."

Kathy, who'd grown quiet, spoke as though in a daze. "Recycling," she said softly. "Wick."

Wick?

"This is a message," Kathy said to Frank, picking up and shaking one of the books. "A coded message!"

He gave her a serious look and a quick, single nod. They both looked at me. I kept my expression neutral. They both understood what she meant by *Wick*, whereas I was new there and did not.

"You could go pay Wick a visit," Frank said. "It would certainly speed this whole thing up, if he is up to something." He patted the erased books. "The longer we let his game play out, the more expensive it gets on our holdings."

Kathy wrinkled her nose. "But he's always so mean to me. Can you come with me, Frank?"

Frank smiled in my direction. "I think Zara's the most in need of fresh air, so you should take her. I insist."

"I'll go," I said.

Kathy rocked from side to side and tucked her sweaty curl behind her ear. "I don't know," she said. "It is the middle of the day."

"Just go," Frank said. "You're no good to us here when you're like this. Take it out on Wick."

She rocked some more.

"Go!" Frank made a shoo gesture. "I'll hold down the fort here. But don't take too long, or I might change us over from the Dewey Decimal to a new system using spine colors. I can see it now. We'll have blue shelves, and green shelves, and red shelves. It'll be so refreshing. Not to mention a visual masterpiece."

Kathy didn't laugh. Librarians usually laugh at jokes about reorganizing by anything that isn't the Dewey Decimal system. It's what passes for humor, when we're not talking about smuggling in wine, or cats, or electric space heaters. This business with the disappearing words had the head librarian riled up.

Frank said, "You two can head out right now. I swear on a stack of all our holy books that I won't get into too much mischief."

Kathy blinked at me, her light-brown eyes shining brightly behind her round glasses. "I'm ready to go when you are."

"I'm as ready as I'll ever be." I grabbed my purse and followed her toward the side door that led to the staff parking area.

Hey, Mr. Finance Wizard, I thought to the new entity in my head. *Do you happen to know anything about library books erasing themselves?*

No response.

Just a coincidence that you showed up here today?

If there had been crickets living in my head, I would have heard nothing but cricket sounds.

CHAPTER 7

I WAS IN the parking lot, opening the passenger side door of Kathy's car when I noticed someone walking by. It was the hat-wearing young woman from the ice cream parlor. Hipster Chick. She had a large tote bag on her shoulder. She walked toward the library's front entrance while withdrawing a hardcover book from the tote bag. It was the rock-star memoir I'd seen on Saturday.

I smacked myself on the forehead. I should have known better. The book I'd looked through that morning must have been another copy we had in circulation. But of course. We often carried multiples of popular new titles. I should have been more confident in my hunch that Hipster Chick wasn't named Margaret. So far, I was a lousy witch detective.

The door of Kathy's car opened with a rusty squeak. It was an older model Honda, brown and pocked with bubbles of rust. She'd given me a ride before, so I was over the initial shock of the vehicle's shabby appearance. She could afford a better car, but this one still ran, got reasonable gas mileage, plus she found it comfortable. Her "nest on wheels," she'd called it. I climbed into the passenger side. There was some clutter on the duct-taped seat that Kathy yanked away just in time. Yarn and... a crochet hook.

"Oh, fluffernuts," she exclaimed.

"I guess I should look before I sit."

"Sorry about that, Zara." She tossed the yarn into the back seat, where it landed on other balls of yarn.

"Kathy, why did you have yarn and a crochet hook on the passenger seat? Don't tell me you crochet and drive."

"That would be illegal," she said, which wasn't the same as saying no.

She threw the car into gear, and we were off. Off to see a man named Wick who was, according to Kathy, always playing games on top of being mean to her. Who could be mean to Kathy? Whooo?

* * *

Kathy drove us past the outskirts of town then turned onto an unpaved road. We passed rolling meadows, farm fields, low fences made of weathered wood, and tall fences made of netted wire designed to keep wildlife on one side. It was a gorgeous day for a drive, with blue skies above and warm breezes all around. Kathy's ancient Honda had no air conditioning, so we rolled the windows down. Kathy was quiet, her eyes on the road ahead and her mind on something that made her scrunch up her face every couple of minutes. Her brown, curly hair swirled around her face, occasionally getting stuck on the arms of her glasses.

I tried not to stare, but I kept sneaking peeks at Kathy, and her sharp-tipped nose. I had no reason to believe she had magical powers—no reason other than the fact she looked so much like an owl. How could she *not* be a bird? If you watch any sort of cartoon show with animals as characters, the librarian is always an owl, and Kathy was the head librarian.

Anthropomorphism is the ascription of human attributes to non-humans. Zoomorphism is the ascription of animal attributes to humans. (No, there won't be a test on this later.) I wondered if Wisteria caused zoomorphism in its residents. Kathy reminded me of an owl. Frank, with his skinny legs and hot-pink hair, reminded me of a flamingo. Then there was little Corvin, who reminded me of a raven. I also had a theory he was the blue jay who'd spoken to me in my back yard the day Zoey and I had moved into the house. But I couldn't exactly go around casting spells to make shifters transform into their animal forms just to satisfy my curiosity. Could I?

The breeze coming in through the windows blew my red hair into my face. The sunshine filtering through made the strands of hair glow orange, right at the same moment I was wondering what animal I resembled. The image of a red fox popped into my head. Scientific name *Vulpes vulpes.* If I could shift into any form, a red fox made the most sense because of their beautiful fur, playfulness, and ability to adapt to new environments. And also because the females are called vixens. How cute is that?

An earthy scent distracted me from my red fox daydreams.

"Oh, fluffernuts," Kathy said. "Roll your window up."

The old car didn't have power windows, so we both rolled up our windows manually. Even with the windows closed, a smell permeated the car's interior. Smell might be too mild of a word. It was a stench.

We passed through a pair of tall, iron gates and into the Wisteria Sanitation Management Station. The title was fancy municipal code for *the dump.*

Kathy looked over at me. "Aren't you glad Frank volunteered you for this mission?"

I pinched my nose. "So glad."

"It's not too bad. The wind usually blows the other way." She returned her attention to the road, and turned down a side road.

"This is the kind of bad smell you can taste in the back of your mouth."

"Oh, Zara. Is it really that bad?"

"I guess my sense of smell has become more sensitive..."*since becoming a witch.* "Since moving to a small town with such clean air."

"That's probably it," she said. "Then again, I've raised three boys who played every sport they could. They crammed all their sweaty equipment into duffle bags, which they left to marinate for days at a time, so my sense of smell might not be as refined as some people's."

I dropped my hand from my nose. "Oh, I've *smelled* things," I said dramatically. I didn't know what I meant by that, but I do have a tendency to keep talking when I'm around people who are clearly stressed.

After a moment, I asked, "So, why are we out here? What's the deal with Wick?"

"All you need to know is he's a quarrelsome man who baits women into arguments. I believe the term is gaslighting. He's a gaslighter."

"And is that gas methane?" I waved my hand under my nose. "I definitely detect some methane in the local environment."

Kathy's mouth relaxed into the smallest of smiles. "It's probably a wild goose chase that we're heading out here, but I've got to trust my intuition, and my intuition is telling me he's up to something."

"What do you mean, *intuition*? Have you got special powers?" I let out a laugh, pretending to be joking even though I was truly fishing.

"Some gifts run in my family. My grandmother, Grandma Kay, would get feelings about things, and more often than not, it would turn out she was right. I haven't predicted half the things she did, but I swear I feel her near me."

I glanced over my shoulder into the back seat. There was no grandmotherly ghost. Just containers filled with twine, fuzzy pipe cleaners, scrapbooks, scissors, and several types of glue, including glitter glue.

When I turned my head back from the back seat, I noticed Kathy was staring at me. Had she seen me jerk my head back to look for Grandma Kay? I smiled at her. When in doubt, smile.

She turned back to the road. "How about you, Zara? Are there any special gifts that run in your family?"

"Gifts?"

"Your aunt is a special lady."

Did Kathy know about the witchcraft in the Riddle family? If she didn't know, she was doing a great job of making me think she did. But I wasn't going to spill anyone's secrets, so I played dumb.

"Zinnia? She sure is a special lady. And, come to think of it, she did give me a gift. A lamp. But it was too, uh, special for the living room, so I made—I mean I *let*— Zoey keep it in her room, where it's nice and safe."

"A lamp," she mused. "Floral?"

"Yes. Why? Do you know something about it?"

She pursed her lips knowingly. "Just a lucky guess."

We turned a corner, and I saw our destination. The road we'd been driving on ended at a corrugated metal building.

"Here we are." Kathy shifted the car into park but didn't turn off the engine.

I asked, "What's the plan, boss? Are you going to hit him with the books until he confesses?"

"I wish. First, I'm going to ask for help. Wick is the town's top ink and paint expert."

"In addition to running the dump?"

"He's in charge of all sorts of things, from garbage pickups to street cleaning. But most importantly, he's the graffiti removal guy. If you ever see graffiti on town property, there's a hotline you can use to call Wick. He *hates* graffiti. He's got all sorts of chemicals for removing it."

"And you think he's got some chemical that removes the ink from pages? And that he's been erasing books to give you a hard time?"

Kathy made an anguished noise. "It sounds ridiculous when you say it out loud, but you've got to know one thing: Wick is a genius. His mind doesn't work like yours or mine."

"Okay."

I looked at the metal building. An empty beer bottle was leaning in the grass next to the corner of the building. I recognized the label from somewhere, but I couldn't place where.

Must be a local brewery.

Kathy turned off the car engine, and pushed open her door with a rusty squeak. "When we get in there, don't let on that you know anything."

"Pretend I know nothing?" I grinned. "Easy peasy lemon squeezy."

We both got out of the brown Honda. Kathy opened the hatchback, grabbed the three library books, and handed them to me to carry in.

We headed toward the waste station's office. The building itself was cute, like an A-framed cottage, but made of galvanized metal. I'd seen houseboats with a similar structure, right down to the round window positioned at the peak.

Kathy knocked on the door.

A man's voice came booming from exterior speakers like the voice of Gandalf.

"YOU MAY ENTER!"

Kathy turned to me, rolling her eyes.

"Vinnie loves being dramatic."

"Vinnie?" The name rang a bell. I took another look at the beer bottle, which rang another bell.

A few weeks ago, my aunt had phoned someone whose name had sounded to me like Viv or Fin or Winnie. Then she'd had this friend, who'd been described as "a cleaner," search through my house for dangers. This person also put up some protective wards. He'd left behind a couple of empty beer bottles with the same label as the one in front of the building.

Zinnia's "cleaner" friend must have been Vinnie Wick. He knew my secret. And I was about to meet him.

CHAPTER 8

WE ENTERED THE metal shack. Inside, on the other side of a desk, was a man who did not match my expectations of someone running a municipal landfill.

This guy resembled a movie mob boss, or the top man in charge of a casino. He was about fifty, clean shaven, and wide shouldered. His hair was shiny black, slicked back and receding on the temples. His eyes were dark and hooded, his nose narrow like a hawk's, and his teeth were small and crooked but very white. Despite the warmth of the day, he wore a lightweight dark sweater over a collared shirt.

Shoot me for jumping to stereotypes, but I'd expected someone with a gray beard and a cigarette dangling from cracked lips. The human equivalent of an old seagull.

When we'd entered, he'd been seated on the other side of a sizable oak desk, facing the door. He didn't get up when he saw us, nor did he invite us to sit—probably because he had only one extra chair for visitors and there were two of us. The metal structure's interior was a single room of about three hundred square feet. What it lacked in guest seating it made up for in filing cabinets. The walls were lined with at least a dozen of them. Something about the alignment of the filing cabinets struck me as odd. They were a little too perfectly straight, like a computer rendering.

Kathy looked at me while waving to the man. "Meet Vincent Wick," she said.

"Hello," I said.

Vincent Wick gave her a sneering smile, flashing only the top row of his gleaming-white teeth. "I see you brought backup, Kathy. You don't trust yourself to be alone with me."

Kathy took off her glasses and squinted at him. "We're here on official library business." Her voice quivered slightly.

"If you say so." He scanned me from head to toe. "And that's why you've brought one of your fellow book pushers."

Book pushers? I squared my shoulders. "I've been called worse."

His prolonged stare made me uncomfortable. I glanced over at the large picture window, which perfectly framed the dump site in a way that made it appear beautiful. From a distance, all the colored bits were like confetti.

He said, "Beautiful, isn't it?"

Was he reading my mind? Was that something "cleaners" did? I kept my eyes on the view. "It's more colorful than I expected."

"It's colorful now, but you're looking at future black gold," he said. "What once was waste will become valuable fertilizer." He paused. "From chaos and decay springs life anew."

I turned to face him, smiling sweetly. "Is that poetry you're reciting, Mr. Wick? Or do you spend a lot of time staring out this window and having deep thoughts about garbage?"

Kathy snorted. I glanced over to find her furiously cleaning her glasses, using a spray-on product from her purse. Cleaning her glasses was a process that could take Kathy several minutes. She'd asked me to play quiet and let her take the lead with Vincent Wick, but she wasn't saying much.

Wick asked, "And what is your name, dear?"

I stared into his dark, hooded eyes. "Don't you already know my name? You seem to know a lot of things. You knew I was a book pusher."

He glanced down at my waist briefly. "Because you're wearing three cardigans, my dear."

I narrowed my eyes at him. *You were in my house. I know you were, but do you know that I know? Are you enjoying this game?*

"My name is Zara Riddle," I said.

"Ah." He tilted his head back. "Zinnia's daughter, or sister, or something like that."

Very good. Almost convincing. "I'm her niece."

"How are you settling into our fine town? Are the restaurants to your liking? Grazie serves the best Italian, but you already knew that."

He knew where I'd been on Saturday night. He'd been spying on me, and now he wanted to throw me off balance. Boy, was he in for disappointment. I'd already sucked a ghost up my nose that day. I wasn't going to get rattled by him name-dropping a restaurant.

Meanwhile, Kathy continued cleaning her glasses.

I stepped toward the desk and put my hand on the corner, encroaching on the man's space. "Mr. Wick, Kathy tells me you're an expert on ink removal."

"Did she now?" He kept his eyes on mine. "I'm sure Ms. Carmichael has told you all sorts of wicked things about me."

"She told me you're the ink expert, which is why we've brought you these." I dropped the trio of books onto his desk. I opened the top one to a page that was missing ten percent of its text.

He looked down his hawk nose at the page. "Someone has vandalized this book," he said.

"Someone or something."

His eyes flicked up. "*Something?* Whatever do you mean?"

The guy probably knew the ink was being erased by magical means, but I had to play along with Kathy's quest. She suspected chemicals, so that was where I'd keep my line of questioning.

"Perhaps a type of industrial cleaning product," I said. "Or something more special?"

"Do you like Sicilian food?"

"Mr. Wick, we just need to know what chemical this prankster is using. Then we can check the local suppliers and find out who has access."

"How industrious," he said. "You're like Watson and Holmes. Tell me, Ms. Riddle, are you Watson?"

I kept going, ignoring his question. "Kathy already tested a few of our book-cleaning supplies, but they're designed to remove pen marks without lifting book ink. We're out of options. Do you have any ideas?" I raised my eyebrows meaningfully. "My aunt didn't have any ideas when I told her about it, but perhaps you do?"

"Oh, I have plenty of ideas."

"How about something slow-acting? For example, a chemical that doesn't react until the book's being read and the surface is exposed to light?"

He frowned and studied the books, flipping through all three, his eyes darting back and forth. He retrieved a magnifying glass from his desk drawer and leaned over the pages. "Interesting," he said.

Kathy finally finished cleaning her glasses and put them on to stare him down. "It's horrible," she said. "We have to pay for replacements out of our budget, which is always getting slashed."

He closed the books. "I have a few notions about this matter, but trust me, it's not worth your time." He opened his desk drawer and pulled out a metal cash box—the kind small businesses use for petty cash. He flipped open the metal lid, counted out a sum of bills and coins, and placed it on the edge of his desk in front of Kathy.

She sputtered. "What's this? Vinnie, I don't need your money."

"Sure, you do. You said so yourself. That sum covers all three titles, plus fifteen percent for the service charge. I'll keep these damaged copies and recycle them."

"Thanks for nothing," she said. "But those books are not for sale."

She reached for the books, but he pulled them back, out of her reach. She started to come around his desk. He quickly grabbed each book and tore it in half along the spine.

Kathy made more sputtering noises.

"Let me take care of this," he said calmly.

"This isn't any of your business, Vinnie."

"Then why did you come here?"

She didn't have an answer for that. She flapped her hands at her sides as she stared at the torn-apart books.

"Vandalism of town assets is technically my business," he said.

We could repair such spine abuse, but what would be the point? The books had been worthlessness even before Vincent Wick ripped them in half.

Kathy grabbed the money, gave me a dark look, and headed for the door. I followed her outside.

The wind must have shifted because the air smelled as sweet and clean as any air I'd ever smelled.

The speakers affixed to the metal building crackled. Vincent's voice boomed out at high volume. "LOVELY TO MEET YOU, ZARA RIDDLE." There was a pause. "ALWAYS A PLEASURE, KATHY CARMICHAEL."

Kathy made a very un-librarian-like gesture with her right hand.

We climbed into Kathy's car. She did a three-point turn at high speed. The gravel of the parking area ground noisily beneath the Honda's tires. Then she hit the accelerator, kicking up gravel from the tires and spraying the metal office building with a machine-gun-like rat-a-tat-tat.

CHAPTER 9

Back at the library, I told Frank about our colorful and fragrant expedition to the dump.

"We didn't accomplish much." I grabbed a tissue and blew my nose for the third time. The garbage stink wouldn't go away. "Not much, unless you count stress-testing my olfactory system."

Frank's eyes had been wide the whole time I'd been talking. Now he looked exactly like the human equivalent of a bottle of pink champagne waiting to be uncorked.

"You're way too excited," I said. "Did you do something naughty while we were gone?"

He snorted. "I know something you don't know."

"About Kathy and Vincent Wick?"

He made a sound like a balloon letting out air. "She told you?"

"She didn't tell me anything, but if I had to guess, I'd say they have a history of fighting over budgets with the town council."

"They used to date," he said.

"That would have been my next guess. Did she tell you that, or did you hear it from the gossip mill?"

"She told me," Frank said. "At the staff barbecue last summer, when she thought the grapefruit punch was nonalcoholic." He rubbed his chin. "Let's see. It was sometime after she started the congo line but before she tried to rip the clothes off the Parks Board employee she thought was a stripper."

I glanced around to make sure nobody was close enough to hear us whispering.

"Kathy knows how to party," I said.

"She claimed it was heat stroke," he said. "She said none of it was true, especially not the stuff about him being a wizard."

My jaw dropped. "A wizard?"

"I know, right? That's a weird thing to say about someone, even if you do have heat stroke."

"Did she mean... an actual wizard? Like he does magic spells and curses?"

Frank frowned and tilted his head. "No," he said slowly. "I assumed she meant a wizard who does tricks at children's birthday parties."

"Those are called magicians."

"What's the difference?"

"A wizard does real magic, whereas magicians do tricks. Illusions."

Frank tilted his head back and mimed a silent laugh. He whispered, "Zara Riddle, you are too funny. Your face right now is so serious." He patted me on the shoulder and looked deeply into my eyes. "Magic isn't real."

"I know that." I rolled my eyes and shrugged off his hand.

"There are no wizards," he said.

"Or witches or werewolves or va—."

"Vampires," he finished for me.

I coughed to clear the frog in my throat. The smell of the garbage dump had really done a number on me.

Or maybe I was feeling the effects of the ghost who'd infiltrated me via my left nostril.

As I thought of the ghost, I remembered the name I'd given him. Mr. Finance Wizard.

If wizards weren't real, then why did I have one living inside my head?

"Frank, if I were to describe a library patron to you, do you think you could guess his name?"

Frank clapped his hands softly. "A game? Let's play."

"It's a man, mid-fifties, average height and build, with gray hair."

"And?"

"That's all I've got."

"That could be anyone. That could be me if I stopped coloring my hair."

"Oh! I know. He's really into personal finance books."

Frank's expression fell. "Again, that could be anyone. This game isn't as fun as I thought it would be."

"Well, thanks for trying. I guess we'd better get back to work."

"If we must," he said dramatically. It was an act, of course. Frank Wonder loved his job as the children's librarian, and everyone loved him.

We both got back to work, and I let my mind puzzle over the mysteries of the day. Luckily, I would be seeing Zinnia after my shift. I couldn't wait to ask her if wizards were real, and if Vincent Wick was one.

CHAPTER 10

AT THE END of my shift, Zoey met me at the library and we walked to my aunt's house together.

Zinnia felt the three of us Riddles should get together as a family regularly. This seemed like a wonderful idea. I wanted to make up for lost time, plus both Zoey and I occasionally enjoyed food that didn't come from a box.

We arrived fashionably late, at five minutes past six. The door opened as we walked up the front steps. My aunt was nowhere to be seen. She must have used magic to let us in. Anyone walking by could have seen. How brazen! I got in trouble for floating one little napkin, but apparently she could do whatever she wanted.

Once inside, Zoey gawked up at the ceiling of the foyer. "Auntie Z sure loves her flowers."

I followed her gaze up and did a double-take. I hadn't noticed before that the ceiling of the foyer had a fresco-style painting of an English garden. The imagery was lovely, and professional quality, but seeing it on the ceiling was strange. It made my *up* feel like *down*, and gave me the disconcerting sensation I was falling.

In a hushed tone, I agreed. "In fact, I'm not entirely sure there's a house underneath all this wallpaper and chintz." I pretended to rap on a wall but didn't let my knuckles make contact. I gasped theatrically. "Zoey, there's no wall here. It's all a magical illusion." I made a spooky hand wave. "We're standing inside a mirage."

Zoey looked at me, her expression brightening the way it did before she dropped some science on a conversation.

"Mirages aren't magic, Mom. They're a naturally occurring optical phenomenon. Light rays are bent to produce a displaced image of distant objects. When people see bodies of water in the desert, it's actually the sky being reflected in mirror image."

I pretended to knock on the wall again. "So, are you saying there's a parallel universe somewhere with this same exact house? With evil twin versions of both of us? If we're evil over there, we definitely have flaxen blonde hair, and you're a cheerleader."

She shook her head. "Never mind."

I looped my arm around her shoulders and gave her a sideways hug. "Don't say never mind. I love it when you go all Wikipedia on me. It makes me feel normal because I do it all the time, too."

"A girl's gotta have some kind of skills," she said. "Especially if she's a so-called witch with zero magical ability."

My chest tightened.

She made a fist and swung her arm in a keep-going gesture. "From here on, I'll be the one reciting book facts and writing up reports, while you fight the forces of evil with actual magic."

I gave her a sympathetic look. My aunt had a theory that my own powers had been delayed because I'd been pregnant with Zoey at the time. Magic had a "mind of its own," and must have chosen to stay dormant rather than disrupt the pregnancy. As far as Zoey's missing powers went, we'd considered the obvious—that Zoey was similarly with child. I'd asked her more than once, "Are you absolutely sure you're not pregnant? You're not in trouble, I promise." This earned me a flurry of eye-rolling along with gagging. Zoey hadn't even been on a date with a boy, let alone any of the other stuff. It was possible the gift had skipped a generation.

But Zinnia wouldn't give up. She felt a spark of magic in Zoey. She was teaching her novice witchcraft lessons anyway. That way, Zoey would know the mechanical side of spells when her abilities kicked in.

I tried to be hopeful, too, but whenever I saw my sweet, kind, brilliant daughter struggle with disappointment, it crushed me. I would have gladly given up all my powers if it meant she could have them. But Zinnia said that such a transfer was impossible. I could give my daughter love, money, and first choice from all boxes of chocolates, but I could never give her the one thing she desperately wanted. Magic.

"Hang in there," I said. "Patience is—"

She stomped her foot. "Stop it."

I frowned. "What's happening? Is this a temper tantrum? Are you the evil mirage-world Zoey? What have you done with my real daughter?"

She stomped again, and groaned through gritted teeth. "Stop telling me to *hang in there*. It's a meaningless platitude that you and Auntie Z say to make yourselves feel better, but it doesn't help me at all."

She gave me a dirty look, then turned to spread the dirt to Zinnia, who stood watching in the hallway. She must have come to see what was taking us so long at the front door.

"We're having some feelings," I explained to my aunt.

"Dinner is waiting," Zinnia said with cool authority.

Zoey huffed and walked past my aunt, toward the kitchen.

"She's upset," Zinnia said. "Which is perfectly understandable, given her situation. Give her some space. You're always trying to micromanage her emotions."

"I am?"

"Yes. And that's fine when they're little, but in order to develop their own boundaries, children need to experience difficult feelings on their own."

I took in a deep breath and let her have it. "I didn't realize you were such an expert on child psychology. It must be from all your real-world experience of having raised... how many children, exactly?" I pretended to rub my chin thoughtfully. "You know, I don't think you have any kids. Not that I can think of."

She was slow to answer. "A wise woman can see more from the bottom of a well than a fool can see from a mountain top."

"Are you calling me a fool?"

"Not at all." She took my elbow and gently directed me toward the smell of food. "The way you climb mountains is admirable, Zara. I certainly have a lot to learn from you."

My irritation was replaced by confusion, and then hunger. Dinner smelled good. If I was a micromanager, then fine. I was ready to micromanage some food into my mouth.

We found Zoey sitting at the table with her hands on her lap. She turned to look out the window rather than make eye contact. I could tell by her body language that she was embarrassed by her outburst, but not enough to apologize. She was probably still arguing with the version of me who lived in her head. I knew because I did the same.

I watched her silently as she stared out the window before shifting to examining strands of her hair. She twisted her hair and scowled at the white-tipped split ends. We were both overdue to get our hair trimmed. I needed to find a hairdresser for both of us.

Zinnia brought in the dinner.

I asked her, "Is there a spell for getting rid of split ends?"

"Certainly," she said. "But I go to a regular hair salon. We must not rely on magic too heavily."

"But you want me to practice spells over and over so I can get good at them. Why not do both? Kill two birds with one stone?"

She arched her eyebrows. "A wise woman can see more from the bottom of a well than a fool can see from a mountain top," she said for the second time that evening. It was no less irritating than the first time.

"I'd rather be on a mountain top than stuck at the bottom of a well."

My daughter made a snorting sound.

"Of course you would," Zinnia said. "How about we eat some dinner now?"

I looked at the bubbling, golden surface of the steaming dish before us. The food smelled like the exact opposite of the Wisteria Sanitation Management Station. I no longer cursed the olfactory sensory neurons in my nose for being so good at their job.

"Thank you so much for dinner," I said. I heaped on more compliments as she heaped the food onto my rose-patterned china plate.

"It's just a simple casserole with green beans," she said. "With hand-made pasta, and fresh herbs from the garden."

"Well, I love anything with cheese on top, and this appears to have two kinds of cheese, so you have my admiration, my gratitude, and a kidney should you ever need one."

My daughter was silent. I kicked the leg of her chair.

Zoey jolted. "Thank you, Auntie Z," she said, still avoiding my eyes. "This is exactly what I need after a long, difficult week."

"But it's only Monday," Zinnia said with a light laugh.

"Oh, right," Zoey said.

Zinnia asked, "Are you having difficulties at your new school? I'm acquainted with the principal. I can speak to him on your behalf, if you'd like."

"Mmm," Zoey said around a mouthful of food, skillfully changing the topic. "This is amazing." She pulled the plate closer to the edge of the table and shifted her chair forward like she meant business. "Never mind me and my school stuff. I'm fine." She flicked her gaze to me briefly. "Mom, you should tell Auntie Z about your exciting trip to the dump today."

"The dump?" Zinnia glanced down at the food and frowned. "If you must," she said.

While we ate, I told her about the other books with missing words. I didn't tell her about the ghost because my daughter was there, and I didn't want her to know about it. Not yet, anyway. So I skipped past that, and told my aunt about my visit to the Wisteria Sanitation Management Station with Kathy.

"He ripped up the books and kept them?" My aunt seemed surprised by this.

"He said vandalism of town property was his business."

"Getting under Kathy's skin is his business."

"They used to be an item?"

Zinnia tilted back her head and looked down her nose at me. "Sounds like you've been digging around a lot today."

"Frank likes to gossip."

"And you like to listen."

I held my hands up. "I can't help it if people enjoy telling me stories. Frank said that Kathy called Wick a wizard."

Zinnia chortled. "That's funny."

"Is he a wizard? He was giving us orders through his speaker system like he was Gandalf the Grey."

"Speakers? That's new."

"Well, is he a wizard? Are wizards real?"

"There are all kinds of wizards," she said. "Vincent Wick is not like the ones in storybooks."

"But he is your cleaner guy, right? He came here to check the house and put up protective wards."

She pinched her lips shut.

"Zinnia, I know it was him."

"You don't know that." She looked down at the food and rearranged the serving dishes.

"Fine," I said. "Is he a shifter?"

Zinnia said gravely, "You would be wise to steer clear of Vincent Wick. The man is descended from a very long line of Wicks. The Wick family has lived in Wisteria since before it was even a town."

"Sure, I'd buy that. His family goes way back. Are they shifters?"

"Whatever makes you think they are?"

"There was a round window in his office building. And you were the one who said shifters like windows that aren't square. Plus he's got a serious hawk vibe going on. Or maybe an eagle vibe?"

"Are you thinking..." She trailed off, glancing at Zoey.

Zoey, who'd been quiet until now, interjected, "Auntie Z, she thinks he's the giant monster bird that attacked her and Chet in the woods."

I forced a light laugh. "Oh, that little incident? I almost forgot all about it. I'm sure it was just an eagle protecting her nest."

"Mom," Zoey said seriously. "I remember how shaken up you were that day."

"You'd be upset, too, if an eagle swooped at you." I waved a hand. "Remember when old Mrs. Pinkman's budgie got out of his cage while you were watering her plants, and pooped on you? You were inconsolable."

Zoey's eyes widened. "That bird was pure evil. His name was Marzipants, and he had it in for me."

"Exactly," I said. "And it was just a budgie. An eagle is much scarier."

Zoey smirked. "I still think the giant bird could have been a shape-shifting garbageman trying to take out the trash."

"Ha ha," I said. "Because I'm the trash. Nice one."

We all laughed, though I knew my daughter wouldn't be joking around if she'd seen the damage the bird had done. At the time, I had downplayed the injuries to keep from scaring her, but now I wasn't so sure about my decision. The rules of being a parent are so contradictory. You want your child to feel safe and secure, but you also want them to be aware of the dangers in the world.

After the laughter died away, Zinnia said, "The Wick family has always been involved with magic, but I don't believe Vincent Wick attacked you. Not even if he were capable of such a thing."

"You should check him," I said. "Test him to see if he can shift into a bird."

"And how do you suggest I do that?"

I shrugged. "There must be some sort of litmus test for detecting magical abilities."

Zoey leaned in with interest. "Is there?"

I continued, "There should be a simple yes-or-no test, like those sticks you pee on to find out if you're pregnant."

The corners of Zinnia's mouth twitched into a smile. "Are you suggesting I should have Vincent Wick urinate onto a plastic stick that detects supernatural abilities?"

"You gotta try something," I said. "It's pretty obvious he's some sort of villain. He's got way too many file cabinets in that office. Why does a garbage dump need so much paperwork?"

"These are all very interesting observations. Have you run your wild theories past Chet?"

I waved one hand dismissively. "Never mind about Chet. Is there any sort of test, pee stick or otherwise?"

My aunt paused as though struggling to not call me a ding-dong.

Finally, she said, "There is no such test. And you ought to be thankful, Zara. If there were such a test, our kind would have been rounded up and exterminated years ago."

"They tried," I said. "Fun fact: Not all witches were burned. Mainly just the ones in France. The ones in New England were hanged."

"That's not really a fun fact," Zoey said.

"It was a fun fact before we became witches," I said.

Zoey's expression grew serious. "They used to drown redheaded babies, too. It's a miracle any of us are around."

I leaned over to tousle her hair. "You're my little miracle." She pulled away before I could get in a good tousling.

My aunt sighed and looked mournfully at the food on her plate. "So much for a pleasant meal without any discussion of murder and mayhem."

"You can't say we're a boring family," I said.

"We are anything but boring," Zoey agreed. "Except for me. I'm a bit boring because I can't do magic."

I pointed at her plate. "Eat your veggies. I hear green beans help bring on magical abilities." I winked at my aunt. The three of us resumed eating.

I'd hoped to get more information from my aunt, but I should have known she'd be her usual secretive self. At least her facial expression had confirmed for me that Vincent Wick was her cleaner, and that he was involved with magic somehow. What had she meant that he was a wizard, but not the kind from storybooks? Did she mean he was a magician at children's parties? No way. No parent would hire a guy who looked like a movie mob boss to entertain their small children, not even with a discount coupon.

Was he a financial wizard, like the ghost I'd seen earlier that day? Probably not. If he were rich, he'd probably spend his days in a place that didn't reek of hot garbage when the wind changed direction.

We finished eating. Zinnia stood and began clearing the dishes using both magic and her hands.

"Girls, please help me tidy up."

Zoey and I exchanged a look. I whispered to my daughter, "I like the two of us being called *girls*."

Zoey said, "And I like doing the dishes when it's at someone else's house. You get to see where everything goes."

My aunt said, "If you like that, you're going to love helping me whip up a batch of bookwyrm dough."

In unison, Zoey and I said, "Bookwyrm dough?"

My aunt smiled. "Yes. Tonight's magic lesson will be a practical one. One of my suppliers mentioned she was nearly out of black scarabyce blood, and I realized what we might use for tonight's lesson."

In unison again, Zoey and I said, "Black scarabyce blood?"

"Not the black scarabyce blood. Oh, no, no, no. That would be dangerous. But it made me think of bookwyrms, so I picked up some supplies. Zara, you can put it to use tomorrow at work."

"Me? But I'm not supposed to do magic at the library."

"That's true," she said. "Forget I even brought it up."

"No, no," I said quickly. "I'm just giving you a hard time because sometimes you're a bit fast and loose with the rules."

She scoffed. "I'm neither fast nor loose, thank you very much."

"Sorry," I said. I bent at the knees and made myself shorter, until I was squatting. "Look at me."

"What are you doing?"

"I'm hiking down from Fool Mountain," I said. "I'm coming all the way down to your Womanly Well of Wisdom."

"You're making fun of me," she said.

"Not on purpose." I straightened up. "I'm the fool. You're the wise woman. I get it now."

Zinnia looked at the plates I'd been levitating. They tipped and spilled food everywhere.

"Maybe we're already moving too quickly with your lessons," she said.

Zoey stepped between us and pressed her palms together in prayer. "Please, Auntie Z, can we make bookwyrm dough? My mother will behave herself, I swear."

"I also swear."

Zinnia threw up both hands. "Fine. I'll probably live to regret this, but I hate to see good ingredients go to waste."

CHAPTER 11

AFTER WE MADE the bookwyrm dough, I got a few minutes alone with my aunt so I could tell her about my new spirit. I also filled her in on what Chet had told me Saturday night at dinner, about needing help with a possible spirit walker.

She didn't look enthused. "Chet specifically said the Riddle family? Not just you alone?"

"Lucky you," I said. "You're getting roped into more X-Files stuff."

"No, thank you." She shook her head. "Tell Chet you found his ghost, and promise you won't do anything dangerous."

"You want me to deal with it on my own? You're not helping? But you're my elder witch. You're supposed to be mentoring me."

"Zara, I do what I can, but I'm not Spirit Charmed like you. To be honest, you already know more about ghosts than I do. I'm not sure how much I can help you at this point."

"What about your coven?"

She gave me a blank look.

"Come on," I said. "I know there must be a coven. You probably call it a book club or something, right?"

The blank look continued.

"Aunt Zinnia, you must know other witches you can talk to."

"It's not that simple." She leaned back and glanced into the kitchen, where Zoey was happily studying a magical book. She turned back to me and spoke in an even softer voice. "I will ask around on your behalf. I'll see if I can find you any more information about being Spirit Charmed."

* * *

Tuesday morning, I arrived at the library with a ball of bookwyrm dough in a Tupperware container. To any outside observer, it was nothing more than a pale green version of the sort of sculpting clay that children play with.

For my mission, I located the rock star memoir that had been returned the previous day. It was on the display table with Frank's other Wonder Picks. Whichever employee had received it back into the library must not have done a thorough flip-through, as they hadn't noticed the pages were missing so many words that some pages were practically blank. I couldn't blame my coworker too harshly, though. The flip-through is mainly to release bookmarks and other debris. It would be impractical to have staff painstakingly checking that all words are where they ought to be.

Next, I took the book with me toward an unoccupied aisle. Along the way, I checked in social sciences for any signs of my ghost. The area was clear.

How ironic that I worked in a library yet had no access to the witchcraft information I really needed. Back when I'd learned about my witch powers, I'd immediately checked under call number 133.4, Philosophy And Psychology > Parapsychology And Occultism > Specific Topics > Witchcraft - Sorcery. Our witchcraft section was sparse, and the few books we carried had the same public domain information and woodcut illustrations of witch burnings. Not fun reading. Not helpful, either.

Once I reached a social sciences aisle with no view of the high-traffic zones, I reached down into the pocket of my loose skirt for the container of bookwyrm dough. I took a good look around to make sure nobody was watching.

This wasn't the first time I'd used magic inside the library. I regularly used my telekinesis to tighten the bows of my lace-up boots without having to bend over. And while I would never float a book down from a tall shelf, I had been using my powers as a power-assist, nudging a row of books to the left or right to free up a book I was retrieving. The telekinesis could speed things up, or make certain book maneuvers less awkward, but using magic didn't save me energy. The power seemingly drew from my body. I'd get just as tired pushing a heavy book cart using magic as I would be from using my arms and core muscles. The only difference was that the magical tiredness spread more widely through my body. Also, I could rejuvenate quickly with a snack. Thus, my magic was limited by my ability to quickly ingest chocolate—so it wasn't a bad trade-off after all.

Using the bookwyrm dough would draw little from my body as it was already charmed by Zinnia. The power was "baked in," so to speak, though the dough hadn't actually been baked.

My hands shook. I glanced around again, feeling ridiculous. It was still early on a Tuesday morning. The library wasn't at all crowded. At opening, we'd had the usual rush of people coming in to claim the best workstations, plus a few patrons with small kids in tow, knocking off their first errand of the day, and now it would be quiet until the lunch-time rush.

I pulled the lid off the container with a POP. The pop was not loud, but it wasn't a typical library sound. I leaned around the corner of the shelves and looked around. Frank stood at the circulation desk. He was visually scanning the main floor. Had he heard the telltale POP?

He tilted his head back and his nose up, sniffing the air. He must have heard the POP. Now he was sniffing for smuggled food. I pulled back into the aisle quickly. Why had I picked a book aisle? I should have taken the book to our repair alcove, and hidden in plain sight. *Too late now.* But I already had the dough in my hand. I could be done within seconds.

Without looking down, I palmed the ball in my right hand and tucked the container back into my pocket. The ball felt smooth and cool, and weirdly refreshing, like dipping your hand into a bag of white flour. Its ingredients were partly magical, yet included household staples such as cornstarch and finely milled white pepper. Zinnia said the cornstarch was for bulk and the white pepper was mainly to keep unsuspecting regular people from eating it. I'd asked her why someone would eat a pale green, raw dough. She'd explained that the main magical ingredient—the bookwyrm dust—was an *attractor*. An attractor is similar to a magnet, but for magic. Attractors serve as binding agents, holding magical compounds together—like how the egg in mayonnaise holds together both oil and vinegar in a suspension.

I brought the dough to my nose and sniffed. It did have a tangy smell, like vinegar, mingled with a mildew aroma, as well as a hint of something floral. Hibiscus? I wondered what it tasted like. Zinnia warned me not to eat it, which I'd laughed at, but now I really needed to know if it tasted the same as it smelled. Would it be sour, or sweet?

I touched the tip of my tongue to the dough.

Big mistake.

The instant my tongue grazed the dough, pain shot through me like an electric jolt. My head flashed with colors and I convulsed, sneezing once, twice, three times.

In the silence following my sneezing fit, the library was more quiet than ever. An unseen woman nearby called out a friendly *gesundheit*.

My body convulsed and I sneezed three more times.

The woman, who seemed to be in the laptop work spaces, asked sweetly, "Are you okay over there?"

"I'll be fine," I called back, my voice croaky. I sneezed once more for good measure.

"That was the last one," I called out breezily, hoping I was right.

I looked down at my right hand expecting to see the pale green ball of dough.

My palm was empty.

Had I accidentally ingested the bookwyrm dough? I started gagging. This was worse than the sneezing, but I got myself under control before it turned into actual retching.

My whole body was damp and hot with panic. I'd assured Zinnia I wouldn't eat the thing, so she hadn't covered the side effects. How bad could it be?

I probed my mouth with my tongue, checking my teeth for signs of the dough, even though I swore I'd barely grazed it with the tip of my tongue. There was a foul taste inside my mouth, but no residue. I decided I couldn't have eaten the dough. Even if my ghost had taken over my body and kicked me out, I would remember the transition happening. The only logical explanation was that I'd dropped the dough while sneezing.

My hands twitched as I started the spell for locating lost objects. Just as quickly as I'd begun, I stopped myself. Zinnia hadn't just told me not to eat the dough. She'd also warned me to never use other spells in conjunction with it. There could be unforeseen interactions, such as when you take a combination of medications.

I stepped back and visually searched the surrounding shelves and the floor. I opened the hardcover memoir I'd brought with me and flipped through the pages. No squashed ball of bookwyrm dough. Just a bunch of blank, wordless areas. How would I explain to my aunt what I'd done? Would it be overkill to visit the hospital and request my stomach get pumped?

Finally, after a several minutes of sweaty panic, I was looking down while turning, my skirt swished out of the way, when I spotted the ball of bookwyrm dough. The pale green blob was on the toe of my right boot. I hadn't felt its landing through the hard leather.

"You cheeky thing," I whispered.

I swear the small bumps and dimples on the dough ball's surface looked exactly like a face, grinning up at me.

With a sharp kick upward, I whipped the ball into the air, palmed it again, and got back on track with my mission.

Following Zinnia's instructions, I rolled the dough out into a log shape. Next, I opened the hardcover rock star memoir to a section that was missing words. I took the bookwyrm log and used it like a rolling pin, rolling it up and down over the blank sections.

Would it work?

I bit my lower lip as I waited to see a reaction. My lower lip felt numb and tingly, but I quickly forgot about that and the horrible taste in my mouth when the magic started to work.

Before my eyes, the missing words all reappeared. Not only did the dough work, but it worked better than expected. The magic was so powerful, it didn't even need to contact every page. It was passing through the book on its own, restoring all the words, dozens of pages deep. Faster and faster I worked, flipping the book entire chapters at a time, rolling the dough across to do its work, and watching in amazement as the words appeared.

The restoration was perfect.

I closed the book with a crisp, satisfied snap.

Where was I again? There were so many books. *Oh, right. The library. Pull yourself together, Zara.*

Reality came back to me in a swooning rush.

My mind felt foggy, as though I'd been in a trance—which I technically had been, since using magical objects puts the user into an altered state just as readily as casting a difficult spell. As I returned to the regular world, the shelves around me loomed high overhead. My eyes blurred, and the whole world seemed to be about to topple over on me. I had the book in one hand and the bookwyrm dough clutched tightly in the other. I steadied myself by leaning my back against one bookcase. I was breathing heavily, panting, and hadn't noticed until now. My mouth felt like something had used it as a litter box. Why was the horrible taste still not washed away? Was my dry mouth caused by using the magic, or my mouth's natural response to having tasted a mixture of cornstarch, white pepper, and the ground-up body casings of magical bookwyrms.

Body casings, I realized with horror. That was the ingredient I hadn't wanted to think about. I had actually tasted the dusty old dead body casings of a magical insect or larva or was it eggs?

I pushed the thought from my mind and put the dough back into the plastic case. I fluffed out my billowy skirts to hide the shape of the container, and walked back toward the library's counter, dropping the perfectly restored book on the table as I walked.

Mission accomplished.

The dough still had plenty of power left in it, so I would simply intercept any books with missing words and restore them as needed. I even had a cover story in case Kathy asked what I was doing. I would tell her the words hadn't been erased or removed at all, but that a white mold was growing on top of the letters, and the dough removed the mold.

No sane librarian would believe such an absurd tale, of course, but Zinnia had taught me something new. A bluffing spell. It would increase my ability to be convincing in a verbal situation. According to my elder witch mentor, the spell increased the witch's charisma as well as the subject's gullibility. The bluffing spell was well above my current ability, and unlikely to work very well in my novice hands, but it was all I had. That and my charming smile.

Frank tapped me on the shoulder. "I'm putting a sushi order for lunch. Do you want some?"

"Count me in," I replied with a happy grin. Sushi would be just the thing to cleanse my palate.

He looked at my mouth. His eyes widened and he let out a strangled cry.

I covered my mouth with my hand. "Is something wrong?"

He made a gagging sound and stepped further away from me. "Good one," he said. "You really got me that time, Zara. I might barf."

"I did?"

"Your lips are really black," he said. "Did you eat one of our stamp pads?"

"Sure," I said slowly. "If that's what it looks like, that must be what I did."

"You'd better wash that ink out of your mouth before Kathy sees. She's been on edge since your trip to see Wick yesterday."

"I'll take care of this right away." I excused myself to go use the staff washroom.

When I saw what had startled Frank, my eyes widened as much as his had. I did look like someone who'd eaten a stamp pad. Or several of them.

My lips were darker than black currant jelly. Not great, but not a disaster. Black lipstick wasn't the most flattering shade on me, but a stranger might assume it was lipstick.

Then I opened my mouth, and nearly gagged. Everything from my teeth to my uvula was a dark, inky black. The inside of my mouth was as murky and terrible as an oil spill.

I turned on the bathroom sink's tap, cupped water in my hands, and started rinsing furiously.

The water I spat out was as clear and pristine as the water from the tap. The blackness inside my mouth didn't lighten at all. I rinsed again and again, but it did nothing for the horror inside my mouth.

CHAPTER 12

WHAT WOULD YOU do if the inside of your mouth, including your teeth, turned as black as the darkest licorice? You'd probably stop eating whatever had caused it. I couldn't solve my problem that easily. I hadn't eaten any bookwyrm dough. All I'd done was touch the tip of my tongue to it. My saliva must have triggered something in the compound. But how? The moisture in my hand hadn't done anything. It seemed spit was a different story.

I phoned my aunt from the bathroom and explained my situation.

"You licked it?"

"I know you warned me not to, but I can't explain it. You've got to give me a spell or a magical mouthwash to reverse this. I'm looking at my mouth in the bathroom mirror right now, and it's like staring into the abyss. What does Nietzsche say? When you stare into the abyss, it stares into you. You become the thing that disturbs you most." I tore my gaze away from my scary reflection. "I'm becoming blackness. I feel it inside me now, spreading. Aunt Zinnia, you've got to help me."

"No."

"You can't help me over the phone? Fair enough. I'll sneak out of here and meet you at your house."

"No."

"I'll meet wherever you want. I'll buy you lunch. Let's go to that Thai place you like."

She didn't answer. I knew she was still there because I could hear her huffy breathing. I had apparently called her while she was busy with some secret business that she wouldn't tell me about even if I asked.

"Fine," I said. "I'll buy you lunch *and* a new pair of boots."

"You owe me a pair anyway. Remember when you stormed out of my house wearing my favorite pair?"

"I'd been recently electrocuted, Aunt Zinnia. I wasn't in full control of myself. The side effects include muscle stiffness, anxiety, and theft of footwear."

She gave no sign of amusement.

I upped the ante. "I'll buy you lunch and three pairs of boots."

"No spell," she said with finality. "You must live through the results of your mistake."

"Are you trying to teach me a lesson?"

"Magic is teaching you this lesson. Not me."

I turned back to my reflection and frowned at my blackened mouth. Frowning only made it worse.

"Some lesson that'll be," I grumbled. "It's going to be so memorable when I get fired, can't make my mortgage payments, and have to move in with you. Then magic will teach you a lesson about not being a very helpful mentor. You'll have two more Riddles living under your roof, eating all your food, and switching the TV channel in the middle of your favorite show, whatever that is. Gardening, maybe? Or cooking?"

"Zara, is the blackness spreading?"

"Yes," I said. "I can feel it in my soul."

"Zara."

I leaned in to the mirror and examined the border of my lips. I could see some regular pink lip skin. The black had been over the edge a few minutes ago.

"No, it's not spreading," I said. "It might even be receding."

"Then you'll have to use the spell of time."

"What?" I perked up. "There's a spell to move time?"

She made a strangled sound. "It's an expression. I meant you need to be patient and wait while the effects wear off over time. That's the spell of time. It makes things change."

"Are you sure? I feel like I'm breathing faster than usual. Or slower. And my stomach feels weird, like I had too many mochas."

"Well, that's what you get for eating bookwyrm dough."

"But I didn't eat it! I only... tasted it. Okay, I see your point."

"It's not going to harm you. The compound is used by witches to restore text that's been damaged by regular wear and tear. Did it at least work on the books?"

"Yes. It worked perfectly. Like magic."

"See? The bookwyrm dough puts ink only where the dough feels it belongs. If the dough restored ink to your mouth, it must have felt that your mouth needed more ink." She chuckled softly.

"The dough felt I should have an extreme goth look?"

"Apparently."

"Wait. Since when does dough have feelings?"

"Magic has a mind of its own, Zara. You know that. Or at least you should because I keep telling you." She sighed heavily into her phone's receiver. Her disappointment in me was as palpable as it was familiar. Sometimes when I was talking to my aunt, my mother didn't seem so dead after all.

"I must have offended the dough in some way," I said. "Should I have given it a name? It looks like a Henry."

Zinnia made a strangled noise. "Don't you dare. Don't go naming that which ought not to be named, and don't go putting things into your mouth. I've got to go now, but please *do* try to keep yourself out of trouble for the remainder of the day."

I gave myself a smile in the bathroom mirror. With my blackened teeth and gums, I looked like a ghoulish creature from a horror movie.

"I'll be a good girl," I said creepily. Or maybe I said it normally, and it was imbued with the creepiness from my appearance. "Zara tries to be a good girl," I said with even more creepiness. "Zara doesn't mean to be a bad witch."

I heard pages riffling on the other side of the phone call.

"Eight to twelve hours," Zinnia said. "The side effects from ingestion of any part of the bookwyrm are said to wear off on human subjects within eight to twelve hours, unless..."

"Unless what?"

"It may become permanent in the event of death, but I don't think we need to worry about that."

I swallowed hard. "Right. Let's not worry about that."

"Did you lose consciousness?"

"No. I didn't even realize anything weird had happened. I did sneeze a few times, but that was it."

"Just sneezing? You're lucky. Your witch powers protected you. If a non-witch had eaten the dough, the results would have been much worse."

I patted the plastic container in my pocket. "Don't worry. I'll keep a close watch on the dough so it doesn't get nibbled on by anyone else."

"I would come to the library right now and take it away for disposal, but I'm a bit busy at the moment."

"Do you want me to throw it out? Flush it down the toilet?"

She gasped. "Don't do that. Proper disposal is another lesson entirely. We'll need a vessel in which to discharge."

"Like nuclear waste?"

"Like *magical* waste."

"Wow. I didn't even know there was such a thing."

"Now you know." She paused. "Until we can properly dispose of the dough, don't let it out of your sight. Promise you'll be careful."

"I promise." I glanced at my extreme-goth mouth. "I've learned my lesson."

"Drink plenty of water."

"Will it speed up recovery?"

"It's always good to stay hydrated." She said goodbye, and I was on my own again.

Just me and my ghoulish black smile.

CHAPTER 13

WITH NO MAGICAL solution to my ghoul-mouth problem, I had to get creative with non-magical tools.

I cleaned off the staff washroom's counter and spread out all the makeup in my purse, plus a few things from the Lost and Found box. I applied a liberal base of opaque skin-toned concealer to cover my stained lips. It worked, but with no pink on my lips, I looked even more terrifying, like a ghost.

I applied a blend of two lipsticks and a lip gloss to put my lips back on. For my teeth, I ducked out to the book repair alcove and grabbed scissors and a roll of the white, cloth-backed tape for repairing book spines. I cut out tooth-sized pieces of white repair tape for my front teeth. The blackness inside my mouth was colorfast, so at least it didn't stain the tape. My gums and tongue were still black. There was nothing I could do about that, but if I kept my talking to a minimum, it was possible nobody would notice.

When I emerged from the washroom, Frank was returning with the sushi. He gave my lips a look but didn't say anything.

Now I had to eat sushi without disturbing the tape on my teeth, or eating the tape. I turned my face down with each bite and made only the minimum number of chews needed to swallow. I was finished with my bento box before Frank had even rubbed the wood burrs from his chopsticks. It wasn't much different from how I normally ate sushi.

After lunch, I performed my librarian duties carefully. I answered patrons' questions by whispering through my hand shyly. If someone gave me a suspicious look, I would cough into my fist and point to a prominently displayed container of cough lozenges. Everyone bought it.

At the end of the day, I punched my time card and left work without much of a goodbye to the others.

I felt terrible for my rudeness, but giving my coworkers a flash of teeth made from book-mending tape would have been much less forgivable.

I walked home quickly, looking forward to brushing my teeth. The glue on the book-mending tape kept melting. It tasted like I'd been sucking on a glue-stick lollipop.

As I rounded the corner onto Beacon Street, I was walking quickly, eager to get home.

I slowed when I caught sight of an attractive male backside. It was Chet, unloading grocery bags from his vehicle. There was a package of powdered miniature donuts at the top of one bag. My mouth immediately watered, which didn't help with the taste of glue-stick lollipop inside my mouth.

Chet saw me walking toward him, and followed my gaze to the groceries. He rearranged the bag's contents to hide the donuts. Too late. I'd seen the sugary treats. Mr. Moore's "traditional" parenting skills weren't so perfect after all. *That's an interesting white vegetable you have there. Is it a new type of turnip?*

I wanted to lay the comment on him, but I bit my blackened tongue.

"Hello," he said. "Just getting back from work?"

I nodded.

"Busy day at the library?"

I gave him a so-so gesture with one hand.

He gave me a suspicious look. "Cat got your tongue?"

I pulled the box of cough lozenges from my pocket and gave them a shake.

He said, "Speaking of cats, why don't you have one? Isn't your type supposed to have a minimum of one cat?"

I raised an eyebrow. Did he mean witch, or librarian, or single woman? And did he *want me* to blast him in his hairy wolf chest with a blue fireball?

"I'm sure you'll get one soon enough," he said. "It's basically inevitable. One of those basic laws of the universe. Your type, and cats." He managed to laugh at his joke without smiling.

I tucked the lozenges back into my pocket and waved goodbye.

"It's been nice talking to you," he said.

He turned back to his groceries. I remained standing on the sidewalk. There was something to talk to him about. His people had been looking for a spirit walker, and the day before, I'd encountered someone who fit the description. But then, it seemed like I'd lost him again right away. Mr. Finance Wizard hadn't made any appearances that day.

There wasn't much to tell Chet, even if I wanted to. And I did *not* want to talk to him. The blackness in my mouth had faded, but my gums were still a sickly shade one might describe on a paint chip as Clarified Bruise. Also, there was a good chance Chet had noticed by now that I'd swiped his clicky pen, and I wasn't ready to give it back. I hadn't even clicked it once for educational purposes.

So, I turned and walked to my house. Chet and I were synchronized, both of us walking up our front steps at the same time. Once I reached the porch, I looked over at him on his porch. His expression shifted, like he wanted to say something but couldn't find the starting word. I waited. He gave me a polite nod, shifted his groceries to one arm, and opened his door. He didn't look back.

I let myself into my house, and finally released the breath I'd been holding. Why did I suddenly feel like crying? I felt like I'd lost something, but how could that be? You can't lose something you never had.

Use the spell of time, I told myself. Tough as I acted on the surface, I had been hurt by Chet's romantic rejection.

Perhaps it was for the best that we'd fizzled before we'd ever caught on fire. It was better than dating, breaking up, and continuing to live next to each other. We wouldn't be plagued by memories of intimate activities as we went about normal neighborly business. We could discuss what kind of wood to use for mending our shared fence without blushing over past conversations about what sort of wood made for the best spanking paddles—not that I'd fantasized about playing wild bedroom games with Chet.

Not much, anyway.

I'd definitely had some daydreams. I'm not made of stone. When he'd shifted into a wolf to save me from the bird monster, he'd achieved mythical status in my heart. There would have to be something wrong with a woman if she didn't have fantasies about a guy like that.

But, like the blackness from the bookwyrm dough, surely the feelings I had for my hot neighbor would eventually fade.

* * *

I found Zoey at the kitchen island, doing her homework. I was using a tissue to wipe the layers of makeup off my lips when I walked in.

She took one look at my mouth and said, "That's not your shade, Mom."

I told her all about my taste-test mishap with the bookwyrm dough. She enjoyed a good laugh at my expense.

"This could have just as easily happened to you," I said defensively.

She squinted and wiped a tear from one eye. "Keep telling yourself that, if it makes you feel any better."

"Zoey, I've seen you put plenty of questionable things into your mouth. The first time I took you to a beach, you tried to eat the dead crabs that were washed up on shore."

"You can't say I'm not a cheap date." She leaned in and took a good look at my mouth, pulling my chin down as though giving me a dental exam. "What did the bookwyrm dough taste like?"

"You know what? I have no idea. Maybe I should taste it again."

We stared at each other before bursting into laughter.

"It will have to stay a mystery," I said. "The magic really took me by surprise. I got a horrible jolt of pain, then I kept sneezing. I'm still a bit dizzy." My tummy rumbled. "But hungry."

"Me, too."

I got rid of the sticky tape, and started hunting around the fridge for dinner. "If you cut the mold off the cheese, it's still safe to eat, right?" I pulled out a chunk of something and took a closer look. "Never mind. That's not even cheese."

"No offense to your kitchen skills, but I think we should do a seance to bring back the ghost of Winona Vander Zalm. Just for a few dinners."

"You must be possessed," I said, narrowing my eyes at her. "My daughter *loves* my creative use of leftovers and condiments."

"Oh, does she? Let's see what you can do."

"Game on." I pulled out several containers of leftovers, and assembled the items that weren't yet fuzzy. I topped it with mango chutney, and tossed the resulting pile of food into the microwave.

"Use the thingie," Zoey said.

"The thingie? Could you be even less specific?"

"The plastic lid thingie. Auntie Z will get mad if you explode the food all over the inside of the microwave. She says we shouldn't microwave so much in the first place, but the least we could do is cover the food so it doesn't look like a burrito crime scene inside there."

With a weary groan, I stopped the microwave, delaying our dinner by at least twenty precious seconds. I started it back up once I'd covered my food with the dome-shaped plastic lid Zinnia had gifted us with the previous week.

With my best redneck voice, I said, "That gosh-darned lady's tryin' to make us all fancy."

"Speaking of fancy, I was thinking about your ghost situation. We should be on the lookout for wealthy ghosts. Their families might give us a reward for passing along messages." She did a double eyebrow lift and grinned devilishly. "This could be our lucky break."

"Since when does my daughter scheme, let alone scheme about extorting the wealthy?"

She didn't even bat an eyelash. "Every witch needs a specialty. Mine must be scheming." She closed her textbooks and pushed them aside to make room for dinner. "Can you really call it extortion if you're providing a valuable service to people in need?"

"My daughter the extortionist. And to think, when you were six, you wanted to be a ballerina."

"I did want to be a ballerina, but then my hopes were dashed when Suzy Wiseacres told me I had the wrong kind of toes, and I'd never be stable *en pointe*, and I'd never get to be a real ballerina because I wasn't born having what it takes." She'd been smiling, but now her face went slack. She was thinking about another disappointment, another ability she didn't have.

"Stupid Suzy Wiseacres," she said bitterly.

"Being a ballerina isn't everything," I said. "They don't get to eat yummy takeout for dinner. No carbs whatsoever. You know, I saw a flock of them once.

Eating. If you could call it eating. I've never seen anything so sad. Did you know that ballerinas gather in a circle and peck at birdseed?"

"Right," Zoey said slowly. "I've heard about that. And they take baths in puddles after the rain."

"That's right. Ballerinas only get puddle baths and bird seed, so I don't know why anyone would want to be one. Plus, after their final performance of Swan Lake for the season, they have to fly south for the winter. Not everyone survives the arduous journey. Several of them are shot by hunters and served at Thanksgiving."

"I think you might be making some of this up."

The microwave beeped. I took out the plate, whipped off the protective plastic lid, and split the serving onto two plates with a magical flourish. She applauded my showmanship.

We both ate right there at the kitchen island, next to piles of homework and mail.

I'd imagined dinner being exactly like this, months earlier when I'd first toured the house.

As our bellies filled with warm food, I forgot about the blackness inside my mouth and simply enjoyed the moment.

What if this is as good as it gets?

That would be fine by me because this was really good. I just had to be careful and not screw it up. Whatever Zinnia told me to do or not do, I'd obey her. Mostly.

CHAPTER 14

AFTER DINNER, ZOEY opened her textbooks again.

"More homework?"

"I'm finished with my assignments, but I just want to double-check everything," she said.

"How about, instead, we go for a walk? There's supposed to be a shortcut around here that takes you straight to a hidden part of the beach."

She looked pointedly at my mouth. "I can't be seen with you in that condition."

"Is it still bad?" I stuck out my tongue and tried to see it by looking straight down. Either my tongue was too short or my cheeks were too round. "Why can't I see my tongue? Don't tell me it's invisible."

"I wish it were invisible. It looks rotten."

"Can you see your tongue? Does your face work any better than mine? I might be defective."

Zoey stuck out her tongue. "You're not defective. It's hard to see the tip of your own tongue."

I stuck my tongue out harder. "Now I really want to see it." I tried again. "I think I see it. Yup. Still brown."

"Ow." She rubbed her cheek. "Tongues aren't meant to stretch that far."

"Maybe there's a spell that can give us snake tongues."

Her eyes widened. "Auntie Z said making physical changes to your body is extremely dangerous."

"I was kidding. I wouldn't want a snake tongue, anyway." At the mention of snakes, I remembered the blonde with the lively hair, and what I'd learned from Chet. "Hey, Zoey, what do you think of gorgons?"

She crossed her arms over her chest. "Blech. I try not to think of gorgons, well, ever. If I see one in a movie, even just a flash, it gives me nightmares for weeks. I don't even like the look of celery root, the way the little snaky bits twist around each other. All writhing around and being... snaky." She shuddered. "Why?"

Because gorgons are real, and one of them lives in our town.

"No reason," I lied. "Just makin' conversation."

She returned her attention to her book.

"Anything good in there?" I asked.

"Are you really so bored that you want to hear about my homework?"

"I'll find something else to do." I got up and checked my smile in the reflection of our brand new, store bought toaster. My teeth had lightened, but only to a rotten brown. My mouth looked human, but the overall effect would still frighten children. I'd have to stay in for the night. What could I do?

"You could work on your special project," Zoey said without looking up from her book.

"Special project?"

"Finish what you started last night."

"Aunt Zinnia wouldn't want me doing anything creative with the bookwyrm dough."

"I mean the special project you started at home last night."

Special project? It had a familiar ring, but I had no recollection of anything specific. We'd come home from Zinnia's around nine o'clock, and then what? Nine was too early for bed. I must have done something.

"*This* special project." Zoey pushed a stack of papers across the kitchen island toward me. "Last night, you swore you'd never let the electric company or anyone else cut us off. You said you were going to organize all the bills and payments into one streamlined system."

"I did?"

Zoey stared at me, her hazel eyes widening. "That wasn't you, was it?"

"What did I say, exactly?"

"You were babbling about all sorts of stuff, like you usually do." She put her chin on her palm and stared at me. "I should have known something was off. You never get that excited about opening the mail."

"I might have been a teensy weensy bit possessed."

"I don't understand. You said Winona Vander Zalm had moved on. Why is she back? And since when does she care about our bills?"

"Here's the thing. There's sort of a new guy in town. Well, a new ghost."

"For how long? When did this happen?"

"Monday, when I was at the library."

"And you're only telling me about it now?"

"I told Aunt Zinnia. It's not a secret. I just didn't want to worry you."

"Mom, you let some guy possess you? He was just here, in the house, talking to me, and I didn't even notice?" She crossed her arms over her chest. "I feel..." She couldn't finish the sentence.

"You and me, both. Think about how I feel. I was possessed last night, and I didn't even notice."

"That would suck."

"It does suck."

She looked at the stack of papers. "On the other hand, he was being helpful."

"By poking into our private business?"

"You did say those bills could use some adult supervision."

I looked at the opened mail. "I did say that."

"You could start working on the bills now, and we can see if he comes back to help."

"Wow. You got over your feelings quickly."

She reached into the stack of papers and plucked out a green envelope. "When a company sends you something in a bright green envelope, that's not good, is it?"

"It could be a very late birthday card for you. From the phone company."

"They wouldn't stamp Final Notice on a very late birthday card."

"Point taken." I cleared away the rest of our dinner dishes, wiped the counter, and took a seat at the kitchen island. I couldn't go out with my monster mouth, so I would make the most of my time at home.

"You'll keep an eye on me?"

"Sure," she said. "I'll call Auntie Z if anything scary happens."

I gave her a sidelong look. "I don't get it. Seeing a CGI gorgon in a movie gives you nightmares for weeks, but you're perfectly happy to sit there while your mother invites a ghost to possess her?"

She shrugged. "He seemed decent enough last night. In fact, he invaded my personal space in the bathroom less than you do." She waved a hand. "Go for it."

"I don't know. This seems different. I'm basically inviting him in."

"Isn't that better? You're the witch. You should be in control."

"You're right. I'm the witch. I'm in control." I placed my hands on the stack of papers, palms down. "What if it doesn't work? Then we'll both feel silly."

"You could always pay that phone bill the regular way. Without being possessed by a ghost."

"Enough crazy talk." I closed my eyes. "Ommmmmm."

"You're meditating?"

I peeked at her with one eye. "You have a better idea?"

She scrunched her face. "I should go somewhere else, so I'm not staring at you. You know what they say. A watched pot never boils."

"Don't go too far. Someone needs to supervise me."

"You'll be fine." She gathered her school materials. "I might take Corvin for a walk."

"And miss all the fun?"

She backed away, leaving the kitchen. "I'll check in on you in a bit." She pointed at the mail. "Pay the phone bill. It's the green envelope."

"Ommmmmm." I closed my eyes.

I heard her walked away. She came back and paused to pat me on the shoulder. "You'll do great," she said. "I believe in you."

I wanted to tell her I believed in her, too, but my mouth went numb. She was floating away, leaving on a wave of gauzy gray water. The surrounding sounds disappeared, as though a gray velvet curtain was being drawn all around me.

"Ommmmmm." All I heard was my own voice.

I felt the dryness of the paper under my fingers, and nothing else. The rest of the world was gone. It was just me and my bills.

And the ghost, or spirit walker.

Hello?

Another *hello* returned, but it was only my own voice echoing.

Mr. Finance Wizard?

Again, the strangely distant echoes.

I no longer felt the dry papers under my hands.

I slipped away.

CHAPTER 15

WEDNESDAY MORNING, I awoke feeling refreshed and invigorated. This was especially surprising considering how early it was. I didn't even feel tempted to use magic to toss my alarm clock across the room. I sat up, switched off the noise, and looked at the sticky note affixed to the front of my LED clock's face.

Haircuts today

Zoey 7:30 a.m.

Zara 8:00 a.m.

Beach Hair Shack

1008 Seahorse Drive

I ran my hand back through my wavy locks. I knew Zoey needed a haircut. Had she booked us appointments, changed my alarm clock time, and written this note?

Since the move, we hadn't found a new salon. This Beach Hair Shack place sounded fun, but something was off. The handwriting was not Zoey's. It appeared to be my own writing. I had zero recollection of writing the sticky note, let alone phoning a salon and making the appointments.

This had to be the work of my ghost. What was Mr. Finance Wizard up to?

I asked, out loud, "Since when does spending money at a hair salon help get your financial budget figured out? Is this a spend-money-to-save-money situation?"

The ghost didn't answer. My head felt clean and tidy, like a fresher version of my usual morning head. Mr. Finance Wizard had left me in better shape than he'd found me, which wasn't too bad at all.

I brushed my teeth before poking my head into Zoey's room. She was already dressed and drawing in her sketchbook on her bed.

"You're up early," I said.

"For the hair appointments."

"You know about that? Did you write the note in my handwriting?"

"No. You told me last night."

I pointed at my chest. "I told you? Me?"

"Don't you remember?"

I shook my head. "You must have been talking to the ghost." I held up the sticky note and wiggled it. "Mr. Finance Wizard must have set this all up."

She closed her sketchbook and set it aside. "That really wasn't you last night?"

I fidgeted with my skirt. "You couldn't tell?"

"I talked to you for a while. You were answering questions." She frowned. "How is that even possible? I thought ghosts weren't able to say things they hadn't said when they were alive. Aren't they supposed to act like recordings? Short phrases at the most? You were talking in lengthy paragraphs last night."

"I don't know. Zinnia did say they're only able to replay old conversations."

"Then your ghost must have known someone named Zoey who needed a haircut."

I rubbed my chin. "Maybe Zinnia was wrong. She did tell me that I probably know more about ghosts than she does. She seemed bummed about it, too."

"I'm not gonna lie. I'm also a bit bummed out that we don't know more about these ghosts."

"But we are learning by experimenting, right? We're like a couple of ghost scientists."

"Ghost scientists," she mused. "Those are two words that do not go together."

"We're the first pair."

"I will alert the Nobel Prize Committee. Did you know there are five? One for each prize?"

"Do I look like I just fell off the apple truck? Of course I know that."

"Turnip truck," she said. "You either fell *off* the turnip truck or fell *out* of the apple tree. Get your idioms straight, Mom."

"I messed that up on purpose so you could gloat all the way to the hairdresser."

She jumped off her bed and clapped her hands. "Yippee!"

I looked down at the note affixed to my fingers. "Do you think this could be a trap? We could walk in the front door and fall down a trap door into a dungeon."

"What's wrong with that? I love dungeons."

"You are a special kind of weird."

"I am. Now let me see your tongue."

I stuck out my tongue.

"Pink again," she reported. "Now open wide and say ah."

"Ah."

She peered in. "Your teeth and gums are ninety-nine percent back to normal. You've got a little staining, but people will just think you're a coffee addict."

"They wouldn't be wrong."

A bird chirped outside. We both turned our heads and checked the time on her bedside clock.

"Time to go," we said in unison.

She laughed while I said, "We can pick up breakfast on our way to the hair place."

Zoey grabbed her book bag and hoisted it onto her shoulder. "You know of a good bakery along the way?"

"This is Wisteria," I said. "There's one on every block."

"We could go to that Gingerbread House of Baking that everyone raves about."

"Or whatever bakery we happen to come across on the way," I said.

There was no need to subject my daughter to meeting a gorgon, on top of everything else.

On our way out, I wrestled her heavy book bag away from her so I could carry it. A mother has to look out for her kid.

* * *

We arrived at the Beach Hair Shack, at 1008 Seahorse Drive, five minutes ahead of our first appointment.

As soon as we saw the place, the name of the salon made perfect sense. It was in a casual, shack-like building with a view of the beach. According to the signs on the front door, they specialized in styling hair to look "tousled by the ocean breezes and kissed by the summer sun."

Zoey breathed excitedly. "That's exactly the look I've always wanted," she said.

"Really? Bleach streaks and bedhead?"

"It's a good thing you're a librarian because nobody would go to your hair salon."

"Ouch."

I pulled open the front door. It was wood-framed screen door that opened with a loud creak. Inside, we found a small waiting area, and only two styling chairs. Nobody else was there.

Zoey whispered to me, "Are they even open?"

I called out, "Hello?"

An interior door creaked open, revealing a glimpse of a lofted bed and kitchenette. The salon space was so tiny because the back half of the building was a residence.

A woman emerged to greet us. She was tiny, barely five feet tall. She had the hair of a mermaid, waist-length and wavy, with a variety of colorful hues ranging from burnt sugar to cherry blossom and daffodil yellow. Some strands were braided and fastened with tiny barrettes that resembled swallowtail butterflies. Judging by the lines on her face, she was fifty years older than me, yet she dressed and moved as fluidly as someone in her twenties.

"Blessed morning to you both," she said with a bow.

"And a blessed morning to you," I replied. "We're the Riddles."

"I know who you are," she said serenely.

"Our first appointment is for seven-thirty. We're not too early, are we?"

"The sun never rises too early," she said.

"Right." I glanced over at Zoey. She looked amused by the eccentric woman. I raised my eyebrows meaningfully. *Do you trust this kooky woman with a pair of scissors near your head?* Zoey shrugged, which I took to mean yes.

The hairdresser was silent. Her eyes were closed, and she was pressing her small hands in front of her chest with palms together, as though in prayer. She looked like a butterfly in repose, with her form-fitting catsuit worn underneath a gauzy silk shawl dyed with teal and ocean blue shades.

I gave Zoey the look again. She shrugged a second time.

The hairdresser opened her eyes and spoke, her voice like tinkling bells. "My name is Morganna Faire, and you must be the Riddle sisters."

Sisters! I nearly cackled. "Close enough for horseshoes and hand grenades."

Zoey, always the stickler for accuracy, corrected her. "We're actually mother and daughter."

Morganna replied, "A blind man should like to see the difference." She pointed at Zoey. "Let's take Mom first."

I let my cackle out as I elbowed my daughter. "Go ahead, *Mom*. Age before beauty."

Zoey's mouth was open. She was used to having people mistake us for sisters, but this was the first time someone had mistaken her for my mother. It served her right for the growth spurt that had made her catch up to me in height.

Morganna beckoned Zoey with fluttering fingers. "Come and take a seat on my magical, mystical, twirly chair." She waved for Zoey to follow her over to one of the two hairdressing stations. The chair looked about sixty years old but freshly upholstered in vinyl the color of green sea glass.

I gave Zoey an enthusiastic shove. "Have fun, *Mom*. I'll sit over here and read magazines, if they have any suitable for teenagers such as myself."

Zoey shot me a dirty look as she walked over to the green chair. Behind her back, Morganna give me a wink to tell me she knew very well which one of us was the mother. I loved our new hairdresser already.

While Zoey and Morganna talked about hairstyles and conditioning routines, I settled on a breezy wicker lounge chair near the front door. I glanced around at my surroundings, trying to piece a story together.

Mr. Finance Wizard must have sent me there for some reason. What could it be? And who was he, anyway? Was he a spirit walker whose body was relaxing in a recliner, still very much alive? Or was he a ghost? If he was a ghost, what unfinished business did he have keeping him around?

Zinnia had told me that ghosts were like the living in some ways. They all reacted differently to change, not unlike how people react differently to retirement. Some retirees embrace leisure activities, whereas others take up leadership roles in service of the community, or get into hobbies that are just as consuming as jobs.

Time would tell what sort of ghost Mr. Finance Wizard was. The haunting seemed benign. The guy had booked me a hair appointment. Very thoughtful. But why had he sent me to this place?

I turned to look behind the seating area. The wall was paneled in old, dry-looking wood, painted a pale green. It was charmingly decorated with sea shells and framed photos that dated back a number of decades, judging by the hairstyles. I saw Morganna in several photos. In one, she was cutting a huge ribbon with oversized scissors. The photo had been taken at the opening of the Beach Hair Shack, five decades ago.

Wow. Even if Morganna Faire had been a young entrepreneur of twenty-five at the time, that made her seventy-five. Now I was even more impressed with the woman's vigor.

I scanned my way over to the handwritten signs taped to the front of the small payment counter. There were the usual notes about walk-ins being welcome, a list of the fees for various services, as well as the types of payment accepted. One sign in particular caught my eye:

Earlybird Special
Wednesdays before 9:00 a.m.
Half-price Cuts

Mystery solved. I reached for some magazines, smiling to myself.

Mr. Finance Wizard had sent us there to save money on our haircuts. According to the other signs, Morganna's regular rates were already very reasonable. Today's visit would cost only a quarter of what we used to spend in our former city. *Keep up the good work, Mr. Finance Wizard.*

With that mystery solved, I lost myself in the fashion magazines. They were a few months out-of-date, but the trends were still new to me. Having spent the last sixteen years supporting myself and my daughter while upgrading my education, I hadn't kept up with hemlines or celebrity style.

As I leafed through the magazines, I chortled to myself. Since when had people become so obsessed with having skinny calves and large buttocks? Oh, but according to the magazines, the large buttocks were only acceptable on musicians, actresses, and reality TV stars. Regular, unfamous women with curvy posteriors were still herded toward A-line skirts and bikini bottoms with fringe, to minimize their shapeliness. At least until the next magazine I picked up.

In that one, there was a feature about regular moms and housewives who were hiring professional photographers to take old-fashioned pin-up style pictures, accentuating their womanly curves. I had to smile at the cute retro images of women climbing stepladders while holding vintage watering jugs.

The static in the air shifted. The creaky screen door opened, and a petite young woman came in. She went straight to the counter. Hipster Chick. I recognized her fedora hat and her designer-label shoulder bag. Her library book was the first I'd seen with missing words. More had sprung up since then, but I had to wonder. Was she connected to the magical outbreak? Was she patient zero?

My mind was buzzing, my ears alert to the soft scuffing sounds of the Hipster Chick's shoes on the old wood floor as she swayed impatiently, waiting to get the hairdresser's attention. Morganna had both hands buried in my daughter's red locks. She glanced over at the visitor and smiled in recognition, but made no movement toward the counter.

I couldn't take my eyes off Hipster Chick. What was she up to? I suspected there were other witches living in town, but Zinnia had tight lips. Was this girl one of them? Could she do magic? I'd screwed up with the bookwyrm. She might have cast a spell that went funny.

Then again, if she were a witch, she wouldn't cast a spell to erase words and then complain about it to strangers. That wasn't logical.

She suddenly whirled to face me. She had a defiant look in her golden brown eyes. When she locked gazes with me, it seemed the wicker chair beneath me gave up, and I was suddenly sinking down, into darkness.

All the air disappeared.

CHAPTER 16

I FOUND MYSELF in darkness. It was glistening and wet, with a thousand eyes. The darkness was continuous, like a tunnel, or a mouth. It was a terrible, gaping chasm that sucked life and love and hope all the way down, down, down. I felt the sinking sensation of loss as the darkness closed around me.

I landed in a slimy place. The walls were slick enough to glisten in the thin light of some window or lamp I couldn't locate. And the walls were moving. Were they breathing? Had I been swallowed whole by some living monstrosity? No, the walls weren't moving as whole parts. Only small segments were moving, shifting around with a rhythm like that of an anthill, or a beehive.

And then, inside this dark space, I was no longer alone. I heard two people talking.

A female was saying, "Project Erasure is coming together faster than planned."

A male with a deep voice replied, "Not fast enough."

"Patience," the female cooed. "No need to rush. Look at where rushing our acquisitions has gotten me." She let out a bitter laugh. "Not to mention letting my emotions lead me right into a trap. I'm such an idiot."

The male didn't argue or offer reassurance. The female kept on laughing bitterly, crazily.

Where was I? This dark place had no smell or temperature. It was a void, containing nothing but these two disembodied voices.

I pulled back, tugging my energy away from the void. I could see a fringe of golden brown, encircling the darkness. Golden brown. And the fringe was a circular. Brown around black, in a circle? Suddenly, I knew.

The last thing I'd seen in the regular world was the brown eyes of Hipster Chick. What's that saying? The eyes are the windows to the soul.

Somehow, I was inside Hipster Chick's eyes, or just beyond them, inside her head. And she had other people inside her head. At least two people. Was this how it worked when I had a spirit inside my head?

The female voice said, "Is it cold in here? I just felt a chill. I think someone's listening."

The male replied, "You're paranoid."

Suddenly, a third voice rang out in the darkness.

"Leave me alone," she cried. It sounded like Hipster Chick. "Go away. I'm not crazy. I'm not crazy." She kept chanting it. "I'm not crazy. I'm not crazy."

The female laughed cruelly. "Keep telling yourself that, sweetheart, for all the good it will do. We're all just a little bit crazy, us females. Isn't that what the world tells us? You find something that makes you happy, and people use it against you."

The male chuckled. "If you say so."

Hipster Chick's chanting finally faded into the background.

The female said to her companion, "I can't wait to get this host erased and take full control of this fresh, young body."

"I'll be next, if it works," said the other one. "It's been years since I enjoyed the pleasures of the physical world. I've been bottled up for far too long."

"I can't wait to see you in person," the female said, practically purring.

"You'll be disappointed. Did you see the hot redhead sitting in the wicker chair? That's my type. Exactly my type."

I heard my own voice in the darkness. "Me? No way. Leave me out of this."

The male laughed. "Zara? How did you get in here?"

"Who are you?" I demanded. My voice was more shrill than theirs, and it echoed like crazy.

He kept laughing. "Oh, you'll find out soon enough. I can't believe you found me."

"I know you," I said. "You're the man I saw in the library. In the financial planning section. You're Mr. Finance Wizard."

"Who?"

"Were you in the Wisteria Public Library on Monday?"

The female interjected, "Why are you even talking to her? She's just a nosy witch who's going to get what's coming to her as soon as I get out of here."

The male chuckled. "Way to tip your hand. Now be quiet and let the grownups talk."

She made a muffled sound, like someone with a gag over their mouth.

"Zara," said the male. "I owe you an apology. I didn't realize you were so strong, or I would have shielded this place."

"That's right," I said. "I'm very powerful, and I know what you're up to."

"And what, exactly, is that?"

"Something bad."

He laughed again. "You don't know, but let me give you a hint. I wasn't in your library on Monday. Let's just say I don't get out much these days."

"If you're not my ghost, who is he? Which one of you is the spirit walker?"

He didn't answer.

"Hello?" My voice echoed in the darkness.

There was a clicking sound, and then the male voice said, "Uh-oh. Party's over. My captor is wise to my tricks."

The female said, "Don't you dare forget me here in the darkness."

"I never forget a favor. Your loyalty and dedication will be rewarded." More clicking sounds. "Everybody out of the pool!"

With a pop of brightness, I was on my way out. I saw the golden brown of Hipster Chick's irises, and then her whole face. She looked both horrified and confused.

I couldn't see my own face, but I was pretty sure my expression matched hers. Did she know I'd been inside her mind? That I knew about the other two entities inside there?

The darkness of the journey still clung to me. I tried to shrug the feeling away, but my shoulders wouldn't move. My body was locked up, frozen, still caught in the dream-like state I must have entered to journey into her mind.

Hipster Chick narrowed her eyes at me. Either she knew I'd been inside her head just now, or she really didn't like the look of me.

And someone was touching me, tapping on my leg.

CHAPTER 17

Hipster Chick gave me one last sneering look before turning her back to me.

The paralysis that had gripped my body suddenly released. The wicker chair squeaked under me as I squirmed in my seat. Sunshine was hitting my face, glaring in my eyes. After the darkness, I'd never been so happy to have sun in my eyes. I breathed in the scent of the ocean mingled with hair styling products.

Someone tapped my thigh again. I looked around. Nobody was there, not even a semitransparent person. I did, however, have a plastic container of bookwyrm dough in the pocket of my skirt. Had it been tapping me?

"Morganna," said Hipster Chick. She was tapping on the counter impatiently. "I left something here yesterday."

"Yes, you did," the hairdresser answered. "You ran out of here." She kept combing and trimming my daughter's hair.

"Sorry," Hipster Chick said. "I don't know what I was thinking. Getting bangs? I must have been crazy. Sometimes the voices in my head tell me to do things."

Morganna gave her a curious look. "Voices in your head?"

"Just an expression." She tapped the counter again. "I just need to get my phone. I left it here, didn't I? My memory has been weird lately, but I'm pretty sure I had it when I got here yesterday but not when I left."

Morganna smiled. "Do you mean that little blue thing that makes the funny noises? I thought you left that squawk box here to drive me crazy."

"That's it! My phone's in a blue case. The screen is all nasty and cracked. Dad's working on something right now, so the budget's a little tight, but things are going to work out."

"I'm surprised you weren't banging on my door before I opened," Morganna said teasingly. "Aren't you young people addicted to your little squawk boxes? Don't you get the shakes when you're separated for more than ten minutes?"

The young woman forced another laugh. "Pretty much," she said.

Morganna excused herself from trimming my daughter's hair, and floated over to the reception desk. She dug around in a drawer before handing over Hipster Chick's phone.

"Here's your squawk box," Morganna said. "Will you tell Perry I send him my best? He needs to get out of the house more. I hardly ever see him anymore."

"You know how he is when he's working on a new project."

"And has he shared with you the details of this new, secret project?"

"Oh... did I say *new* project? I meant that he's dabbling on a bunch of random things." She tucked the phone into her bag and took a few steps backward.

Morganna came out from behind the counter and took tentative steps toward the girl. "Josephine, are you sleeping well? You have dark circles under your eyes. They're darker than yesterday."

"No, they're not any darker," Hipster Chick—real name Josephine—said defensively.

"Wait here," Morganna said soothingly. "I'll give you a sea salt candle holder. It will help you sleep. You do know those voices in your head aren't real, don't you?"

"I'm fine, really," Josephine said, sounding irritated.

"You're tense." Morganna grabbed her by the wrist. "And your pulse is racing."

Josephine yanked her hand away and took a few more steps backward. She stepped on my toes, lost her balance, and fell backward, right onto my lap.

Suddenly, I felt a surprising jolt of familiarity. I knew this girl. I hadn't even known her name was Josephine until just now, yet I *knew* her. I knew she wouldn't take a bath unless her rubber ducky was there, and she wouldn't go to bed unless she had her stuffed bunny, and she wouldn't eat breakfast cereal unless it was brand-name. I knew her the way a parent would.

The girl jumped up, spewing apologies. "I'm so clumsy," she said to me.

"And forgetful," I said with surprising vehemence. My mouth moved with a mind of its own. "Little Jo, head in the clouds, leaving things behind everywhere she goes."

She gave me a startled look. And for good reason. A complete stranger had just scolded her, seemingly with knowledge of her bad habits.

But I couldn't explain myself. *Hey, Josephine, I'm a witch, and I'm possessed by a ghost right now—a ghost who apparently knows you well. Also, I was just inside your head, and I heard those two people in there, a man and a woman, scheming about stealing bodies, starting with yours. What do you think of that? That can't be good. Are you a witch, too? Should we team up and solve this mystery together?*

But I couldn't say that. I couldn't say anything.

As we stared at each other, her shock shifted to irritation. "What are you looking at, lady?" She crossed her arms and gave me an angry look. "I apologized for tripping over your feet. What more do you want?"

The look on her face triggered something in my ghost.

Mr. Finance Wizard took over for a good scolding. "Just for you to finally learn from your mistakes," he said with my mouth.

"You sound just like my father," she said. "Do you know him?"

"Your father is a sensible man," the ghost replied.

"I don't get it. Who are you, lady? Are you dating my dad?"

The ghost gave control back to me. "Yes," I said. "I mean no."

Everyone was staring at me. Morganna. Josephine. Zoey, who was still sitting in the hairdressing chair.

Was I dating Josephine's father? Yes or no? I smiled at the other three women. "It's complicated."

"How..." Josephine blinked repeatedly and swooned. She caught herself on the counter, barely, and as she caught her breath, she gave us confused looks.

"Jo?" Morganna looked concerned.

"What are we talking about?" Josephine kept blinking and forcing her eyes to open wider. "I can't remember what I'm doing. Why am I even here? I keep forgetting. My mind's being erased. Is this what it feels like to be crazy?"

Morganna handed her a bottle of water. "Drink this, Jo. You're probably dehydrated. You young people drink too much coffee."

Josephine thanked her and took a sip.

I flipped open a magazine and pretended to be reading it, minding my own business.

Josephine said to Morganna, "I'm trying to get my life together. Honestly, I really am."

"I know," the hairdresser said. "Soon everything will be different."

"I've been so forgetful lately."

Morganna spoke softly. "Forgetfulness is no sin. If anything, forgetfulness is the cure for our sorrows." Her eyes wrinkled with truth and wisdom as she smiled.

Josephine set the empty water bottle on the counter and straightened her hipster hat. "I hate to disagree with you, Morganna, but *money* is the only cure for our sorrows."

She walked toward the door, pausing to look at me. "Sorry again for... I don't know. Something."

"No problem," I said. The poor thing.

And then she was gone with whatever crazy stuff was happening inside her head.

Morganna was back with Zoey, cooing over what a lovely head of red hair she had.

Zoey caught my eye in the mirror and silently mouthed the words *what was that*?

I mouthed the word *ghost*.

My daughter nodded, looking concerned for all of three seconds, and then went back to chatting with Morganna about texturizing her hair to control the natural wave.

I sighed and looked down at the magazine on my lap.

The pages of the magazine were entirely blank. White. I flipped through the magazine. Every page was either partially or completely blank.

I rolled up the magazine and slipped it into my purse for examining later. I picked up another magazine and flipped through. It was normal. I picked up two more and riffled through. All the other magazines appeared to be intact.

I thought of the secret thing the two voices in Jo's head had been discussing before I'd spoken up and blown my cover.

The female said, "Project Erasure is coming together faster than planned."

Then the male said it wasn't fast enough.

Project Erasure.

At least I had a name. That was something. I had a lot of *somethings*.

First, I had words being erased, from library books, business cards, and magazines. At least two of those things were connected to Josephine, aka Hipster Chick. Was she my patient zero?

Second, I knew she had voices inside her head. Ones that were real enough for me to hear. A man and a woman who were plotting to erase bodies.

Third, I knew Josephine's father was working on something to get her money.

Fourth, I had a strong hunch her father was the semitransparent man I called Mr. Finance Wizard.

So, how did all these things add up? Was Mr. Wizard working on an invention that let people travel outside of their bodies? That had to be it. And then other people would steal the bodies when they were empty. Sure. That sounded... exactly like the plot of a sci-fi horror movie.

Who was the crazy one now?

It was a shame the voices in Josephine's head hadn't named their secret project something more informative. Just plain Erasure was so vague. They could have called it something more self-descriptive, such as Project Erasure of Voting Ballots, or Project Erasure of Valuable Picasso Paintings.

I wondered, if I could erase anything in the world, where would I start? The comments section under YouTube videos? Then billboards and outdoor advertising. Would it work on freckles?

My thoughts were disrupted by the hairdresser calling out, "Next!"

Morganna had finished trimming Zoey's hair and was calling me to her chair.

I walked over and climbed into the green seat.

Morganna wrapped a protective plastic cape around me. She paused as though frozen, staring down at her hand. I watched her as she walked over to the sink, washed her hands, and continued to stare at her right hand, lifting it up and down slowly, tracking it with her eyes.

I rotated my chair and looked over at Zoey. She hadn't noticed the hairdresser's strange behavior because she was using her phone to take photos of herself with new haircut. I wondered if she was taking the pictures for new friends, or her old friends Francie and Jade back in the city.

Morganna returned, still staring at her hand.

I asked, "Is everything okay? Your friend seemed upset about something."

"Little Jo will be fine," Morganna said. "She's always had a flair for the dramatic. That's how it always has been with the daughters of Amora."

"Amora? I don't know her. Does she have a big family?"

Morganna laughed. "Very big. Some say everyone's related to her, one way or another."

She combed my hair and sprayed on water to dampen it for cutting.

"This woman," I said. "Amora..."

Morganna laughed again. "It's a very old story. I will tell you another time. And I think you will find yourself in this tale, as a daughter of Mahra."

"Right."

"Shh. Let me focus. Quiet your mind, little fox."

I raised an eyebrow at her in the mirror. I understood now why Morganna's haircuts were so cheap. You have to offer a bargain if you're going to be so nutty.

As she worked, she kept glancing at the top of her right hand and letting her gaze linger.

Finally, I had to ask, "Is there something wrong with your hand?"

"Do you know how people say they'd know something like the back of their hand? I was just thinking about what an odd expression that is."

"Most idioms are a bit odd."

"I don't know the back of my hand very well at all. Once upon a time, I had a little fairy tattooed on the back of my hand, and now it's gone."

Another clue. Project Erasure strikes again!

"Has it been erased?"

"No, silly." She whipped her tiny hands up into my hair and began massaging my scalp. "It must have faded away over the years, so slowly that I never noticed."

Or maybe something blew through here and erased your tattoo. We're lucky it didn't take our minds.

Morganna Faire smiled at me in the mirror.

CHAPTER 18

"I LOVE MY new beach hair," Zoey cooed as we left the Beach Hair Shack.

"If I were to tell you that was a half-price bargain haircut, would you love it more or less?"

"Even more," she said.

"Me, too."

She looked over at me and tilted her head. "Yours looks more like bedhead. You should have let her put in more styling mud." She twirled one of her tiny braids, which Morganna had fastened with a butterfly elastic. "And a few mermaid braids."

"Bohemian doesn't suit me," I said. "My look is more classic."

"Classic what?"

I fluffed out my voluminous skirts and kicked up my laced boots. "Classic Anne of Green Gables," I said.

"You're right! How did I never see this before? You could move to Prince Edward Island and become a celebrity Anne performer. They're always in need of genuine redheads. You already have the wardrobe."

"You want to move again? We're barely unpacked."

"No," she said hesitantly. "Wisteria is great. But..." She trailed off.

"But what?"

"Nothing." She looked around, whipping her fluffy beach hair. "What street are we on?"

We stopped to read the street signs and figure out which way to turn for the high school. We resumed walking. Zoey continued to fluff her hair and whip her head to make it fly out. She didn't care that it was a half-price hairdo.

After a few minutes, she asked, "What was going on back there, anyway?" She lowered her voice. "Did you get a visit from your new ghost?"

The sun slipped behind a cloud. As my skin cooled without the sunshine, I thought of the interior of Jo's mind. Had I felt things wriggling around in that darkness? The walls had been, like the inside of a machine, but one that was alive. What did you call a living machine? A brain. *Well, duh.* If I'd been inside Hipster Chick's head, I'd been wandering around her brain, which was both alive, and a machine... of sorts.

"Mom?" Zoey sounded concerned. "What happened?"

"Nothing for you to worry about," I said lightly. "Let me deal with the odd ghost or two, and you keep on getting those stellar grades at school."

"Sure thing." She sped up, pulling away from me. She walked faster and faster.

"Hey," I called after her. "I'm not really dressed for jogging!"

She turned and walked backward, facing me. "The library's that way." She pointed to a side street. "I can make it to school on my own."

"Too embarrassed to be seen with your mother?"

"Of course not. It's just that there's no need for you to backtrack."

"I don't mind."

"Thanks for the haircut." She turned and picked up the pace, moving way faster than I wanted to move that early in the morning. "Have fun at work, and I'll see you at home!"

I waved goodbye, not that she noticed.

As she rounded the corner, I caught a glimpse of the twelve-year-old version of her, insisting she could walk the last few blocks to school on her own. She'd always been so independent. I would agree, and then follow at a distance, just to make sure she was safe.

Even now that she was sixteen, I felt the urge to follow, to keep her in my sight. As I watched after her, my heart did that mother thing and broke just a little. My baby appreciated me, but she didn't *need* me.

One day, when I was gone, how would Zoey remember me? How would she remember today? Would it be the beautiful sunny day she got beach hair at a kooky lady's wooden shack, or the day her mother wasn't a very good mother because she was busy talking to ghosts and getting sucked into other people's business?

* * *

By the time I got to work, I'd forgotten about my hair, as well as the weird stuff at Morganna's. All that stuffed paled in comparison to worrying about being good mother. Ghosts? Take a number. I was too busy trying to find work-life balance. No. Work-life-*magic* balance.

I went straight to the staff lounge and made the day's first pot of coffee.

Frank came in, took one look at me, and made a comment about the sort of activities one might engage in to rumple up one's hair.

"It's not bedhead," I said. "Or whatever else you're thinking. I went to a hairdresser, and she backcombed it for a beach-tousled look."

"Beach-tousled? More like bed-wrestled."

I snorted. "People with one-track minds see what they want to see."

Frank poured a coffee and squinted at me with one eye. He had a tough time keeping both eyes open before his first cup of coffee. "Why would you get a haircut this early, anyway?"

"Early bird special. I got a great deal."

"Great deal or not, you'd never catch me up that early. My beauty sleep is worth more than money."

I gave him a half shrug. "Not everyone can afford to be as beautiful as you, Frank Wonder."

He struck a Southern Belle pose.

He fixed up his coffee the way he liked it. "Who gave you that bedhead? I mean beach-tousled locks?"

"A woman named Morganna Faire. She's got a half-price Wednesday morning special."

"Morganna Faire? But her rates are already so reasonable."

"You know her?"

"Everyone knows Morganna. She's been around here forever. She might even be older than Winona Vander Zalm was. They used to go out together sometimes."

"They were friends?"

"I don't know what they were, but they gave me the heebie jeebies whenever I saw them together. Maybe it was ageism or sexism or both. Maybe I should wash my mouth out with soap immediately, but they always looked to me like a pair of witches in search of a third witch, so they could form a triad, and stir up some cauldrons together."

"Frank, I don't know if that's ageism, but it's not very nice."

He hung his head. "I'll go wash my mouth out with soap."

"No need, sir. I'm letting you off with a warning." I gave him a serious look. "This time."

We finished our coffee then punched in our time cards with two loud KERCHUNKS. It was strange that a quiet place like a library had such a loud time card system, but I did enjoy how satisfying it felt to punch in or out. The loud KERCHUNK stirred up the pride I felt in my job. I always stood taller when I was "on the clock."

We unlocked the front door, went through the day's opening procedures, and got to work.

A while later, I started researching something for myself. I didn't like doing personal research while I was working, but it would have roused more suspicion if I'd used the computer terminals on my coffee break.

I had to know more about the young woman I'd seen at the hairdresser's. She was connected not just to a library book with disappearing words, but also a blanked magazine, and now a missing tattoo. Plus she was my only solid lead on Mr. Finance Wizard.

According to our computer, we had three copies of the rock-star memoir. One had been checked out and returned by someone named Josephine Pressman. Our system didn't have anything as high-tech as photos associated with patron accounts but it had to be her.

I glanced over my shoulder to make sure nobody was around to witness what I was about to do.

As a professional librarian, I take confidentiality very seriously. No person wants their internet search history to be public knowledge. The same is true of their reading history. People will borrow books they wouldn't be caught dead with on their shelves at home. While I might find it amusing to know that a certain patron has paid for two copies of *Fifty Shades of You-Know-What* due to dropping both books into her bathtub, that's for me (and Frank) to giggle over, and not for the general public.

On a more serious note, there are instances where checkout history needs to stay secret and the stakes are higher than social embarrassment. For example, just that morning, I helped an unwed young lady with a newborn baby in her arms find some books about paternity testing and parental rights. An hour later, I helped a worried-looking fifty-something man check out several relationship books, including, coincidentally enough, one titled *Rebuilding Your Marriage After an Affair*. He kept twisting his wedding band nervously while I processed his stack of books.

"They really have a book for everything," he'd said, and I agreed.

"This is for a friend," he insisted, and again, I agreed. As he left, I wished him a good day and the best of luck. "I'll probably be back for some of your divorce books," he said heavily. I assured him I would help as much as I could, should it come to that. My promise seemed to lift his chin a few degrees.

And isn't this exactly what most of us want from our careers? Not just a paycheck, but the opportunity to lift someone's chin a few degrees.

But I digress.

Back to my amateur sleuthing.

Not only did I locate Josephine Pressman in our database, but there was another Pressman named Perry. He resided at the same address as Josephine. The account history went back a good forty years. He was the father. According to our records, Perry Pressman's book history included a vast number of titles about stock trading and personal finance. He had to be the ghost, or spirit walker, I'd been calling Mr. Finance Wizard.

I jotted down his address. The pen was slippery in my hand. I was sweating.

I did an internet search on Perry Pressman. After some cross-referencing to narrow the results, I found the guy.

Perry Pressman, a long-time resident of Wisteria, was the founder and editor of the Penny Pincher Gazette, a local classified advertisement circular and coupon guide.

Penny Pincher? That must have been what the semitransparent man meant when he'd pinched his fingers together during our mimed conversation. He'd been pinching imaginary pennies.

The Penny Pincher Gazette shut down two years ago due to "changing technologies in the coupon industry." In other words, the internet. There was a photo accompanying the article. A jolt of recognition shot through me. This was the man I'd seen on Monday. I'd already felt certain I'd found my guy, but seeing the photo cranked it up a level.

In the photo, he wore a plaid, button-up shirt, faded from repeated washing but crisply ironed. He had narrow shoulders and a rectangular face, angular with loose neck folds. His gray hair tufted up over one ear, as though he'd cut it himself and missed a spot. Given his love of pinching pennies, he probably did cut his own hair.

Was he dead? There was no obituary. And Morganna had asked Josephine about him.

He had to be the spirit walker Chet was looking for.

Unless... he had died elsewhere and his family didn't know yet. The young woman did have other things on her mind. And inside her mind. She might not have noticed her father was missing. What if that was the thing she was worried about forgetting?

Loose puzzle pieces clicked together, and my mind created a story to explain everything.

Sometimes a traumatic event can cause memory loss. What if Perry had died, and only Josephine knew? What if his body was lying somewhere, decaying, and his daughter was wandering around town being forgetful and hearing voices in her head? She might have been trying to erase her own memories.

I looked down at the scrap of paper with the Pressman address. I had half a mind to toss it into the garbage and forget about the matter. The man's daughter would eventually figure things out. And if the voices in her head were of her own creation, she needed the kind of help that didn't come from a witch.

Then again, what if a witch was exactly what she needed? Perry had come to me for a reason.

No. He'd come to the *library* for a reason. Perhaps he'd just happened to bump into me.

Ugh. I didn't know. Thinking about it wasn't getting me anywhere.

I grabbed my phone and called Chet's number.

CHAPTER 19

I WALKED INTO Dreamland Coffee and looked around for Chet. I'd phoned him from the library to talk about his spirit walker case, but he'd refused to discuss it over the phone. We arranged to meet at a coffee shop on the outskirts of town. I'd taken a taxi to get there on time, and ended up early. He wasn't there yet.

The coffee shop was quiet, with a big crowd of seniors clearing out just as I arrived. I chatted with the owner, a woman named Maisy, while she steamed a latte for me. Then I took my mug over to a quiet corner and waited for Chet to arrive.

The front door opened. An older woman with very long, gray hair walked in. She paused to give some verbal commands to her companions, two very large dogs, who sat obediently outside the door. She walked up to the front counter and ordered a mint mocha, and a smoked-meat sandwich.

I couldn't stop staring at her, especially her hair. It fell down below her waist, and seemed far too gray for her age. She turned her head and met my gaze. She jerked her head slightly, as though jolted by recognition. Did she know me? I didn't know her. She looked away quickly.

The door opened again, and Chet walked in.

The gray-haired woman turned to him, smiling. "Moore," she said gruffly. "I hope Jasper and Coco didn't give you a hard time."

"Those little puppies? Not at all."

"How are you? I almost hate to ask, but how's your father? I haven't seen him around much."

Chet glanced over at me, nodded, then looked at the woman again. "Don is about as well as can be expected. He has his good days and his bad days. Sometimes I feel like I'm raising two kids."

"They call it the Sandwich Generation," she said. "Looking after aging parents plus children. I feel for you, I really do."

His shoulders lifted up in a shrug and didn't come down. "Life doesn't always work out as planned."

"Right. About, uh... has there been any change?"

"No change."

"Such a shame." She made several tsk-tsk sounds. "Such a shame," she repeated.

Chet cleared his throat and looked past her, at the food waiting on the counter. "I'll let you get to your meal," he said gruffly. "Good to see you again."

The woman took her plate and mug, gave me a quick glance, and went outside to sit at a sidewalk table. Her two enormous dogs begged for scraps. She lovingly fed them bits of meat from her sandwich.

Chet joined me at my table. He had a mug of black coffee.

"What's the plan?" I asked. "Are we here to spy on that lady? Who is she?"

"Zara, you're the one who called me. You said you might have seen the person I'm looking for?"

I kept staring through the window at the gray-haired woman sitting outside. She looked so familiar. Her angular face and her narrow nose reminded me of someone.

Chet waved a hand in front of my face. "Never mind about her."

"Is that lady a witch? A shifter? She looked at me like she knew who I was. Did you tell her about me?"

He sighed. "I believe she's friends with your aunt," he said. "She probably recognized the family likeness."

"Great," I said. "Anyone who knows my aunt and what she is just has to take one look at me and they know all my secrets, too. What's the use in me trying to be careful? I might as well buy a pointy hat and start carrying a broom."

He looked at me over his coffee mug as he lifted it to his lips. "Tough day?"

"I've been struggling with work-life-magic balance."

"Did something happen with Zoey?"

"She didn't want me to walk her all the way to school."

"Ouch."

"My baby doesn't need me."

"Is that all?"

"You'll see, Chet. You'll see when Corvin doesn't need you anymore. You'll see..." I trailed off, remembering that our situations were not exactly the same. He had a parent who also needed his care. I was being rude.

"Never mind my grumbling," I said with a quick smile. "A cup of coffee is all I need." I lifted my cup and bumped it against his mug. "Cheers."

Amusement flickered in his green eyes. "Cheers."

We sipped our drinks, then I set up the sound bubble spell to be sure we had our privacy. The interior of the coffee shop was empty, and the owner had disappeared into the back room, but it was good practice to not get comfortable blabbing about magic and ghosts without protection.

I told Chet about everything that had happened recently. There had been the disappearing ink on Saturday, the appearance of Perry Pressman at the library on Monday and my subsequent possession, then the strange encounter with his daughter, Josephine, at the hairdresser's.

Chet stopped me. "You went in through her eyes, into her mind? And you heard two other people in there, talking about a machine?"

"They didn't say it was a machine. The female called it Project Erasure."

"What did she sound like? Young? Old? Weak? Strong?"

I had to think about it. "Old? I'm not sure. The way she mocked Josephine, it wasn't the way another woman of the same age would. I'd say she was at least a generation older than the host."

Chet's eyebrows raised. He gave me an appreciative look. "That's very good deductive reasoning," he said. "You'd make a fine agent, Riddle."

"You think?"

He gazed into my eyes. "We would make a great team. You and I."

"Hunting down ghosts and monsters?"

"Someone's gotta do it."

I chortled. "Like I need another job."

"You wouldn't like it, anyway." He slouched and looked down at his coffee. "It's a tough line of work."

"Cheer up. At least I found your spirit walker."

He slouched even more. "No. You haven't."

"Perry Pressman isn't your guy?"

"Not even close."

"So, he's not a spirit walker? He's not doing astral projection, roaming around as a disembodied spirit while his body's safe and sound at home in a recliner?"

"It sounds to me like he's just a standard ghost."

"Just a standard ghost. Huh. I don't know why I feel so disappointed. He's only the second ghost I've met so far. Is it normal to get jaded so quickly once you know magic's real?"

"I wouldn't know," Chet said.

"You've always known about magic? Ever since you were young?"

He nodded. "I don't know what it's like to not know. You're lucky that you get to experience the world both ways."

"Lucky me." I took another sip of my latte. The coffee at Dreamland was good. "Now, what do you suppose I should do about my standard ghost? My aunt says they stick around for a reason. He's probably been murdered or something awful like that. Sometime after Saturday, when he was on the phone with his daughter, assuming she hadn't hallucinated the phone call."

"Did you hear the phone ring, or buzz?"

I closed my eyes and thought back. "I'm pretty sure there was an incoming call. I remember the screen was cracked." I opened my eyes. "Sorry I'm not a better eyewitness."

"You're doing fine. When I get back to the office, I'll start up a case file and get someone to pop by his house to check for signs of a body. You may be right about his daughter being in denial."

"Do you think she killed him? She was talking about money. She might have been eager to get her hands on her inheritance, or maybe a life insurance policy. That's always a good motive. Remember, that's why I thought you might have killed your neighbor."

He frowned. "You did?"

"Just for a minute. Barely. Anyone with half a brain would have at least considered the possibility."

He stared into his black coffee. "Things are not always as they seem. Pressman might have died of natural causes. He could be decomposing in a room of the house where his daughter doesn't usually go. She might be, as you guessed, in complete denial. There's a type of shock people go into when they can't let go." He flicked his eyes up to meet mine. "And can you blame them? It's hard to let go."

"It can be hard to let go."

He kept staring into his black coffee like it was a place he wanted to go.

"What's going on, Chet?"

"What do you mean?"

"You seem even more tense and uncomfortable than usual."

He made a face. "What do you mean, *than usual*? I'm always easygoing. I'm laid-back."

I burst out laughing. He didn't. I stopped and stared at him.

"Oh, you're not kidding," I said. "You actually believe you're laid-back."

"Considering all the responsibilities I have, I'm Mr. Chill."

I stifled more laughter. "Mr. Chill. Yes, I see it now."

He pulled back in his chair, shaking his head. "I shouldn't have gotten you involved in any of this."

"Too late. I'm here, and you're stuck with me. What's the deal with the disappearing ink? If Perry's dead, and he's the one doing that, does it have something to do with his name?"

Chet looked down at the table and frowned.

"Perry Pressman," I said. "Pressman is the title of the person who runs a printing press. And those printing presses use ink. It's kind of poetic, in a way. Do you think ghosts are always so metaphorical?"

Chet flicked some stray crumbs off our table.

"You're not listening," I said. "You don't have any interest whatsoever in my ghost or the disappearing ink."

"I'll start a case," he muttered. "I'll get someone to look into it."

"What about the two people I heard talking inside the daughter's head? Is one of them your spirit walker?"

"Those voices weren't real. The girl's probably crazy. Forget about what you thought you heard, and don't go digging around inside people's heads. You won't like what you find."

I waved my hand in front of his face. "Is that why you're staring at those crumbs like they're a Van Gogh? Are you afraid to make eye contact with me? Do you think I'll crawl in through your beautiful green eyes and start digging around?"

He jerked his chin up and met my eyes with a fiery vengeance. He was daring me to climb through his open windows, straight into him.

And me, being the headstrong witch I am, I tried. I really tried.

Okay, Mr. Chill, what are you hiding?

I saw eyes. Nothing else. I remembered something I forgot to do at work. I wondered what Zinnia was doing. I thought about what I might eat for dinner. Then I remembered a couple more things I forgot to do at work.

My phone buzzed.

I was thankful to end our staring contest to check my phone.

Aunt Zinnia: *I have that information you wanted.*

Did she mean the information about being Spirit Charmed? She was always careful to not use words such as *spells* or *magic* in her messages.

I texted back: *Could you be even more cloak and dagger?*

She wrote back: *What? Who said anything about daggers? Just come to my house when you can.*

I replied that I would see her shortly.

Chet was watching me with interest. "Who was that?"

"The pope."

He shook his head. "Are all witches so sarcastic?"

"Just the fun ones."

CHAPTER 20

Zinnia greeted me at her front door. She wore a voluminous green skirt, paired with a cream blouse and a fitted vest in a tapestry-like fabric decorated with purple blossoms.

"No skort today," I said.

"It's been washed, if you'd like to borrow it."

I pointed to her vest. "Where did you get this? The fabric looks so familiar."

"I sewed it myself."

"Did you shoot a chesterfield and skin its hide for raw materials?"

She sniffed and led me through the house.

I got a closer at the back of her vest. "What are these purple flowers? Thistles? Why do I know this fabric?"

She turned to face me. "Because it's the same fabric I also used to upholster my ottoman."

"I knew it," I exclaimed. "That ottoman made quite an impression on me last time I was here. Literally. I fell asleep for a minute, and when I woke up, there was an imprint of the thistles on my cheek."

She unbuttoned the vest and tossed it on top of the ottoman. "Happy now?"

With a flick of my wrist, I commanded the vest to flap up into the air like a moth. It circled the room three times before settling back down on the ottoman, aligning the print patterns perfectly so that it disappeared against the furniture, like a mottled insect resting in its natural habitat.

Zinnia said only, "Your fine motor control is improving."

"And your outfit is actually cute, minus the vest. You have a great figure. You should show it off more. Maybe a certain Detective Bentley would take notice."

"The last thing the Riddle family needs is a cop sniffing around."

"Even if he is handsome, and capable, with steely gray eyes that peer deeply into your soul?"

"His eyes are rather steely," she agreed.

"When was the last time you went on a date?"

"I should ask the same of you."

"Hah! The answer is five minutes ago. I had coffee with an eligible bachelor."

"Chet Moore dropped you off here. Was it him? Are you two back on again?"

"Again? We were never *on* in the first place. But we did have a pretty intense staring contest over coffee just now. I tried to enter his mind through his eyes, using them as windows."

She gasped. "Tell me you didn't. That's an extremely advanced spell."

"Don't worry. Nothing happened. Not with Chet, anyway."

"You entered someone else?"

"Not on purpose. Earlier today, I was innocently waiting to get a haircut when I might have taken a wrong turn and ended up in somebody else's head. It gave me a taste of what it must feel like to be a ghost, actually."

Her eyes widened, and she seemed to struggle for words before finally saying, "Floopy doop."

I bit my tongue to keep from laughing. *Floopy doop*? I couldn't wait to tell Zoey that one.

"You'll tell me everything," she said. "But first, let me take care of what I was doing before you arrived."

"Can I watch?"

"Even better. You can help."

My aunt led me into her kitchen

"Holy sweatpants!" I looked around, gawking. "What's with the horticulture emporium? Where did your kitchen go, Aunt Zinnia?"

Her kitchen looked like a cross between a florist, and an apothecary shop, and a museum of weird artifacts. There were bundles of herbs hanging from strings criss-crossing the kitchen, and plants of various colors everywhere. Her oven was on, and something was audibly crackling inside. The air smelled like a blend of spicy curry, hot apple cider, and those pine-tree shaped car air fresheners.

My aunt smiled as she set a row of empty glass jars on the counter. "My supplier was clearing out some greenhouses to make room for a new crop," she said. "And I figured, why not? It doesn't hurt to stock up."

"Is any of this edible?"

"That depends." She narrowed her eyes at me. "Zara, have you been eating things you're not supposed to?"

I held up my hand. "I haven't even touched the bookwyrm dough today, much less tasted it. I swear."

"Good."

I reached into my bag and pulled out the takeout I'd picked up on the way over. Chet had recommended a place that had a half-price Wednesday special. Mr. Finance Wizard would have been proud of our penny pinching.

"I picked us up some sushi," I said. "Are there any safe zones where I can put this?" All around us, every flat surface contained some kind of plant, bowl, or measuring apparatus.

Zinnia cleared a space on the counter, moving a stone mortar and pestle.

"You can set it there, but keep the lids on until we eat, for safety." She used her hands to crumble some large, sparkly leaves into a clean jar.

"Are all of these things for casting spells?"

She tucked a strand of red hair behind her ear. "Some of it's for cooking," she said.

I poked at a dangling bundle that looked like black barbed wire sprouting red berries. The bundle twisted, recoiling from my touch. I jerked my hand back.

"That one's not for cooking," she said.

"I should hope not. It looks like it would cause indigestion."

She chuckled. "Indigestion would be the least of your worries."

"Oh?" I reached out to poke it again. The red berries looked so plump and delicious.

"Don't," she barked. "Don't touch anything."

I put my hands behind my back and used only my eyes to examine the twisting tendrils. "Are these tentacles?"

"I'm not entirely sure what they are, exactly, but I'll find a good use for them some day."

"You make up your own spells?"

Her hazel eyes twinkled with amusement, revealing a lighter side I rarely saw. "Oh, I dabble a bit, with this and that."

"Is that your specialty? Something to do with herbs?"

"Yes. I'm Kitchen Bewitched."

I blinked in surprise. I hadn't expected a straight answer, much less one so corny sounding. Kitchen Bewitched? Spirit Charmed? Who thought up these things?

"Good to know," I said with a straight face.

"Some specialties run in families," she said. "Zoey doesn't strike me as the Kitchen Bewitched type. I asked her to help me prepare some crudités. She used a pair of scissors instead of a knife, and she cut the vegetables into the most awkward shapes."

"Awkward crudités," I said. "That's our Zoey."

"She is a very quick learner, though. As soon as those powers kick in, she'll have us both on our toes."

"I hope so."

I was distracted by the black barbed-wire with the red berries. The bundle hanging over me undulated in a suggestive, come hither manner. What was that scent? Licorice? I stood on my toes and leaned in to take a sniff.

Suddenly, the tendrils yanked back, formed a hand shape, and slapped me across the cheek.

I gasped, "Why you little—"

Zinnia barked, "Don't!"

I rubbed my cheek. "But I didn't do anything."

"You didn't?"

"That thing was asking me to get closer. I just wanted to smell it."

"Do not sniff the ingredients," Zinnia said. "Do not touch, poke, or otherwise agitate the ingredients. Magic has a mind of its own, and magical items are not to be taunted."

"I wasn't taunting anything."

"Just being human is a way of taunting something that is not."

"Oh."

"Those are Black Startwists. They can be very good listeners, but they are excitable."

"Sounds like a few people I know."

She continued putting dried sparkly bits into jars. "Let me see your cheek."

I dropped my hand away. "Is it bad?"

"The venom will wear off in a few minutes. Try not to get slapped again."

"I'll try not to... taunt the magical ingredients."

"Here, keep yourself out of trouble by reading the information I got for you." She nodded toward the refrigerator door, where a magnet was pulling away from a loose sheet of paper. Zinnia used her magic to float the paper over to me.

The top of the page read:

Top Five FAQs About Being Spyryt Chyrmed

I looked up at Zinnia. "Spyryt Chyrmed? With three Y's?"

She didn't take her eyes off her ingredients. Now she had a row of ant-like creatures marching around the counter in a figure eight formation.

"Never mind the Y's," she said. "The person who put that up was either taking artistic license or misspelling the term on purpose to keep it from search engine results. Or just being weird for the sake of being weird. Some people are like that."

"Some of my favorite people are like that."

"Yes, well, it takes all types to make the world go 'round."

I looked over the sheet of paper. It was a standard-sized photocopy of a page that had originally been printed on an old dot-matrix printer. At the very bottom was a footer listing the address of the website. I couldn't believe what I was seeing, and I'd just been slapped across the cheek by tentacle herbs.

"Aunt Zinnia, you got a list of witchcraft FAQs off a Geocities website?" I shook the page. "Are you kidding me? Geocities?"

"The information isn't online anymore, of course. It's all been scrubbed. But back in the mid-nineties, a few things got up and circulated. It was actually a wonderful time for us. A golden age of witchcraft. But it couldn't last. We had to lock down the information before it fell into the wrong hands."

"Ah, to be a witch in the mid-nineties. Ah, to have a Geocities address."

"What do you know about Geocities?"

"I know that when Yahoo bought it out, Geocities was the third-most visited website on the World Wide Web."

Zinnia gave me a surprised, pleased smile. "You must be a wonderful librarian. Wisteria is very lucky to have you."

I beamed. First Chet, and now my aunt. I was getting a lot of compliments today, and not just about my hair.

Zinnia asked, "Didn't you do something interesting on the internet at one point? Something in entertainment?"

"I dabbled a bit, in this and that." Today was not the day to explain to my aunt what a camgirl was. Most people associated the term with stripping, but it was different during those early days. It was a more innocent time, when webcams were more about community than nudity. Ah, the late nineties and early two-thousands. When the internet was still trying to figure out what it was for.

My aunt seemed focused on her marching herb parade. She waved to dismiss me. "Go ahead and read in the living room. I'll be done shortly."

I took the takeout sushi and waved goodbye to the Black Startwists from a distance.

In case you're dying to know about the FAQs for Being "Spyryt Chyrmed," it's included below. I've resisted the urge to change the Y's to their proper letters. I've also left the Unnecessary Capitalization of Terms intact. *You're wylcyme.*

Top Five FAQs About Being Spyryt Chyrmed

1. Who are these Spyryts that some Wytches attract?

For now, we will only concern ourselves with the Spyryts of humans. These entities of pure energy come from the deceased (usually but not always). They may be recent or ancient. The age of the city you live in will affect the vintage of your Spyryts, since they usually stay within a twenty mile radius of where they died. Most people, when they die, move on to the next plane of existence without lingering. It seems that only those who had some connection to Magyck stick around. Kinda makes you go hmmm about your own future, doesn't it?

2. What do they want?

What do we all want? To live a little more! Some Spyryts wish to share their wisdom, spend more time with family and friends, or to see and do things they enjoyed when they were alive. Occasionally, you will encounter an entity seeking justice or vengeance. You must NOT, I repeat, you MUST NOT get involved in these errands, as they will be very annoying, not to mention dangerous. The police will not be sympathetic if you are caught breaking and entering into homes. Claiming that a "ghost made you do it" will only get you a stay in the loony bin. Trust me on this one.

3. When will they move on?

When they are good and ready. Some spells can speed up the process. Please consult your Elders before attempting any direct communications with the Spyryts. You don't want to accidentally conjure a portal to a Demon Dymensyon and release Hell on Earth! Nobody likes a Wytch who gets into trouble she can't handle or sets off the Apocalypse.

4. Where do they go in between their Communions with the Chyrmed?

My theory is long naps. Stay with me for a minute while I explain. These Spyryts, like some of our respected Elders, experience memory loss and confusion. Without the concrete structure of their bodies, even time loses its linear nature. While their knowledge seems to stay intact, their short-term memory is as slippery as a handful of tadpoles.

5. How do I make money off being Spyryt Chyrmed?

There are many ways a modern Wytch can earn a living from her powers, without being burned at the stake! Please email Beatrizz Riddle today (click here!) for more details. It's not Amway.

Love and Light,

Bea.

Click here for a list of my favorite World Wide Web links. Happy surfing!

"I wish I could click your favorite links, Bea," I said to the paper. "But I'm a few years late to the party."

Zinnia came into the room, applying a bandage to one finger. "Did you say something, Zara?"

"Just talking to Bea."

Zinnia glanced around. "Is she here now? Hello? Beatrizz?"

"Aunt Zinnia, I was talking to myself. Nobody else is here. Do you know the woman who wrote this?"

Zinnia was slow to answer and careful with her words. "She's a cousin of mine. Well, a second cousin. That would make her your second cousin once removed." She licked her lips. "And that's all I can say for now."

"I hope I get to meet her one day."

"In time," Zinnia said vaguely.

I reached for my purse and pulled out the magazine I'd taken from the hairdresser that morning. "Look at this." I showed her the blank pages. "Whatever has been erasing things is still at it."

"Apparently."

"It also removed something else," I said. "The tattoo from my hairdresser's hand."

"A tattoo? You must be joking."

"For a change, no." I explained how Zoey and I had visited Morganna Faire at the Beach Hair Shack that morning, where I'd seen Josephine Pressman and been sucked into her mind, right through her eyes.

My aunt nodded and looked up at my hair. "Yes, that would explain your appearance. And here I thought you slept in the woods last night."

I told her the rest, right up to and including my meeting with Chet.

When I was done, she gave me a worried look. "You won't leave this thing alone, will you?"

"It's different now. This isn't just me being curious about some disappearing ink. A ghost has come to me for help, and I have to help a ghost who needs it, so they can move on. Isn't that basically what Beatrizz here is getting at?" I waved the photocopied paper.

"It's your specialty, and your calling."

"Let's start by dropping by the Pressman house. I've already got the address."

She blinked. I thought for sure she was going to say no, but instead, she said, "Let's eat that sushi before we set out."

CHAPTER 21

WE DID THE sensible thing and ate our sushi before setting out. We couldn't go sleuthing while hungry, after all.

I phoned Zoey to check in with her. She sounded suspicious and slightly hurt that I was at Zinnia's house without her.

"You'll come with me next time," I promised, shoving a sushi roll into my mouth. "This was just a spur-of-the-moment thing."

"Are you eating sushi?"

"Wow, do you have good hearing," I said.

"You make specific noises when you stuff a big California roll in your mouth."

"I find it strange that you know that and I don't."

"Whatever. If you're having sushi, I'm having Pop-Tarts for dinner."

"Okay," I said. "Don't eat them in the tub."

"I'll be careful."

We said goodbye, and I finished my sushi.

Zinnia went upstairs to get ready while I cleaned up the takeout. As I shook the leftover wasabi paste into the compost bucket, I thought of the compost's future destination, on the pile outside Vincent Wick's office. Kathy might have suspected he was involved with the disappearing ink, but I didn't think he was.

Even if Wick had been erasing the text from the library books, he couldn't have removed the tattoo from Morganna's hand. No chemical solvent would do that without damaging the skin.

Zinnia came downstairs and met me in the living room.

I took one look at her and said, "You're not going dressed like that."

"Why not? Whatever is wrong with what I'm wearing?" She fluffed out her voluminous green skirt. It was eerily similar to the one I wore that day, my Anne of Green Gables look. I'd gotten an excellent deal on the outfit during a theater company's wardrobe sale fundraiser. Those sales were where I got all my best clothes.

"You look like my twin," I said.

"So?"

"We already get plenty of funny looks when we're out together. Shouldn't we try to keep a low profile?"

Zinnia nodded. "I can put on a disguise. I know the perfect spell."

"I was thinking about jeans, or a hat or a scarf, but a spell is even better." I rubbed my hands. "Let's see what you've got."

She made a tsk-tsk noise and shook her head. "It's well above your skill level, so I'm afraid I can't teach this one to you yet."

"Not even a sneak peek? I'll be super careful."

She gave me a stern look. "Zara, wait right here by the door. Don't do anything or touch anything. Give me five minutes upstairs. Alone."

I groaned but I did as I was told, albeit with a grumpy look on my face. I leaned back against the wall, my hands in my pockets to avoid touching anything that might get me in trouble.

I slowed my breathing and listened for sounds coming from upstairs. I heard a few floor creaks, but no spells.

At least the prospect of learning this disguise spell was something to look forward to. The spells I'd been practicing for my lessons were unimpressive yet fiddly.

For example, the most recent one was a spell for checking the ripeness of muskmelon, also known as the North American Cantaloupe. Sounds like a pretty good spell, right? If you truly love cantaloupe, it's about as handy as a spell can be. Unfortunately, everything about it, from the phrasing of the words to the intricate hand gestures, was terribly convoluted. The spell took ten minutes to cast. Ten minutes *per cantaloupe*. Sure, it did identify the sweetness level using the Percent Sucrose Equivalent scale of zero to fifteen, but a non-magical person could do a passable job by sniffing the dimple on the blossom side in two seconds flat.

The cantaloupe spell was how I knew that, despite some mid-nineties internet leakage, the secret of magic had not been discovered by the world at large. If people really knew, the expression "it happened as if by magic" would mean that some ordinary, simple task took ten aggravating minutes longer than necessary.

The creaking sounds upstairs had stopped.

"Aunt Zinnia? Are you taking a nap up there?"

No response.

There was a knock on her front door. I turned and peered through the side window. Standing on the front porch was an old man with stooped posture.

My aunt had instructed me to not touch anything, but the old guy knocked again, and I couldn't exactly leave him standing out there.

I opened the door and said hello.

The stooped man had a cane in one hand, and a black eye patch over one eye. His white hair was uneven and patchy, as though he was molting. He wore dark green slacks that struck me as familiar, though I couldn't put my finger on why.

Spitting from one side of his mouth as he talked, he said, "You're not Zinnia Riddle. What have you done with her, witch?"

I took a step back and called for my aunt over my shoulder. "Zinnia? There's a gentleman here to see you."

The old man thrust his cane forward and stepped inside the house without an invitation. He gave me a dirty look with his one good eye.

"You've done something to Zinnia," he spat. "Something evil." He took a few more steps toward me, moving quickly for someone in his condition. In a blink, he'd raised his cane and pointed it at me. My heart began to pound wildly.

"Witch, we have ways of making you talk," he growled.

CHAPTER 22

"Talk?" I flashed my eyes at him. "Joke's on you, mister, because I *love* to talk."

And then, grabbing the cane with my magic, I wrenched it from his gnarled hands and tossed it aside. The cane clattered to the floor.

"Let's talk," I said.

The man let out a sigh that sounded surprisingly feminine. He straightened up smoothly, like an elastic being stretched. The air around him shimmered, and he transformed into my aunt. Or, should I say, *back* into my aunt.

I didn't know whether to laugh or cry. So I clapped slowly.

"Good one," I said. "That was quite the performance, Aunt Zinnia. You really got me. My heart was beating like a little bunny's. Go ahead and take a bow."

She didn't take a bow. Her face still bore the angry expression the old man had glared at me with.

"Great disguise," I said. "I guess you transformed upstairs, went out the fire escape, and came around to surprise me. Well, consider me surprised." I looked down at her green skirt, which was the same shade the man's trousers had been. "I knew his pants looked familiar, but you fooled me completely."

Zinnia pursed her lips into a tight-lipped frown as she shook her head slowly. "And you gave yourself away. You gave away your secrets with such little provocation."

"I was under attack," I said.

"You were under no such attack."

"He stormed in here, looking for trouble. There was a gleam in his eye. In your eye."

"Zara, a wise witch doesn't reveal herself. Not for a gleam. Not for a look. Not for a bad feeling."

"All I did was yank away his cane."

"With magic!"

"Did I? It all happened so quickly. Are you sure?"

She gave me a motherly look. Specifically, the look my own mother used to give me when we both knew I was in deep trouble.

I shook my finger at her. "You're lucky you didn't get a couple of blue fireballs in the chest."

"Zara Riddle, don't look so pleased with yourself. To the outside observer, an old man did nothing more than point the rubber tip of his cane at you, and you let him see your witch powers."

"You're right." I hung my head in shame. "That is what happened."

"It's not entirely your fault. You didn't learn your skills in the correct order. You should have built up slowly to your defensive magic. But you didn't have a chance, because that bird thing attacked you in the woods."

"That's right," I agreed. "Let's blame this all on the bird thing."

She reached into the pocket of her skirt and pulled out a foil-wrapped chocolate Easter egg. "Here. You'll thank me later."

I unwrapped the egg and tossed it into my mouth. My mouth had been watering for dessert ever since the sushi. The chocolate went down very easily.

"Never mind later," I said. "I'll thank you right now. This chocolate is delicious. Do I taste cinnamon?"

"No," she said coolly. "You're tasting Black Startwists, along with a few other things."

My esophagus felt warm suddenly. I coughed. "What?"

"The spell in that egg should be taking effect now. You might feel a bit lightheaded."

"You drugged me?"

"I gave you a chocolate egg with drugs inside it. Technically, you drugged yourself."

I turned and ran into the kitchen. I spat the chocolate residue from my mouth into the sink, and stuck my finger down my throat.

"Don't bother vomiting," Zinnia said. "The spell is already at work, and you'll only waste perfectly good chocolate."

I cupped handfuls of water to my mouth and rinsed repeatedly. Now my throat was going from hot to numb. Was that better, or worse?

I tried using my magic to open a cupboard door to get a water glass. The cupboard stayed shut. I tried lifting the sponge at the back of the sink. Not even a wiggle.

"My powers," I said. "I can't move things."

I wheeled around to face my aunt. Words and anger bubbled up. If I knew how to summon a fire-breathing dragon, I might have.

Zinnia's face shifted—not through witch magic, but by something primal. Time shifted, losing its linearity.

In my aunt's face, I saw her sister. My mother. Throwing me out of the house that had been my only home. "You've got your wish," she'd said. "Go, and be free of me." She sent me away with nothing but the clothes on my back. And all, as she claimed, for my own good. *You'll thank me later*, she'd said. Well, I hadn't then, and I wouldn't now. Why would I thank someone for hurting me?

I opened my mouth to tell the woman standing before me what I thought of her punishment. Before I could get the first word out, she reached up and caught my face softly with both palms. She gave me a look that was tender and disarming. My mother was standing before me. Her familiar hazel eyes looked back at me.

Mom?

"Zara, I'm sorry," she said softly.

"No," I said. "You don't get to apologize. You're dead."

"Zara?"

The face in front of me shifted. It was my aunt. It was just Zinnia.

I whispered, "What's happening?"

"The spell has some strange side effects."

"Does it bring back the dead? I could have sworn you were my mother just now."

"Oh, Zara, if I could bring back my sister for both of us, you know I would. But she made her choices."

I shrugged off the uncomfortable feeling all this heartfelt talk was giving me. "It would be a bad idea anyway," I said. "I've read that book. *Pet Cemetery*. Some barriers aren't meant to be crossed."

"True. Barriers exist for a reason."

I looked at the kitchen sponge again, trying to lift it. Again, not even a wiggle. And the effort of trying made me feel exhausted.

"My magic's gone," I said. "Is it really that easy to get rid of someone's magic?"

"The spell will wear off in a few days."

"A few days?"

"You've got to understand it wasn't my choice. You did this to yourself."

I crossed my arms. "That's a big, steaming pile of floopy doop, and you know it."

"Oh, I'm quite serious. A witch cannot take away another witch's powers."

"Unless she makes her eat a poisoned chocolate egg."

Zinnia tilted her head and smiled. "You grounded yourself, Zara. Deep down, you know that you needed some reining in. You want to have your powers grounded."

I tapped my fingers on my arm. "Is that so? And did I want them to be grounded for a few days? Wouldn't one day have been sufficient?"

"I don't make the rules," she said. "Besides, you were overdue to face this particular challenge."

"Challenge? Is this part of the initiation rites I have to get through before I can meet the other witches in your coven?"

Her eyes widened. "I don't know why you insist that I'm part of some coven. Not everything you read about witches in storybooks is true, Zara. Look in a mirror. Neither of us have big, warty noses. Nor do we have black cats, or ride around on broomsticks for that matter."

"As soon as I get my powers back, I'm riding a broomstick over town with three cats on the back."

My aunt gasped, "Don't you dare."

We stared at each other, then she let her breath out. "Oh. We're back to joking around again."

"I can't stay angry at you, Aunt Zinnia. You've taken me under your wing and tried to teach me. This grounding is the right punishment. I could use the break from ghosts and things."

"Oh, I'm afraid it won't stop the ghosts."

I groaned. "Seriously?" My mouth felt cottony, and she was right about the lightheadedness. Whatever had been in the chocolate egg was dulling my senses along with shorting out my magical circuits.

"We grounded *you*, Zara, not all the ghosts in existence. That would be ridiculous."

"Yeah." I forced a laugh. "That *would* be ridiculous."

"It won't be long," she said. "Just a few days, maybe less."

"What do you mean, maybe less? Time off for good behavior?"

"Sure."

"You don't know how long, do you? Aunt Zinnia, you put a spell on me without knowing the exact effects."

She rubbed her hands together. They sounded dry, in need of hand lotion. "We really should get going," she said.

"Going?" I'd forgotten our plans to visit the Pressman residence. It all came flooding back to me. And I didn't want to go. I didn't want to knock on someone's door and fish for information. I wanted to go home and pull the covers over my head until my magic came back.

"We should go now," she said. "Let's not dilly dally and waste the light."

I followed her to the house and to the door. I'd gotten used to using my telekinetic magic to do little things, such as twist doorknobs. I nearly walked face-first into her door. I had to use my hand to turn the knob the non-magical way.

"Wait," I said, pausing in the front entryway. "Shouldn't you put your old-man disguise back on?"

"Not yet," she said. "I can still turn on the glamour today, but my energy won't last forever. It's like a battery. You don't want to waste if you don't need to."

"Understood. Are you up to this?"

"If we go now, yes. The closer we get to my bedtime, the more difficult it is for me to focus."

"Same for me." I'd noticed that my concentration waned around bedtime. That was when I'd drop teacups and other objects. But if I stayed up well past my bedtime, I'd start to get a second wind, a new burst of energy.

Whenever I did magic in the dead of night, it felt different. More powerful, but darker. Like my aunt when she was teaching me a lesson.

We got into Zinnia's car, with her at the wheel.

The Pressman house wasn't far away. Driving in the car, we would be there in under ten minutes.

I wondered how quickly we could get there by broomstick. Just as a thought experiment. Not that I would actually do such a thing. Not without my witchy trio of cats, anyway.

CHAPTER 23

THE PRESSMAN HOUSE was plain and boxy, the sort of Bland Builder's Special I'd almost forgot existed. Wisteria residents preferred their houses quaint and colorful, with breezy wrap-around porches and lush front gardens. This house didn't even have a single blade of grass. The lawn was entirely gravel. It looked like one big driveway.

Zinnia parked on the street and turned off the car engine. We sat quietly, sizing up the place.

"I know this house," I said. "We walked by it on Saturday, on our way to get ice cream."

"You have an excellent memory."

"I don't usually remember every house I walk past, but this one struck me as particularly sad."

"It is a bit sad. We shouldn't judge, but this is not much of a castle to come home to." She made a tsk noise. "There's no lawn at all."

Something shifted gears inside me, and I took another direction. "Lawns are a waste of resources. The average household spends over a thousand dollars annually on landscaping, which returns not one single cent of profit or agricultural production."

She turned to me. "What was that?"

"A fun fact, I guess. Fun facts pop into my head sometimes."

"Frequently?"

"A few times a day. It's a librarian thing. Lots of librarians do it."

"What do these fun facts feel like?"

"You know how sometimes you'll be doing something else while there's a quiz show on TV, and the host will ask a question, and you get the answer in your head? It pops up there, almost like credits on a movie screen, and you don't know *how* you know something, but you do?"

"That happens to everyone on occasion, but what you said just now was different. Your voice changed."

"Like I was possessed?"

"Yes and no. What you said just now about people wasting money on lawns, I read that exact quote in an old issue of the Penny Pincher Gazette."

"My fun fact came from Perry Pressman."

"Residual knowledge," she said. "How fascinating."

"Residual knowledge makes it sound so... messy. Are you saying my ghosts are leaving behind fun facts in my head?"

"So it seems."

I nodded at the house. "The good news is we've found our ghost. Mr. Finance Wizard is Perry Pressman. Do you think his body's in the house?"

She didn't respond. She seemed to be puzzling over something. "Zara, do you suppose all this residual knowledge will stick around forever?"

"I've still got song lyrics up there from twenty years ago, so why not? At this rate, I'm a few hundred ghost possessions away from becoming the World Champion on Jeopardy. Like that cat-loving youth services librarian from Wilmington, North Carolina, who cleaned up the cash and won over hearts. When she said her favorite hobby was knitting, every librarian from coast to coast jumped up and fist pumped the air."

My aunt sucked in air between her teeth. "Not Jeopardy. No, no, no. We must never draw the public's attention to ourselves."

"It was a joke, Aunt Zinnia." I turned to the window and looked at the plain house again.

When I turned back to Zinnia, she'd been replaced by an old man with mangy-looking white hair and a black eye patch over one eye.

I made a shocked noise. "Holy sweatpants! A little warning might have been nice."

In the croaky old man voice, she said, "Wait in the car."

"I'm not going with you?"

"It could be dangerous. Trust me. I have a plan."

"Do I really have to wait in the car? Is this part of my punishment?"

"I'm just being practical. You saw the daughter this morning, so she'll be suspicious if you show up on her front doorstep. How would you even explain what you're doing here?"

"Library survey?"

"Wait in the car. And slide down so she doesn't see you."

"Can't you throw some of your disguise spell over me, too?"

"It doesn't work that way. I could, however, turn you into a tree, or a shrub. If you absolutely *must* be part of this."

"Great." I reached for the door handle and paused. "Wait. Do you mean you'd *turn me into* a shrub, or that you'd *disguise me* as one?"

The old man's one good eye blinked at me. "What do you think?"

"It's just that..." I scratched my head. "Remember on Saturday, when you said you had a dream that you killed me? I know you said your dreams can be metaphorical, but..."

The good eye blinked again.

"I don't want to be *turned into* a shrub."

"The spell is just a glamour. An illusion. I'm not really an old man right now. Do you see this ring?" The old man held up one wrinkly hand. There was a gold ring on his pinkie. "That's real. It's the power source for the glamour."

"Neat! Do I get to wear some funky magical jewelry to power my shrub disguise? Like a cool amulet?"

"Just open the door and grab any old twig or branch."

"For my glamour? But that's not very glamour-ous, ha-ha. See what I did there?"

Another one-eyed blink. "My energy is running down, so get out and make your puns while you're finding a twig."

I flung open the car door and got to work. There was nothing growing in the Pressmans' yard, so I had to traipse over to the neighbor's leafy green yard. I yanked a twig off a bush, and Zinnia cast the spell. I didn't feel any different.

She said, "Now act more like a shrub."

I looked down. My legs were gone, replaced with a mass of shrubbery. I lifted one leg, bending at the knee, and wiggled my foot. What I saw with my eyes was a branch quivering as though blown in the wind.

"You're not a very convincing shrug," Zinnia said. "Are you doing the Hokey Pokey?"

"Just getting acquainted with how the glamour works."

"Stop jiggling around so much. It will hide some of your movements, but I can still see you goofing around in there."

"Can you guess what I'm doing now?" I made a rude gesture while sticking out my tongue.

"Behave yourself."

Or what? Would I get double grounded?

Instead of giving her sass, I said, "Yes, Aunt Zinnia." I knew better than to push my luck. She was teaching me new magic and helping with my ghost. I did appreciate my elder witch. "Good luck," I said.

My aunt walked up to the front door of the Pressman residence. She lifted her fist to knock on the door but paused.

I whispered, "Is something wrong?"

She didn't move. Was she afraid? Or was there a glitch in her glamour so it only looked like she was frozen?

I leaned back—slowly and as shrub-like as possible—and looked around the house and then up. The Pressman house had an attic floor, with a window. Standing in the window, looking down at the front step, was the same man I'd seen in the personal finance section of the library, and in the newspaper article. Perry Pressman.

He looked solid, and alive. My "ghost" was alive. How could that be?

CHAPTER 24

THE MAN IN the attic window glared down at my aunt. His rectangular face looked skinnier than it had appeared in his newspaper photo. His hooded eyes were dark holes.

I shivered, my leaves rustling around me. The sun was setting. With the day turning to night, our fun excursion suddenly felt dangerous.

The man in the window stepped back, disappearing from sight.

I looked over at my aunt and waved a branch to get her attention.

She hadn't knocked on the door yet. Instead, she had opened the household's mailbox and was sorting through the envelopes. She seemed to be in no hurry at all.

On the car ride over, she had told me her plan. She would pass herself off as an old college friend of Perry Pressman's, just passing through town and hoping to see the man. She would see what Josephine said, and then pretend to faint in order to get invited inside. Then she would snoop around and continue asking questions, improvising. If all went well, she might even ascertain what business of Perry's might remain unfinished.

That was Plan A, anyway.

We didn't have a Plan B, unless you counted running to the car and driving away as a plan.

We also hadn't discussed was what she'd do if her "old college friend" Perry came to the door. And we hadn't discussed my aunt going through their mail.

I whisper-yelled to Old-Man-Zinnia, "Someone was in the attic. It looked like Perry Pressman, only he wasn't a ghost."

Old-Man-Zinnia dropped the mail back in the box, and walked over to me. The gravel that covered the front yard crunched under her feet, but not in sync with her movement. The glamour's audio track was slightly out of whack.

But the voice worked perfectly. "No condolence cards in the mail," she said, spitting her words in the elderly male voice.

"I know. I just saw him upstairs, in the attic window. He looked solid."

Old-Man-Zinnia looked up. "But there's a reflection on the glass. It's dusk now, so it's hard to see in, and even if you did, he would have been backlit. Are you sure it wasn't your imagination?"

"I know what I saw. He was solid."

"Zara, things are never clear during the transition between day and night. Shadows walk from tree to tree, and hawks take flight to nowhere. It is the time when webbed things manifest, when bats unfurl from gathering mist and cloak the world in quiet darkness."

"And dusk is the time when you start waxing poetic, apparently. Could you *be* any weirder?"

The one good eye blinked back at me. "Says the talking bush."

Something clawed at my hair. "Speaking of bush concerns, birds are landing on me," I said. "Or possibly bats. I'm too scared to look. Can we move this along? If Perry Pressman is still alive, then he's a spirit walker. I'll report him to Chet."

Old-Man-Zinnia adjusted her eye patch. "Did you read through all the recent obituaries for alternatives? Maybe your ghost is someone who's just similar to Perry. Does the man have a brother? An identical twin?"

"You got me." I'd been overconfident because identifying the Pressmans had happened so easily. But mostly, I hadn't read the obituaries because I hadn't thought of it.

"You're Spirit Charmed, Zara. Checking the obituaries should be your top priority. You ought to be reading them first thing in the morning, along with your coffee."

"A great start to any day: caffeine and death."

Old-Man-Zinnia let out a mannish harrumph sound. "Well, since we're already here, I'll go knock on the door and see what we shall see."

Old-Man-Zinnia knocked on the door and waited, both gnarled hands resting on the cane. Was the cane a physical prop, conjured from nothingness into solid matter? I hadn't heard the tip of the cane strike the gravel. If the cane wasn't real, then technically I hadn't broken the rules by magically moving it. Magic telekinesis on a magic glamour canceled itself out. That would make Zinnia's grounding of my powers unfair and possibly illegal. I would consider taking up the matter with her coven of peers, if only I knew who they were.

The front door opened. A man appeared. It was Perry Pressman.

I couldn't hear their words, but the tone of the conversation sounded pleasant enough. To any onlooker, they were just two older fellows, having a neighborly chat.

The two walked off the front step and meandered across the gravel front yard. The pea gravel crunched under their feet. Perry Pressman wore an old-fashioned men's fedora. Weirdly, he wore it perched on the back of his head, the way a fashionable young woman might wear it. The last two times I'd seen his daughter, she'd been wearing a hat the same way.

As they neared me, I was better able to hear their conversation.

Old-Man-Zinnia asked gruffly, "What about maintenance? I can't bend over like I used to. Blood pressure drops, and I'm liable to fall and smash up my nose again."

"Maintenance isn't so bad," Perry said. "You can top up the gravel every few years if you like, but all it really needs is a bit of elbow grease and a ten-dollar rake from the hardware store. You'll save yourself a few thousand by going with gravel instead of asphalt and turf. Plus it has a pleasing, rustic look." Perry knelt down and gave his gravel driveway a loving pat.

Old-Man-Zinnia cleared her throat. "Thanks for the good advice, neighbor. Do you have any young people living with you to help with the raking? I live alone, so maybe I could hire one of yours."

Perry straightened up, stumbled, and fell against Old-Man-Zinnia. She caught the man and quickly righted him again.

"Oops," Perry said, clutching his hat with both hands. "Sorry about that. It seems I've had one of those blood pressure drops you mentioned."

"You should see a doctor about that. How are you feeling? Have you got any other symptoms? Taking any new medication?"

Perry groaned as he dropped one arm limply to the side. He kept one hand fixed to his hat, still mounted on the back of his head.

"Huh? New medication? Who are you?"

Old-Man-Zinnia chuckled self-consciously. "I'm, uh, retired now, but I used to work in the medical field. Is there anything you'd like some help with?"

"There's absolutely nothing wrong with me," Perry said defensively. "Now, if you'll excuse me, I'm very busy with my work."

"And what kind of work is that?" Old-Man-Zinnia shook one gnarled finger at Perry. "Say, aren't you the fellow who used to run that coupon newspaper? The one with the classifieds?"

"The Penny Pincher has been shut down." Perry backed away stiffly.

"The Penny Pincher! Now, that was a great little paper." Old-Man-Zinnia's voice crackled as though glitching. Her speech sounded more feminine now. "Now, what was that catchy tagline? The Penny Pincher Gazette. The most valuable thing printed today, besides money."

"You remembered." He sounded surprised.

"Such a shame the paper's gone now. But I suppose it was inevitable, now that everyone's got the internet, not to mention cheap shipping from the big online stores. Of course, those stores don't want you to save money, they just want you to spend, spend, spend. Then they'll get you some credit cards so you can keep going. Why worry about tomorrow when you can have everything you want today?"

Perry's arms jerked. He replied with an angry tone, spitting out his words. "The people in this town didn't appreciate good advice when they had it. All they read these days is garbage on the internet that wouldn't be worth printing on paper anyway."

"There's no accounting for taste. Your gazette was a valuable service to the community."

Perry softened. "Thanks for being a fan, anyway. See you around, neighbor."

Behind him, another figure appeared in the doorway. It was Hipster Chick, his daughter Josephine.

"Dad? I thought you were upstairs napping. Are you feeling better?"

He said, "Fine. Why does everyone keep asking me what's wrong? I'm in the best shape of my life."

"Sure, Dad." She didn't sound convinced.

Perry waved goodbye to my aunt and went back inside his house with his daughter.

Old-Man-Zinnia came over to where I was standing still, doing my best to impersonate a bush.

The sun had set, and the murky twilight gave everything an underwater look.

She was breathing hard as she shimmered back to her regular Aunt Zinnia form. Her pale skin looked sweaty and waxen.

I looked down to find my body was no longer twigs and leaves. I made eye contact with a sparrow on my shoulder. It must have thought it had found a warm roost for the night. The bird startled and fluttered away.

"Something's wrong," Zinnia said. Her clipped words made my blood run cold.

I climbed over the low fence separating the yards and rushed to her side.

"What's wrong?"

She coughed and slumped against me. I caught her in my arms.

"Tell me what to do," I said. Panic rose in my chest.

"Home," she said hoarsely. "You drive. Get me home."

I draped one of her clammy arms across my shoulders and guided her toward the car.

"Easy does it," I coaxed. "One foot in front of the other."

She continued to stumble and weave. It didn't help that she had her head turned so she could stare at the Pressman house.

I followed her gaze, up to the attic window.

Two shadows stood framed in the window, not moving.

"They're watching us," I whispered. "It's two people, but it feels like the house itself is watching us."

"It's happening," she said, her voice barely a croak.

I pulled open the passenger side door and folded her in. As I was about to close the door, her body jerked, her eyes rolled up, and she made a hissing sound.

"Zinnia?" I shook her. "Open your eyes. Look at me. Wake up! Do I need to take you to the hospital?" I pressed my hand against her forehead. She was burning up.

"Home," she moaned.

"I'm taking you to the emergency room."

"Don't," she whispered. "I'll kill you."

I pulled away from her and took a step back, nearly tripping over the sidewalk.

"Zara, take me home." She curled up in the passenger seat.

CHAPTER 25

"Go home to your daughter," Zinnia said for the fourth time as she waved tiredly.

"Aunt Zinnia, I'm taking care of you. Even though you threatened to kill me if I took you to the hospital."

"I'm okay. Go home." She wiggled inside her cocoon of blankets.

I'd taken her straight home from the Pressman house. Now she was bundled up on her floral-print sofa, snuggled up with two laundry baskets' worth of pillows and blankets. She had recovered from her mysterious dizziness, but she wasn't back to her old self yet. She had been trying to reassure me everything was fine, but I didn't buy it for a minute.

"You need more water," I said. "Blended with ice, lemon, and salt. Now, that might sound like a margarita, but there's no tequila. It's a Poor Man's Gatorade." I knocked on my head. "Another fun fact. Do you think it's from Winona Vander Zalm?"

"No. She would never make a Poor Man's Anything. That recipe sounds like something from the Penny Pincher Gazette."

I knocked on my head again. "Hello? Mr. Finance Wizard? If you're not Perry Pressman, then who the heck are you? Thanks for the Poor Man's Gatorade recipe, but I'd appreciate a little more cooperation from you."

"Perhaps there never was a ghost."

"That recipe didn't just pop into my head from nowhere."

"Not from nowhere, no. But perhaps your witch powers have activated other pools of knowledge within your brain. From books you've read, documentaries you've watched."

"You mean I'm getting smarter?"

Zinnia pulled herself upright. "Zara Riddle, it is possible that the entity you call Mr. Finance Wizard is, in fact, you. You possess the knowledge to fix your financial problems."

"If you saw my credit card statement, you wouldn't say that."

"Are you having money problems?" She looked worried.

"You say money *problems*, I say money *adventures*. Anyone can cook breakfast with working electricity. It takes an Iron Chef to make do without."

I checked the temperature of her forehead using my hand. She was still weak and clammy, but at least she wasn't running a fever.

She pushed my hand away. "I'm fine, Zara. It was the glamour spell. I've never had two of them running at once like that. It wore me out faster than I expected."

"Believe whatever you want, but I saw the way you looked at that house. I felt it, and you felt it, too. The house itself was alive. We were looking at it, and it was looking at us. It's like Nietzsche says, when you stare into the abyss, it stares into you."

She gave me a sideways look. "When I was talking to Mr. Pressman, I did have the sensation I was looking through him."

"Did it happen when you looked into his eyes?"

"Yes."

"Were you looking through him into another dimension?"

"More like... this is going to sound odd, but it was as if I was looking at the inside of his hat."

"That does sound odd. His hat? Do you suppose the Pressmans have magical hats?"

"Magical hats do exist, but they're very rare."

I had nothing to say to that. I digested the information.

"There's more," she said. "I sensed his thoughts. He was thinking about a machine." She pulled the blankets tighter around herself and whispered, "A bad machine."

"Project Erasure."

The room was so quiet, I could hear a clock ticking somewhere.

"His last name is Pressman," I said. "Do you think he's working on a printing press that, um, works in reverse? Sucking the ink out of things?"

"It's a preposterous idea," Zinnia said. "Then again, people don't use magic to do *regular* things."

I nodded. "People use magic to do *preposterous* things."

She gave me a weak smile. "You are learning."

I grinned. *Zara tries to be a good novice witch.*

She licked her lips. "I would like some of that Poor Man's Gatorade."

I jumped up and went to her kitchen. She still had masses of plants strung from the ceiling beams. I avoided eye contact with the face-slapping tentacles. I triple-checked the labels on the salt and sugar containers to be certain I wasn't making some magic cocktail that would turn us into weasels.

I loaded the drinks onto a tray and brought them out to Zinnia.

My aunt didn't even react to me entering the room. I dropped the tray and checked her pulse. She was still alive, just sleeping.

I tucked the blanket around her, cleaned up the spilled drink, and went to sit in the kitchen so I could stick around a bit in case she woke and needed me.

I made a second batch of Poor Man's Gatorade, alternatively named the Less-Fun Margarita. I sipped it and thought about Perry Pressman and his daughter.

The motto of his Penny Pincher Gazette had been *The most valuable thing printed today, besides money.*

Was he using a magic-infused printing press to print counterfeit money? Why would the machine suck the ink from people's tattoos and books? Was it just the quirky way magic behaved?

I remembered something he'd said to my aunt as they stood on his gravel yard. *"The people in this town didn't appreciate good advice when they had it. All they read is garbage."*

"Revenge," I said to myself. He wanted to make money by taking away from the people of Wisteria, by taking away things they loved, such as library books and tattoos.

Something at the edge of my vision wriggled. It was the bundle of black barbed-wire hanging from the ceiling, getting excited. Did they think I was talking to them?

"I wasn't talking to you," I said.

The black barbed-wire tentacles quivered and beckoned me to continue.

So, despite my better judgment, I did. I told the Black Startwists my wacky theory about Perry and his plans to get back at the town for not supporting his business.

The magical herbs made encouraging gestures, and what appeared to be a thumbs-up.

"You're a good listener," I said. "Do you know much about dating? Specifically, about the dating habits of single fathers who happen to be shifters?"

The tentacles spread apart and then tousled themselves into breezy beach hair.

"I'll take that as a yes?"

The tentacles relaxed into a pose that reminded me of a person resting his chin on his hands, saying *do go on, love. Tell me more.*

And so I did. Keeping my voice low so I didn't disturb my aunt, I told the tentacles about all the dark, weak thoughts I had, the ones that I wouldn't dare burden other people with.

I shared my fears. That I worried I had screwed up my life beyond salvage many years ago. That all around me were people who seemed to understand what life was all about, who made plans and looked forward to things. I stood outside, looking in through the glass, wondering where they found the time.

Other people celebrated milestones I couldn't relate to. Meanwhile, I was so busy getting through the chaos from one minute to the next, always promising myself that any day now I was going to get my act together, but I was always too busy or too distracted or too something, and I never did. Whenever good things happened in my life—and I was grateful that they did—it happened by accident, almost in spite of my plans. The truth was, I felt more comfortable when things were going wrong because that was what I felt I deserved.

"And now, I've barely got a minute to myself," I told the listening tentacles. "I have three full-time jobs. Mother, librarian, witch."

The tentacles balled up all but four finger-like extremities.

"You're right," I said. "Four jobs, if you include being an unpaid personal assistant to ghosts."

The fingers gestured for me to go on, so I went on for a while. Quite a while. My throat became hoarse. When I looked up, the black barbed-wire tentacles had gone limp. A few of the shiny red berries had fallen off.

I had bored it to sleep. Or possibly to death. I didn't dare wake it to find out.

"Hint taken." I tidied up the kitchen.

The taste of the Poor Man's Gatorade had given me a wicked craving for real margaritas, with real tequila.

I checked on my aunt one more time, then locked up using the spare key she kept in a rock. This was no Hide-a-Key plastic rock from a hardware store, but an actual rock, hollowed out by magic to contain a slide-out drawer that only opened for people it trusted. How the rock knew who was to be trusted was anyone's guess.

I headed toward home. The sun had set hours ago, but the night was the warmest of the year so far.

Talking to the tentacle herbs had unburdened me, and now I wanted company.

When I reached Beacon Street, I walked right up to the blue house where the Moores lived and rang the doorbell.

CHAPTER 26

From within the Moore house, I heard someone who sounded an awful lot like my daughter yelling, "Doorbell!"

Zoey opened the door.

"Hey! I have one at home just like you," I said. "You two should meet."

She rolled her eyes. "Mr. Moore invited me over for dinner," she said. "He said I should eat something more nutritious than Pop-Tarts."

"Well, that's easy. Eating the cardboard box they come in would be more nutritious than Pop-Tarts."

She frowned. "That's weird. Mr. Moore literally said the exact same thing to me."

"We both buy our bad parent-humor jokes at the same store."

"Apparently." She didn't move from the doorway.

"Wasn't dinner a few hours ago?"

"I'm helping Corvin with his homework."

Corvin appeared behind her. He seemed to have materialized there soundlessly, the weird little imp.

"Hi, Corvin. What kind of homework are you and Zoey working on?"

He stared up at me with his big, dark-green eyes. "You owe me one."

I glanced at Zoey and then back at the little boy. "Oh, really? What do I owe you for?"

He raised his fist and waved his thumb up and down.

"What's that? Thumb wars?"

He shook his head.

"Okay," I said with a shrug. "I guess I owe you one of... something yet to be determined."

He nodded.

Zoey shifted over, blocking my view of him, and none too soon. The boy gave me the heebie jeebies.

"There's plenty of food left over," she said. "You could probably come in and eat some of it. Actually, you'd be doing the Moores a favor since there's not much room in their fridge."

"Thanks, but I've already eaten," I said, even though my sushi had been digested hours ago. My stomach, the traitor, growled.

Truthfully, I was hungry, but I wasn't in the mood to be around the entire Moore family. I'd come to invite Chet over to my porch, but I hadn't thought it through. Chet came with Grampa Don and Corvin.

"Just come in," Zoey said. "Grampa Don could use some help with his jigsaw puzzle."

"Tempting offer," I lied. "But I'll have to pass."

She narrowed her hazel eyes. "You're worn out from learning new spells with Auntie Z." She looked me up and down. "You look different. You're full of magic."

I had to laugh. "Oh, Zoey, you are brilliant, but you could not be more wrong. She grounded me, took away my powers, and then turned me into a bush."

"What?"

"Well, it was more of a shrub. And she didn't turn me into anything. That would be bad. It was just a glamour, an illusion."

"You learned how to do glamours? Was there special jewelry?"

I backed away, retreating down the steps of the porch. "I'll tell you when I see you back at home. Tell the Moores I said hello, and don't forget to thank them for feeding you."

"Come in and tell them yourself. Mr. Moore wanted to talk to you anyway."

I pretended not to hear her, and kept going. Zoey exhibited "selective hearing" when she didn't like my suggestions, so I was simply borrowing from her playbook.

* * *

I got ready to dig into a little dish we called Whistler. It was a peaked mountain of mixed takeout leftovers, topped with crumbled potato chips.

The doorbell chimed.

"Nobody home," I called out. "Also, I gave at the office, I'm not a registered voter, and the purple welts that cover fifty percent of my body are extremely contagious."

The person on my porch leaned over and called into the house through a screen window. "Zara? It's me, Chet."

"Did I say fifty percent? The purple welts have spread to ninety percent of my body."

"Can I come in?"

"You probably could if you tried a little harder. The door's not locked."

He let himself in. He found me in the kitchen, excavating my snowy mountain of leftovers.

"I don't see any purple welts," he said.

"They've retreated to my bathing suit areas, and now they're layered up, so they're *really* purple."

He looked down and pinched the bridge of his nose. "Is everyone this colorful where you're from?"

"Of course not. I would have never left and moved here."

He looked up at me. "Your hair's different."

"It's the same as it was a few hours ago, when you saw me at Dreamland Coffee."

"No. It's messier now."

"That makes sense. There were some birds in it, hunkering down for the night. I had to evict them."

He raised an eyebrow.

I waved for a glass of water. Nothing moved. *Right. I'm grounded. No magic.* I got up and poured myself a glass manually.

"Can I offer you one of these?" I waved my glass. "House special. We have it on tap."

"No, thanks." He stared at my food. His lean cheeks bore a dark shadow, making his face appear longer and more angular but still handsome. I returned to my seat and got back to eating. He watched the food go into my mouth. I chewed self-consciously.

He said, "You told your daughter you weren't hungry. You lied to her."

I wiped crushed potato chips from the corner of my mouth. "Just a little white lie."

"Do you lie to your daughter a lot?"

"Do you listen in other people's conversations a lot?"

"You were in my house."

"I was *on* your porch, just outside your house, which is not the same."

"Are you always this infuriating?"

"According to other members of the Riddle family, yes." I stabbed my food with my fork. "If you came over here to heckle me while I eat, go ahead and take a seat."

The corner of his mouth twitched. "I'll try to behave myself."

"Why start now?"

He winced. "Am I really that awful?"

"Your attitude could be improved by a bottle of tequila. You didn't happen to read my mind and bring over a bottle of *Jose Cuervo*, did you?"

"Who told you I could read minds?"

"Can you read minds?" I guiltily thought of the clicky pen I had stuck it in a drawer upstairs.

"Not exactly," he said. "I don't read minds, but I can sense other things." He studied me, his nostrils flaring. His eyes flicked down to my lower legs. I was sitting on a stool with my legs crossed. My skirt had ridden up, so he could see my bare legs from the thighs down. And if he could see my skin, he could probably smell it.

"Stop sniffing me," I said. "Not without my permission."

"How did you know?"

I smoothed my skirt down over my knees. "Bad doggie," I said.

"Witch."

"What else can you pick up on with your keen shifter senses?" Did he know that I was currently powerless, grounded for being irresponsible with my magic?

He replied, his voice low and smoky, "I can tell that you're in need of a drink right now, and I don't mean that glass of tap water."

Where had this sexy, flirty version of Chet been on Saturday, during our date?

"Go on," I said, curious to see where this would go.

"Let's see how well I can read you." With his eyes on me, he moved around the kitchen, stopping in front of one cabinet, and then another.

I clapped girlishly. "Oh, goody. A parlor trick. People do not appreciate old-fashioned parlor tricks like they used to."

He circled the kitchen twice, returning to the cupboard where I kept wine. With his eyes still locked on mine, he whipped open the cabinet.

"Here's the wine," he said. "I read it in your body language."

I raised my eyebrows and kept eating. Was my body language also telling him he'd been inside my kitchen a few times now and saw inside the cupboards? Was my body language telling him he was full of himself? Or were my eyes telling him where to find the wine glasses?

He found the wine glasses. He didn't need a corkscrew. He popped out a wolf talon and pulled out the cork the way he had after my last dinner party. I made a small noise to let him know I was duly impressed. He poured two glasses of wine, grabbed a fork, and joined me at the kitchen island.

Without asking permission, he took a bite of my food. He'd presumably eaten with his family and my daughter, over at his house, but here he was stealing my food.

He took another bite.

And I let him.

He looked into my eyes as he chewed. When I stared back at him, the rest of his face faded away. The whole world went dim, and it was just those eyes.

Was my body language telling him I found his food theft simultaneously aggravating and sexy? Or that dueling over the remaining bites on the plate was more intimate than I'd been with a man in years? That watching him lick his lips in such close proximity to my lips made me unable to think of anything but kissing him?

We finished the plate of food and sipped the wine. The bottle he'd opened was a dessert wine, a housewarming gift. It was still warm from the cupboard, and as sweet as Mountain Dew, but it was the best wine I'd ever had.

Chet picked up the plate and forks. "Save your magic. I've got this."

He loaded the plate and forks into the dishwasher. He put the plate in facing the wrong direction, according to Zoey's dishwasher rules, but I wasn't about to complain. Is there anything more delicious than the sight of a man loading the dishwasher, even if he is doing it wrong?

"Now we just need dessert," he said.

"Who are you, and what have you done with Chet?" I clapped my hands. "Oh, I get it. This is Mr. Chill. You've rolled him out and dusted him off so I can see how easygoing you truly are."

"It's not an act."

"Who cares? I like it. I'm not complaining."

"Good. Now, for dessert..."

He rummaged through my pantry cupboards. I liked the Mr. Chill side of Chet. Especially the way his lightweight waffle-knit shirt hugged his body and showed off the contrast between his muscular shoulders and slim waist. Whether it was the magic of Wisteria or his shifter powers, something was keeping the guy in peak physical condition. I had a feeling it would take an awful lot of physical activity to wear him out. A whole lot of sweaty...

"What?" He spun around. "Did you say something?"

Was he reading my mind?

"Fig newtons," I said. "Check the back of the middle shelf. Zoey and I buy the ones we don't like, so they last longer."

He grabbed the box without taking his eyes off mine. He repeated my words, his voice as low as a growl. "So they last longer?"

My cheeks felt hot. I'd been thinking about sweaty physical activity too much. Everything was a double entendre and the real double entendres were quadruple entendres.

"Where shall we take these?" His eyes flicked up at the ceiling briefly.

Up? To the floor with the bedrooms? Bad doggie.

"Living room," I said, leading the way. "Don't forget the wine. We'll need it to wash down those fig newtons. When I said we buy the ones we don't like, I wasn't kidding. They're terrible."

"You're really selling me on these fig newtons."

We moved into the living room, where he stared at the sofa for a good thirty seconds before wisely settling into a chair. Who knew what kind of dangers might have befallen him if he'd chosen the sofa? He could have gotten... some of my face on his face. Not to mention the very real specter of sofa-burn.

I settled on the sofa by myself, and we ripped into the box of fig newtons. He filled my wine glass.

"Hey, that's a new bottle," I said. "I didn't even see you open it."

"I'm quick and efficient."

"And sneaky." I took a sip. "Either this wine is better, or I'm tipsy. A few more glasses and I'll be astrally projecting." I struggled over the pronunciation of the term. "So, are you going to tell me more about this spirit walker guy of yours? Are you sure it's not Perry Pressman? We went by his house tonight, and the dude is living."

"Living?" He smirked.

"If you could call it that. The dude's not living it up, not like the two of us, but he's up and walking. Zinnia talked to him."

"She did? When I dropped you off at her house, you promised you'd stay out of trouble."

I snorted. "You're not the boss of me."

Mr. Chill completely disappeared. "You both need to stay away from the Pressmans. I don't know what they're up to, but he's made some questionable purchases lately. We believe he's working on something inside the house."

"What are you going to do about it? Raid the house?"

He blinked. "That's none of your concern."

"I want to come with you. I want to see this machine of his."

He shook his head. "That's not going to happen."

I made puppy-dog eyes. "I could watch from a safe distance."

He relaxed his clenched jaw and took a sip of his wine. "Actually, that might not be the worst idea you've had."

"Uh, thanks."

"Your powers could come in handy."

"Yes. My powers. The ones that I definitely have right now."

He gave me a sidelong look. "You're funny when you drink."

"That's offensive." I pointed an accusing finger at him. "I'm funny all the time."

"Yes. That's what your daughter says you believe."

I glanced in the direction of the front door. At any moment, my daughter could return. She would probably make big eyes and call me a Turbo-flirter if she saw how I was behaving.

"Thanks for taking care of her tonight," I said. "How was dinner over at your house?"

"The usual," he said. "I won't bore you with the ins and outs of getting kids to eat more vegetables by hiding them in other foods."

I clutched a fig newton to my chest. "How could a person do such a thing?"

"You wouldn't say that if you tasted my zucchini chocolate cake."

He looked down at my feet. I'd taken off my boots and socks when I'd arrived home, so my feet were bare. I was sitting with my legs pulled up to one side on the cushion next to me. I wiggled my toes. He didn't look away.

"What else do you bake?" I asked lightly.

His gaze traveled up to my bare shins. "I've got a great recipe for banana bread, but the bananas have to be ripe." The wine was affecting him, too. His words were slightly slurred. "Really ripe and sweet."

I folded my legs and pulled my feet closer, so I could cover them with the hem of my skirt.

He looked away from me. "You can hide a lot of veggies in smoothies," he said.

"Oh?"

The conversation turned to smoothies, and stayed there. Chet discussed the merits of raw kale versus spinach in blended beverages. He talked about various health studies, and never knowing which foods or technologies were currently poisoning the country's youth or readying them for the future.

I told him about some of the wacky cleansing diets people came to the library to borrow books about. We both laughed, and I shifted on the sofa, exposing my legs again.

He looked down at my bare legs and stopped talking.

The living room was so very quiet, even the air seemed to stop circulating.

I got the weirdest idea he was going to offer to massage my feet. Any minute now. And what if he did? How could I refuse? How could I accept?

I imagined his powerful hands on me, his long fingers encircling my ankles, his palms cupping my heels as he drew my feet toward his lap. Even seated in the chair across from me, he wasn't that far away. If I straightened my legs and angled my body a few degrees, I could do magic without magic—I could make the space between us disappear.

I shifted my position on the couch, taking pleasure in noting how he couldn't look away from my bare ankles, or the few inches of calf visible below my long skirt. I pointed my toes, uncrossed and recrossed my legs. He watched without moving. He seemed to have stopped breathing.

The house creaked.

He jerked his head up, his gaze off my legs. "Raw kale is packed with nutrients!"

"Okay." If I ever needed to kill romantic tension, talking about raw kale seemed to do the trick.

"The organic is more expensive, but not by much," he said, looking at the ceiling now. "Do you shop at the Golden Apple Market? They have the best prices on produce."

"Sure, sure." I nodded while he went on about the Golden Apple Market. *Best prices on produce.*

Something fuzzy rubbed up against the inside of my head, like a cat announcing its presence with a tickle on your shin. My tongue felt thick and heavy. Too much wine? Yes, but also something else.

"They really have great coupons," Chet said, his eyes resting anywhere but on me. "Two for one, sometimes even three for one. And if you buy in bulk..."

My head swam. *Two for one. Three for one.*

Dimly, I realized what was happening. I wasn't being bored to sleep. Another mind was squeezing into my head, fuzzing everything. Mr. Finance Wizard. He must have been drawn by all the talk about coupons and discounts. Either him, or a demon who was summoned by bargains!

Chet was still talking. He'd moved on to weekend early bird specials. I tried to interrupt him, to tell him about the ghost, but my mouth wasn't working, and he wouldn't meet my gaze.

The fuzziness filled my awareness with white noise.

I was squeezed out, squished into oblivion.

CHAPTER 27

THURSDAY MORNING, I woke up in the same skirt and blouse I'd been wearing the previous night. I was in my bed, though I didn't remember climbing in.

I did, however, remember Chet talking about discounts at grocery stores. That bargain talk had summoned my wacky penny-pinching ghost, the one who was possibly a relative of Perry Pressman's.

I wondered how Mr. Finance Wizard handled flirting with attractive neighbors while drinking wine and eating the world's worst fig newtons. That couldn't have gone well. The next time I saw Chet, it was going to be awkward. More than usual. Thinking about it made my head... buzz?

My head was really buzzing away. No, scratch that. It was my alarm clock. And it sounded particularly annoying that morning. I rolled out of bed and switched it off manually.

"You're lucky my powers are still grounded," I said menacingly. "Or you might have finally gotten your wish to fly. Straight out my window."

A voice down the hall called out, "It's about time you shut that thing off."

"And a chirpy good morning to you, too, sunshine."

She grumbled, "Too early for sarcasm."

"If it's too early for sarcasm, it's also too early for eye rolling. So, just stop it. I can hear your eyes rolling. I can hear them rattling through the walls."

She groaned and muttered something, presumably snarky.

Zoey and I took turns being the annoying morning person. We didn't have a set schedule for switching back and forth, but it seemed to work out about fifty-fifty.

I rubbed my eyes and looked around for Post-It notes. Had my ghost made plans for me, like he had the day before? If he had, he had neglected to leave me a sticky notes.

I got myself showered, put on fresh clothes, and went downstairs. The kitchen looked the way I expected. I opened the dishwasher. Zoey had corrected Chet's placement of the plate. What a cute little weirdo.

The wine glasses had been hand-washed, and sat on a tea towel next to the sink. Chet must have done that. I'd bought wine glasses with short stems specifically so they could go in the top rack of the dishwasher. On the plus side, that meant he hadn't run screaming from the house.

I went to check the living room. What was I looking for? Claw marks in the sofa? The furniture was no more shredded than it had been the day before.

So, how had Chet and I left things the night before? Had he even noticed he was sharing kale smoothie tips with a ghost?

The coffee maker let out its happy hiss to let me know the morning's first pot was ready. I poured a mug and pondered how interesting it was people called making coffee "brewing." The verb implied a magical transformation. But with coffee, the real magic happened with the drinking, not the percolating.

Upstairs, the shower started running. Zoey was getting ready for school.

I wanted to know what I'd gotten up to the night before, and she was the nearest eyewitness.

I brought my mug of coffee up to the bathroom, and took a seat on the sink counter. Zoey wouldn't mind. Some of our best conversations had happened through the shower curtain. We had gotten a clear shower curtain once, with rubber duckies, but we soon realized nudity didn't help casual conversation. Ever since then, only opaque curtains.

I started the conversation by sharing my thoughts about coffee and brewing.

"You should write that down for your memoir," she said.

"Nice."

"Do you think this honey shampoo contains actual honey? I think that would be a bad idea because honey is sticky, and a person typically uses shampoo to make their hair the exact opposite of sticky."

"That shampoo was expensive, so it had better contain whatever we paid for."

"Expensive?" The water splashed noisily as she moved around inside the shower. "Are we having money problems?"

"Why do you ask? Is this about the electric bill? Zoey, I've got things under control now. Sort of."

"I think I should get an after-school job for a while, to help out."

"You already have a job. Your job is getting good grades at school."

I sipped my coffee and turned to look at myself in the mirror. I nearly did a spit-take. I looked rough, with bloodshot eyes and dark circles. Getting possessed was evidently the opposite of getting beauty sleep. I wondered if my aunt's cousin had any beauty tips to counter being Spirit Charmed. Or if she looked twice her age. Perish the thought.

Zoey said, "Maybe I could tutor Corvin."

"That could work. I could talk to his father about it." I used my elbow to rub an ugly smudge off the mirror. It didn't work. The smudge was my face.

Casually, I asked, "What time did you get home from the Moore house last night?"

"Ten o'clock. I was helping Corvin with a science project. Grampa Don wouldn't let him use the hot glue gun unsupervised. He gave us a whole speech about gun control, and I'm not sure he was entirely joking."

"Grampa Don is quite the wild card," I said.

"He's fun. He makes me miss Pawpaw. Is he going to come visit us soon?"

I groaned. "That's all I need."

"It's too bad he missed my birthday."

"Well, it's too bad he always misses people's birthdays, but that's what happens when you're a..." I took a deep breath and let it go. I had more pressing concerns than my fair-weather father.

"Zoey, do you happen to remember what your dear old mother was doing when you got home last night?"

"I don't know. You were in your bedroom with the door closed."

"Alone?"

"What?" She turned off the shower, wrapped herself in a towel, and yanked the curtain back. "You didn't! With Mr. Moore? Is that where he was?"

"No! I was alone. I just wonder if you heard me talking to myself, or talking to a ghost. That's all."

She regarded me with suspicion. "I checked in on you at eleven o'clock, right before I went to bed. I opened the door, and you were already under your covers. Just one lump, so you must have been alone."

"Or so it seemed." I waggled my eyebrows. "Perhaps someone was in there with me, but he turned into a tiny little French bulldog, and was snuggled up close where you couldn't see him."

She wiped her eyes with the edge of her towel. "Mom, you're not nearly as funny first thing in the morning as you think you are."

"No one ever is."

I jumped off the vanity and headed for the door.

"Wait," she said. "There's a reason I went in to check on you last night. I thought you were calling out to me. You were saying something like, 'I want to see my baby.' I thought you were singing a song. You kept saying it over and over, but I don't know what song that is."

I smiled to cover for the chill that ran up my spine. "And so you came to check on me because you're my baby. That's so sweet of you."

"Do you think it was a ghost?"

"It might have been. I'm afraid Mr. Finance Wizard took over for a while last night. That's why I asked you about what you might have seen me doing."

She wrinkled her brow, sending shower water streaming down the sides of her face. "You were also saying some other stuff, but it wasn't as weird. You were just talking about croissants and donuts and cake."

"Ah. My usual sleep-talking topics."

"You did mention gingerbread, though, and I know that's not your favorite."

"Interesting." I stepped away from the door and waved her through. "Get ready for school. You can't wear that towel all day."

She rolled her eyes and left.

I turned to consult my reflection in the mirror. *I want to see my baby?* As far as sleep-talking went, that was pretty creepy.

The gingerbread, though, gave me an idea. I might have been talking about the Gingerbread House of Baking. I'd been meaning to check out the bakery. I heard the pastries were excellent, plus I wanted to gawk at the owners. I'd never met a gorgon before.

CHAPTER 28

THE GINGERBREAD HOUSE of Baking was decorated to look exactly like a gingerbread house. There were giant sugared gumdrops, white swirls of "frosting," and gum balls the size of baseballs. It was all Styrofoam and wood, of course, but very well done. The interior was sparkling and white, with the treats taking center stage.

The man behind the counter yawned as he greeted me. We hadn't been introduced, but I was certain he was Jordan Taub.

"That newborn of yours must be keeping you up," I said.

He rubbed his eye with his knuckles. "Is it that obvious?"

I looked left and right. "Any photos of the new... what did you have?"

Jordan suddenly looked very awake. "A boy," he said, staring intently at me.

"How wonderful. I've never had one of those before. Just a girl. She's sixteen now. Quite the handful. Won't let me walk her all the way to school. This is going to sound crazy, but you should treasure these sleepless nights. Your little guy will be all grown up way too soon."

He gave me a wary look. "Can I get you something?"

"Croissants," I said.

He boxed them up quickly, fastened the box with a peppermint-striped ribbon, and held out his hand for payment.

I reached for my credit card and pulled out shards of plastic.

"Oops," I said. "Something happened to this one."

"Looks like someone cut up your credit card."

"Why would someone do—" The answer came to me immediately. This was the work of Mr. Finance Wizard.

I gathered up the remnants of a couple credit cards. "Do you have a garbage can?"

The baker chuckled. "I've been there," he said knowingly. He picked up a bin and we both swept the pieces into the trash.

"I guess my next credit card statements will be lighter on ink," I said.

"Whatever works," he said. "My wife used to freeze her credit cards in a block of ice."

The bells on the door chimed, and someone came in behind me. Jordan eyed the newcomer and stood at attention. I saw military training shining through his casual baker persona.

He tapped one hand on the box of croissants. "So, it'll be cash today?"

I took the hint and reached for my cash. "Sure. Let's hope I didn't shred everything last night in my eagerness to..." I stared in disbelief at the blank rectangles of paper sitting in the compartment where I kept my bills. My money had been erased. The baker leaned over and plucked the paper from my hands.

"What's this?" he asked. "Did you leave your cash out in the sun?"

"Looks that way, doesn't it?" I held out my hand, and he gave the erased bills back. Would my bookwyrm be able to restore the ink? I would have to try later.

The other customer—a man—said, "Those papers look an awful lot like low-denomination bills that have been washed for counterfeiting."

I turned to find Detective Bentley, from the Wisteria Police Department, looking as serious and steely-eyed as ever. He wore a dark gray suit that matched his hair. He looked rested and ready to nab bad guys and counterfeiters.

"You got me," I said to Bentley with a laugh. "These are for my counterfeiting machine. Oops, and now you know I'm running a crime ring here in Wisteria."

Bentley raised an eyebrow. "I'm listening."

"It's a whole thing," I said, drawing a rainbow shape in the air with one hand. "When I go crime ring, I go all the way. I've got counterfeiting, drugs, houses of ill repute, and even some rum runners. I know rum running hasn't been cool since the end of prohibition, but I'm trying to bring it back."

"Rum running?"

"Hey! What's going on over there across the street?" I pointed to the window behind Bentley and made a shocked face. "Do you think those guys with the masks and the big sacks of money just robbed a bank?"

Detective Bentley whipped around. I folded the erased money and tucked the wad into my bra. I glanced over at the baker and winked. He didn't make a peep. He was yawning again and probably hadn't seen anything.

"What sacks of money?" Bentley to face me again. "You're up to something."

"Just one of my hilarious pranks," I said, winking.

I turned to the baker and asked, "How do you feel about opening a tab for me? I work at the library, so you know where to find me, plus you know I'll be an excellent customer."

He slid the box toward me. "Take these, on the house."

"I promise I'll pay for them the next visit."

"Sure. I'll start a tab for you." He scratched his stubbly chin. "But I can't quite remember your name."

Detective Bentley said, "She's Zara Riddle."

I gave the cop a dirty look. Did he think I was going to give a fake name just to get free croissants?

Jordan stifled a yawn. "Right. I knew it was something starting with a Z. Like Zinnia."

"A lot like Zinnia," I said through a tight smile.

The baker wrote on a slip of paper.

I leaned over and said, "Go ahead and put Detective Bentley's order on my tab as well? I'll pay for his donut."

"My donut?" Bentley sounded indignant.

I grabbed my box of croissants and patted Bentley on the bicep. He was all muscle underneath the gray suit. "Keep up the good work, Detective, and I'll see you around."

"Let's hope not," he said.

As I left with my box of croissants, I heard the detective order a donut with rainbow sprinkles before asking, "Have you folks had any suspicious graffiti recently?"

My ears pricked up. I set my box on the counter by the window and bent down to re-tie my laces.

"Graffiti? No. More like the opposite," Jordan said. "There were a bunch of tags on the dumpsters in the alley, and this morning they looked as clean as new."

"Have you spoken to the waste removal service? They might have replaced the bins."

"They didn't. Yesterday's garbage and recycling was still in there. I know because my wife tossed in a few stinky diapers last night, and they're still around. It looks like someone came along and just erased the graffiti without touching the paint."

"That is strange," Bentley said. "Mind if I take a look?"

"Right this way." Jordan led the detective through the bakery to the back door.

I looked around the bakery for signs of anything else strange. Everything seemed normal enough for a bakery. The business cards had ink on them. I took a handful and left.

I would have to report to Zinnia that whatever was erasing ink around town wasn't stopping. Now it had spread to the graffiti on garbage bins and, more importantly, my money.

CHAPTER 29

FRANK TOOK ONE of the croissants and gave me a devilish smile. "And it's not even Fresh Pastry Friday," he said. "You're spoiling us."

"Why not have fresh pastry every day? It's not like limiting it to Friday keeps us from eating it. We just nibble on the stale stuff all week."

"You're preaching to the choir, Little Miss Muffet." He waggled his pink eyebrows.

"Did you call me Little Miss Muffet?"

Frank made a mischievous face.

I gave him one of my Mom's Onto You looks. "What are you up to, Frank Wonder?"

He used his index finger to make a dimple in one cheek. "You'll see."

"Oh, dear. I'm so frightened." He had no idea that I regularly got possessed by ghosts, and that one had recently wiped out my money. Frank's mischief was way down on my list of things to worry about. Way, way down.

Before we opened the doors to the public, I checked my bank and credit card statements online. How bad could it be? I braced myself for the worst.

My most recent credit purchases were the haircuts at the Beach Hair Shack and last night's sushi takeout. The balance owing was about what I expected. I didn't see anything out of the ordinary. I clicked into the security log report and found that I'd been logged in for two hours the previous night, accessing every single one of my banking reports.

I had no recollection of doing this. And two hours was far too long for me. Typically, whenever I logged in to pay my bills, I held my breath, treating it like a trip to a port-a-potty at an outdoor music festival—in and out before I passed out.

So, what was my ghost up to? I hoped he wasn't getting my information ready for some Nigerian prince to transfer millions of dollars through my account.

The ghost did have a point about my credit cards. I had too many, and it was hard to track all the balances. But carrying cash around wasn't ideal. I contacted the bank and ordered a replacement for one of the cards.

Then I pulled out the photocopied FAQ from Beatrizz Riddle and re-read it, paying special attention to point three:

When will they move on?

When they are good and ready. Some spells can speed up the process. Please consult your Elders before attempting any direct communications with the Spyryts. You don't want to accidentally conjure a portal to a Demon Dymensyon and release Hell on Earth! Nobody likes a Wytch who gets into trouble she can't handle or sets off the Apocalypse.

No, Beatrizz, nobody likes a witch who sets off the Apocalypse.

* * *

I skipped my coffee break and stayed on the computer. Last night's visit to the Pressman residence hadn't turned up a body, but perhaps some computer searches would, so to speak. If Perry wasn't haunting me, who the heck was it?

There were no other Pressmans living in Wisteria, and far too many outside our town.

I tried another tactic. Some digging in the database revealed that another person had once shared Perry's home address. Her name had been Jasmine Pressman, but it was now Jasmine Carter. She had to be his ex-wife. Her date of birth matched up.

Jasmine Carter still lived in Wisteria, in an apartment building.

I searched for obituaries of Carters, looking for anyone on Josephine's mother's side who might be my ghost. I found a grandmother who'd passed away three years earlier. She might have been the one who scolded "Little Jo" for being absentminded.

The grandmother lived her whole life in Wisteria, and accomplished many things. She was a beloved member of the community and a talented artist, specializing in the mediums of wood carving and watercolors. She did not, however, seem to have any work experience in the financial sectors. If she had ghosted her way up my nostril, I'd have spent last night carving bear figurines from driftwood instead of hacking up my credit cards.

I read the final line: *She is survived by her daughter, Jasmine Carter, and her granddaughter, Josephine Pressman.*

A tear came to my eye. Obituaries always hit me hard, even those of strangers. The best ones made me happy and sad at the same time.

I imagined my own obituary. *Zara Riddle is survived by her daughter Zoey and her many grandchildren, great-grandchildren, and loved ones who are too numerous to mention by name.* Thinking of my many chubby-cheeked, redheaded descendants made me misty-eyed. I blew my nose and went to the washroom to freshen up. I returned to the computer at the front desk and got back to my investigation.

Inspiration had struck when I was washing my hands in the washroom. I was on the right track with the

Pressman family, but I had to get my hands dirty. I had to break a few rules.

I picked up the library's phone and called Jasmine Carter. She picked up the phone after one ring.

"Good morning, Ms. Carter," I said. "How are you?"

"Fine," she said slowly. "Do I have books overdue? I'm reading one of those House of Hallows books at the moment, but I should be done in a few days. I always bring the books back right away if I know there's a waiting list."

"Your account is in good standing. We're just conducting a study for the benefit of the library. Do you have a few minutes to help?"

"Why, of course!" She sounded eager, and pleased to be asked. This was a woman who appreciated her town's library. I liked her already.

"Ms. Carter, do you find that our summer hours meet your needs?"

"Well, sometimes I wish the library was open a little later on Thursdays because that's when I play pickleball at the recreation center. But then again I suppose you can't please everyone, can you?" She laughed lightly. "And I'm always sweaty after pickleball, so I'd want to go straight home most nights." She laughed self-consciously. "Oh, dear. I'm not helping at all, am I?"

"This is all very good," I said. "Pickleball sounds like fun."

"You'd love it! Pickleball is excellent for all ages." She went on to explain the rules to me.

After a few minutes of her pickleball recruitment pitch, I interrupted. "Ms. Carter, your voice sounds so familiar, and not just from the library."

"Oh?"

"Is it possible we've met recently? Say, at a memorial?"

"Hmm."

I leaned forward on the counter expectantly, gripping the phone tighter.

"Probably not," she said. "I'm fortunate to have not attended any funerals since my mother passed three years back. Knock wood." I heard her tapping on something.

I nodded. She hadn't lost a family member or close friend in three years, which was good for her, but a dead end for me.

"Well, thank you so much for your time," I said.

"That's all you've got? It's not much of a survey. All I've done is try to recruit you for the pickleball league."

Now it was my turn to laugh self-consciously. "I suppose it isn't much of a survey." I fumbled around with some papers in front of me. "Oh! I've just flipped the paper over and there are a few more questions after all." I glanced around to make sure my coworkers weren't listening. Frank was near the library's public computer terminals. He winked at me.

I made up a new survey question on the spot. "Ms. Carter, we're planning to paint the library's exterior. How do you feel about the color blue?"

"Isn't the library mostly concrete? Why would you paint it?"

You're a sharp one, Ms. Carter. "Just the doors," I said. "We are considering a light shade of blue."

"That would be fine," she said. "Blue is nice. Darker, or lighter."

"And we might change the grassy area to a rock garden, and the rock garden to grass."

"I don't see why you'd bother spending money on that when you could add it to the book budget."

"Right. Actually, the survey question about the rock garden was actually a trick question. Of course we wouldn't do anything so foolish." I used the back of my hand to wipe the sweat from my brow. Frank was still watching me from across the library, and this fake-survey ruse was getting increasingly complicated to keep up.

Now I understood why Zinnia had been so exhausted by the glamour spells.

"Okay," Ms. Carter said, sounding dubious.

"What sort of books would you like to see more of? Additional copies of our most popular epic fantasy series?"

"Occult," she said. "Nonfiction."

Was she talking about witchcraft? Did this woman know more about me than the fact I was calling her from the library?

"I'll make a note of that," I said calmly. "I'm writing your comments right here, on the form. Occult books. Anything specific?"

"Oh, this is so embarrassing. I should tell you, my ex-husband is the one to blame for my interest in such tawdry things. He gave me a book about crystal skulls and aura photography and astral projection, and I've been hooked ever since. But you folks have almost nothing on the topic. Your occult section has a few titles about the Egyptian pyramids, but it's so dry. I've had to get my occult fix at the bookstores, and that can really add up. I try to not be a cheapskate, but years of being married to a penny pincher have had an effect on me."

Now we were getting somewhere. "I know a man just like that. A real financial wizard. Have you ever had someone in your life who cut up your credit cards?"

She squealed. "At least twice! Honestly, my ex-husband truly meant well, but he was so heavy handed."

"Your ex-husband cut up your credit cards?" Why did every clue keep pointing to Perry Pressman when the man was still alive?"

"He sure did. I swear, our daughter Josephine went the exact opposite direction, just to rebel. The girl is a magician. That's what Perry always said. A magician! If you want to see a dollar disappear, put it in her palm."

There was a scratchy, light tap on my shoulder. I turned to find a giant spider the size of my hand, hanging in the air.

I dropped the phone. If my magic had been functioning, I might have given my secrets away by flinging the spider away.

I took a closer look. The spider was rubber. A simple Halloween decoration, suspended from fishing line. The line ran along the ceiling, all the way to the computer terminals, where Frank stood grinning at me. He raised and lowered his hand. The spider made a corresponding jaunt up and down in the air.

This was why he'd called me Little Miss Muffet earlier. He must have spent an hour prepping this particular gem. He couldn't have looked more pleased.

I grabbed some scissors and cut the line before the spider could take another victim.

I picked up the phone. Jasmine Carter was still talking, unaware of the phone having been dropped.

"Perry was always so fascinated about the intersection between humans and technology, and how the two things might be merged someday in the future. I told him, 'Perry, I hope to God we don't all become robots in my lifetime. That's not my idea of scientific advancement.' And he told me that saving money was only going to be a concern for people for just a few more years. Once the machines gained human capabilities, they'd be able to do all our menial labor, and we'd all become members of the leisure class. He thought the future looked pretty darn rosy, but if you ask me, people get bored if they don't have anything meaningful to do. I mean, just imagine! Idle hands are the devil's workshop!"

She paused, waiting for a response.

"Devil's workshop," I said. "That would be a good name for a heavy metal band."

"I suppose it would be."

"Speaking of workshops, does your ex-husband build things? Inventions?"

She was quiet so long, I worried I'd gotten too aggressive and lost her.

When she finally answered, her voice was brittle. "I told Perry I couldn't live in the same house with anything that was an atrocity to our Lord and Maker. It would be like inviting demons to come inside."

"You believe in demons?"

"I'm a good Christian woman! Of course I believe in the existence of demons. Without evil, there is no reason for salvation."

"I guess I never considered that."

She coughed. "Oh, look at the time. I have to go. Thanks so much for calling me today."

The line clicked. She was gone.

I hung up the phone and stared at it. Jasmine Carter condemned her husband's interests in combining humans and machines because it was an abomination against God. And yet she was keenly interested in borrowing library books about occult matters. Humans are funny creatures. Simultaneously attracted and repulsed by that which fascinates us.

I picked up the spider Frank had scared me with. With its cartoonish fangs, the spider was both ugly and cute at the same time.

And how about the mysterious Perry Pressman? His ex-wife practically ratted him out as the builder of atrocities.

Ghost or not, he was up to something.

Something wicked.

I used my cell phone to message Chet: *When is the raid, and can I come?*

CHAPTER 30

My boss came by and stopped to frown at a stack of books that had been growing throughout the day.

Kathy didn't know it, but our ink problem hadn't gone away. Several more blanked-out books and magazines had surfaced in the overnight returns. I'd instructed the support staff to intercept the damaged books and put them into a stack for me. I planned to use my bookwyrm dough to restore the words, and then carry on as though nothing was wrong.

Kathy patted the stack accusingly. "Who put these books here?"

"Those are my little project." I grabbed the stack with a weary sigh. "I'll get these fixed up and back in circulation in no time."

"Fixed up? Are they damaged?"

Yes, but I couldn't tell her that. I wrinkled my nose. "Sticky covers, I'm afraid. Someone put a Popsicle through the return slot. Luckily it only dribbled on a few before we caught it."

"Someone put a Popsicle through the return slot?" Kathy's eyes expanded to fill her glasses. She couldn't have looked more alarmed if I'd reported a picnic basket full of Anthrax and lit firecrackers.

She hooted, "Whooo would do such a thing?"

I held the stack of books tightly to my chest. "I don't know who, but if I ever catch them, I'll be sure and let you know."

As I walked away, I heard Kathy muttering about medieval torture devices.

Once I was in the repairs alcove, I reached into my pocket and pulled out the container of bookwyrm dough. I plopped it into my hand. It felt warmer than I expected.

I held the pale green ball up to eye level and asked, "Are you ready to do your job, little guy?"

The bookwyrm dough seemed to wiggle in anticipation. I wasn't seeing things. I'd also felt it shift on the palm of my hand.

"Did you just wiggle?"

The ball of dough pulsed in my hand. Then it pulsed again, this time rocking from side to side.

"Okay," I said. "I did *not* just imagine that."

The ball of dough vibrated. It was emitting a noise.

"What's that, little guy?"

I held it up to my ear, where it made a sound like tee-hee-hee.

Shocked, I held it in front of my eyes again. "Excuse me, but did you just say *tee-hee-hee*?"

A tiny slit appeared within the dough, and then two dots above it. If that wasn't a mouth and eyes, I didn't know what was.

A small but clear voice said, "Tee-hee-hee."

I nearly dropped the thing.

"You're alive?"

It made a soft sound that translated in my head as *I dunno*.

"If you're alive, how do you feel about being rolled into a snake-shaped log, then up and down on these damaged book pages?"

It made a chattering sound that might have meant pleasure. The eyes blinked up at me, and its slit of a mouth curved into a smile.

"I'll take that as a positive response," I said. "You enjoy being useful. Having a purpose."

It made another sound I heard as *Whee!*

I sandwiched the ball between my hands and gave it a roll. It elongated, just like a ball of dough would. The eyes and mouth were gone. Had I imagined our conversation?

I rolled the dough until I had a handy-sized log. The dough didn't complain or giggle.

I got to work fixing the erased pages. All it took was a smooth roll of the bookwyrm dough—or should I say *the bookwyrm*, on one page, and the text would reappear throughout the entire tome. The books that were affected showed no pattern. The titles varied from children's picture books to photography manuals and infrequently borrowed guides for home improvement projects.

In just a few minutes, I'd finished half the stack. Strangely, the bookwyrm seemed to be growing in size. If someone else had been present in the alcove with me, I almost certainly would have made some very distasteful jokes, given the particular shape of the bookwyrm as well as its propensity to grow under my touch. It would have been stranger to *not* make such jokes, but I digress.

The bookwyrm's face didn't reappear, nor did it make any more noises. By the time I'd finished repairing the entire stack of books, the bookwyrm had grown by about fifteen percent. I opened the plastic container, balled the dough up, and plopped it in. The fit was tight.

"Thanks for the help, little guy," I whispered.

The lump grew a single, tiny hole, from which it emitted a cheery whistle.

"Shh," I said. "Keep it down in there."

It whistled again, but quieter.

I attempted to put the lid on top, but I couldn't get a seal on the rim. The bookwyrm had outgrown its container.

"You chubby little rascal," I said. "What am I supposed to do now?"

It made the *I dunno* sound.

"I could chop off a little bit of you."

It emitted a high pitched chirp of horror, which grew in volume to an alarm warble.

I slapped my hand over the top of the pale green lump. This worked to muffle the sound.

"Just kidding about the chopping, little buddy. How about you wait right here for me and I'll go ransack the staff kitchen for a bigger container for you? Can you be quiet?"

The warble died down and the bookwyrm went quiet. I took my hand away, expecting the worst. Would it grow fangs and bite me?

The bookwyrm was as silent and inert as a regular ball of dough in a plastic container.

"Good bookwyrm," I said.

It chirped once.

"This is my life now," I whispered to myself with a sigh. "Stay here and don't make a peep."

Eyes and a mouth appeared. "Peep," it said softly.

"I'm serious," I said, shaking my finger. "Just remember, I'm much bigger than you. And I'm a witch."

The bookwyrm gasped and sucked its eyes and mouth back into itself with a pop.

I grabbed the re-inked books, gave the bookwyrm a stern look of warning, and left it in the alcove while I went to find a larger container.

It took me two minutes to put the books out for shelving, and then eight minutes to gather an assortment of clean containers from the staff lounge.

A total of only ten minutes. Ten minutes.

And in that short amount of time, the bookwyrm got into a heap of trouble.

I returned to the cleaning alcove to find my coworker Frank Wonder crumpled limply on the floor.

Frank was breathing, but his whole face was blacker than black licorice. The black extended across his scalp, showing at the roots of his dyed-pink hair. I checked the inside of his mouth. Black as well, from teeth to tongue. He'd been inked.

Frank must have entered the alcove, seen the bookwyrm, and then what? Had he licked it? What had given him the idea to do such a thing?

I wheeled around to face the bookwyrm. It was still in the base of the plastic container.

"What did you do?"

The bookwyrm formed two eyes and a mouth. It made an innocent *I dunno* sound.

"Right. If you didn't do this, who did? Was it some *other* bookwyrm?"

The tiny eyes narrowed and it emitted a hiss.

"Bad bookwyrm," I said. "Bad."

It hissed again, this time louder, and spraying little balls of dough from its mouth.

"That's enough out of you for one day." I transferred it into an empty plastic container, face down so I didn't get spat on. The container had once held onion chip dip, and still smelled of it. The bookwyrm moaned in protest. I slapped on the lid and pressed it shut.

Once sealed inside the container, the bookwyrm made a mournful, recalcitrant sound.

"Don't just say you're sorry," I told it. "*Show me* you're sorry. Tell me how to make Frank's face go back to regular color."

The bookwyrm made another *I dunno* sound. It went on to warble innocently that it only knew how to put ink on things, not how to remove it.

"How convenient," I said dryly.

Frank continued to lie unconscious on the floor, no help at all.

CHAPTER 31

WHO DO YOU call when your coworker mistakes your magic dough for something tasty and gets knocked unconscious by a full face inking?

If you have an aunt who's a witch, you call her. Well, first you consider calling 9-1-1, and then you imagine their questions, and *then* you call your aunt.

Zinnia got to the library in ten minutes flat. I let her in through the staff door and into the book cleaning alcove to take a look at poor, limp, inked-up Frank.

"We have to get the bookwyrm ink off his face," Zinnia said.

"You think?" I blinked at her. "I thought we'd dye the rest of him to match."

"All black?" She seemed to consider the idea. "There's really nothing I can say right now that doesn't tread dangerously near offensiveness."

"Speaking of dangerous, check this out." I pushed up one of his eyelids to reveal all-black eyeballs. "That's got to affect a person's vision."

"He shouldn't be woken up in this state."

"That's why I haven't tried."

She performed a cursory physical exam and pondered the problem for a minute.

"Let's get him out of the library," she finally said. "We've got options, but they should happen elsewhere."

"You grab his hands and I'll get his feet."

She twitched her nose. "I can take him by myself."

"He's skinny, but he still weighs more than you."

She whispered something in Witch Tongue. Then she grabbed Frank by the torso and tossed him over her shoulder as easily as a bath towel.

"Holy sweatpants. You're stronger than you look."

She waved a hand as she explained, "Your coworker just temporarily lost most of his body weight. I cast a body-buoyancy spell."

"You made him lose weight? Frank's going to be so bummed he missed out on this."

She shook her head. "He can never know about this. Understand?"

I nodded and mimed zipping my lips.

She leaned out of the alcove to check the pathway to the staff exit. The book repair alcove was near the staff lounge, but she would be exposed as soon as she walked out. I wondered what kind of magic she'd use for the escape. As bad as I felt for Frank, I was excited to see what Zinnia would do next.

"Zara, go cause a distraction," she said.

"Why? Don't you have a cloaking spell? Something like the bush glamour, to make you blend into your background?"

"A smart witch must never, ever use a spell when she can use her head." She gave me a shove out of the alcove.

I walked over to the circulation counter, pulled Frank's plastic spider out of a drawer, and proceeded to cause a distraction. The shrieking and hand waving, although humiliating, would provide Zinnia with the necessary cover to get my limp coworker out of the building. Inside a quiet library, a little screaming goes a long way.

Kathy Carmichael came running to save me. She stabbed a letter opener through the plastic spider and into the book beneath it. She blinked at me in shock.

"You saved my life," I said.

"Whooo would put a big plastic spider in the book return?"

"Probably the same jerk who return-slotted the Popsicle."

Her eyes expanded behind her round glasses. If she'd been a cartoon, steam would have been coming out of her ears.

Through gritted teeth, Kathy said, "Vincent Wick. Have you seen him around?"

"Not, uh, lately." I glanced over to make sure my aunt was gone. The alcove was empty. Either Zinnia had turned invisible, or she'd made it out safely with Frank.

I gingerly took the stabbed plastic spider away from Kathy. "No need for an autopsy," I said. "What makes you think this plastic spider is the work of Vincent Wick?"

"Who else? He's always around whenever there's trouble. He's like a..." Her face went through a series of unpleasant expressions.

"Like a wizard?"

She frowned. "Not exactly. More like a lightning rod for trouble."

"What kind of trouble?"

Kathy scrunched her pointy nose. "He gets his birds to swoop on people."

"What? His birds?"

She waved a hand. "Just his falcons. He trains them. The town has a couple of falcons who keep other birds away from the airport runways."

"How big are these falcons?" *And do they attack witches and shifters going for an innocent walk in the park?*

"Oh, forget I said anything. Vincent Wick is all bark, no bite. He doesn't cause the trouble. He prefers to sit back and watch." She glanced around. "Have you seen Frank? He was mending a book spine but I haven't seen him around."

I reached for my stomach and began moaning. "Oh, no!"

"What's wrong?"

"Frank was sick, and now I think I've got whatever he has." I groaned. "We should not have shared that odd-smelling tuna sandwich for lunch. He was making some horrible sounds in the staff washroom. I'm scared to go in there, but I don't know how much longer I can last."

Kathy backed away, all the way to the hand sanitizer dispenser. She squirted foam liberally onto both hands.

"Zara, you can go home early," she said. "And tell Frank the same. We can't risk all three of us getting stomach flu at the same time."

Grimacing, I thanked her and made my exit. The truth was, my stomach did hurt. I felt terrible about what had happened to Frank. It was my fault for leaving the bookwyrm unattended.

I grabbed my purse and went outside to find Zinnia. I found her car in the parking lot, but no sign of my aunt.

"Psst." The sound came from the bushes. I found her hunching over Frank's limp, partly blackened body.

"There were people in the parking lot," Zinnia said.

"It's all clear now. But don't do a fireman's carry. We'll do it together, one arm over each of us."

"First give me your hand." She reached out. I put my hand in hers, and she gave it a squeeze. A tingle of electricity buzzed from my hand throughout my body. After a full day of being grounded and having no power, the magic was intoxicating.

"Don't pull," she said crossly. "I'm trying to draw power *from* you. Just relax."

I let my hand go limp. I'd thought she was giving me my powers back, but no such luck.

She explained, "I need to borrow some of your strength so I can cast a complicated spell. If it works, it should keep him sleeping for the next several hours. He might suffer some brain damage, but I'm sure you can cover for him at work while he heals."

"Did you say brain damage? Can't you just fix him? Cast a spell to turn his face back to... face color?"

"Face color is not a color, and no, I cannot."

"You're doing this on purpose to punish me," I said. "You're making this more difficult than it needs to be. But I get it, okay? Lesson learned. I was careless and left the bookwyrm out where a regular person could get their hands on it. I'll take my forty lashes, but don't punish Frank." I crouched over his prone body and placed my free hand on his forehead. "Plus he's already so warped. Brain damage is the last thing Frank needs."

Zinnia sighed and released my hand. "Very well then." She reached into her purse, pulled out a vial of pills, and shook out two. "Crush these up between his teeth. There are plenty of ways to knock someone out that don't involve magic. I suppose I should take my own advice about not resorting to magic when regular ways will work."

I took two pills from her hand. "Drugs?" I popped my head up over the edge of the bushes and looked around before crouching down again to stare at my aunt, who'd apparently gone crazy. "We're talking about drugging and kidnapping my coworker. We're breaking all kinds of librarian codes, not to mention laws."

"There's nothing else we can do. The bookwyrm ink will take time to deal with, and as soon as he wakes up, he's going to have all kinds of questions."

We both looked down at Frank, who was still unconscious.

"We can pretend it was a prank," I said. I didn't want to drug my friend.

She gave me a motherly look. "We must be brave and do what needs to be done."

Reluctantly, I popped the pills into Frank's inky mouth. I worked his jaw to crush them. I rubbed his neck, and he swallowed without waking up.

Zinnia arched her eyebrows. "You've got a real knack with human manipulation."

"Thanks, I guess."

We carried Frank across the parking lot, and loaded him into the back seat of Zinnia's car.

"You put on his seat belt while I make a phone call," she said.

"Who are you calling?"

She gave me a look that said *you'll see.*

While I got Frank secured in the back, Zinnia made her call.

She spoke slowly and clearly into the phone. "I need a cleanup." She paused, listening. "I'm in my vehicle right now, but I'll be at my residence within ten minutes."

She ended the call, tossed her phone into her purse, and started the car engine.

Something about the set of her jaw made me refrain from peppering her with questions.

After a few minutes, once we were on our way to her house, she spoke.

"Zara, sometimes even good witches do bad things. Whatever happens tonight, please do as I say without question. Everything's going to be fine."

She was saying the right words, but the tone of her voice gave me no comfort.

I turned to check on poor Frank. His pink eyebrows looked like two fuzzy caterpillars. He looked so helpless. What did *cleanup* mean?

CHAPTER 32

"WHAT RAID?" ZINNIA asked. We were nearly at her house, and hadn't spoken for several minutes.

"Huh? I didn't say anything."

"Oh." She kept her eyes on the road ahead and smiled knowingly.

My phone buzzed. I pulled it out and saw a new message.

Chet Moore: *The raid is happening tonight. I'll pick you up.*

"That's eerie," I said to my aunt. I explained how she must have gotten a premonition about my incoming text message.

"My future sight is not that impressive," she said. "I can sense when someone's calling, but only a few seconds before they do."

"It's better than nothing."

She snorted and glanced over at the phone in my hands. "So, are you going to answer my question? What raid?"

I told her what I knew about Chet's people starting a case on the Pressmans and digging into their business. She seemed relieved.

"I'm glad to hear someone's looking in on the Pressmans. I can't wait to dispose of that rotten bookwyrm and get life back to... whatever passes for normal around here."

"Can I get my magic back in time for the raid?"

"What do you think?"

I groaned and slumped in my seat like a grounded teenager pouting.

We pulled onto her street. Her usual parking spot in front of her house was already taken by a white cargo van. The side was marked Wisteria Department of Sanitation. As we pulled up behind the van, the back doors opened and a man stepped out.

Vincent Wick.

"I knew it," I whispered.

Zinnia shot me a warning look. "Pretend you didn't know until just now."

I stared at Wick and made a shocked face for his benefit. "Your cleaner is Vincent Wick?" I gasped for good measure.

Vincent Wick squinted in the bright afternoon sunshine. He had the desperate look of a rat caught raiding the kitchen. With his shiny-black hair and tanned skin, he looked waxen and artificial.

He opened the back door of Zinnia's car, and slid in next to Frank.

"Two Riddles in one place," he said, grinning.

I opened my mouth to say something, but Zinnia gave me a magical kick in the shin. Right. She'd told me to stay quiet and do as I was told.

"It's your lucky day," Zinnia said to Wick cheerfully. "Can you help us?"

Wick turned to Frank's unconscious body. "Let's see how far the affliction extends." He tugged at Frank's shirt collar. The ink ended halfway down Frank's neck. The edge of the blackness was irregular, like a birthmark.

"Interesting," Vincent said. "Was this an accident with pashylar paste?"

"Bookwyrm dough," Zinnia answered.

"Of course." He patted Frank's hair. "But how did it make all his hair go pink?"

I interjected, "It was like that before. Frank dyes it pink."

Vincent didn't react to my input. He said, "You two can load him into the van." He reached under Frank and pulled out his wallet. He checked Frank's driver's license. "His residence is an apartment. Not ideal, but I'll drop him at this address. He won't be in to work tomorrow." He glanced in my direction briefly. "I trust you can cover for him."

"Sure," I said. "Will he be back on Monday?"

Vincent turned away from me, opened the door, and stepped out of the car.

I leaned over and asked Zinnia, "Is Frank really going to come back to work on Monday? Or is he going to get *cleaned up* all the way into someone's concrete foundation?"

"Everything will be fine." She gave me a look that was almost reassuring.

We got out of the car and transferred Frank, whose head lolled from side to side limply, into the van.

The inside of Wick's van was filled with equipment, electronics of some kind. I tried to get a look, but Zinnia pushed me away.

"Go and wait in the house," she commanded.

Now, I'd like to say I did as she asked. She was, after all, my elder witch. Plus she knew best. The sensible thing would have been to use her magical key-hiding rock to let myself into her house, then wait there for future orders.

That's what I should have done. And if I had, she probably wouldn't have killed me.

But what I actually did was walked toward her front door, then as soon as she and Vincent got into the back of the van, I doubled back to the van.

Standing at the corner of the bumper, with my ear at the edge of the door's hinge side, I could hear their conversation.

Vincent Wick said, "It's been a long time, Zinnia."

"Not that long. You set up those wards for me barely a month ago."

"I mean it's been a long time since we worked on a cleanup job together."

"No way. I'm leaving Pinkie with you. I've got to watch after my niece. You wouldn't believe the trouble she gets herself into. She's probably burning my house down right now."

Wick chuckled. "I don't smell smoke."

Zinnia chuckled as well. "Not yet. Give her a few minutes."

"What else is new with you?"

"Never mind me. Shouldn't you be getting this one back to your wizard lair?"

"Come now. There's always time for a little gossip between old friends."

She snorted. "Right."

"I bet you haven't heard the latest about Dorothy Tibbits."

"I've heard she's claiming that we framed her for murder, and forced a false confession."

"That she did, but there's more. Help me get Pinkie onto this cot." The van rocked as they moved around inside.

"What else is Tibbits saying?"

"Not much. She's in a coma. The doctors are saying it was a stroke or an aneurysm, but I think you and I know differently."

Zinnia replied coolly, "I do not appreciate what you are implying."

"It wasn't your doing?" The van rocked again. "No cheeky little witcher-i-doo spell or curse?"

"Absolutely not."

"Sure." He chuckled again. "But listen. If you ever get yourself into deep, deep trouble, I hope I'm the first one you call."

"Sure," she said begrudgingly. "First things first. What do you know about local flareups?"

"I can neither confirm nor deny reports of local flareups. This guy's face looks like a simple accident."

"Vincent, I've seen bookwyrm dough accidents before. This one knocked him out cold, and my reversal spell doesn't even lighten the ink. Here, watch." They were silent, presumably observing as Zinnia performed a spell —a spell she'd pretended to not know two days earlier. *That witch!*

"Hmm," he said. "That is troubling."

"See? It's definitely a flareup, or a power surge. Something big and powerful is surfacing."

"In Wisteria? Nothing new there."

"Come on, Vincent. There's no need for you to shut me out like some civilian. What are you seeing on your end? And don't tell me *nothing*, because I know you see everything."

"The Department has been tracking some unexplained surges. Nothing for you to worry about."

"That's what they always say. Why do they shut us out?"

He guffawed. "You witches, with your erratic magic, do more harm than good. Just look at this innocent man. He'll be lucky if he's not permanently debilitated. Now that this town's got two more Riddles, it's a miracle the place isn't a smoldering pile of rubble."

"Give me a little credit, will you? Speaking of family members, what's yours up to?"

"I don't know what you mean."

Zinnia sighed. "She's been more secretive than usual. I think there's a change in crop coming in. And she was cleaned out of black scarabyce blood. It might be innocent enough, but I fear we may have a flying monkey situation."

Vincent laughed. "Flying monkeys?"

"Not *actual* flying monkeys, of course. But large quantities of black scarabyce blood can be used to prevent tissue rejection."

"You think someone's sticking together strange new creatures?" He laughed again, a low, mocking laugh. "I'll put out an APB on Dr. Frankenstein and that other guy, Dr. Moreau."

"Forget I said anything." She sounded huffy.

"You're barking up the wrong tree. Look a little closer to home. There's a heat signature coming off your novice. All the dials have been off the charts since the day she rolled into town. Whatever's happening, she's involved."

"Zara *has* been connected to the objects that were erased," she said slowly. "But no. She's a good witch. She's tries so hard to be good, and she *is* good. I vouch for her."

"Do you?" There was a tapping sound, fingers on a computer keyboard. "Have a look at this reading. Your niece is standing just outside that door, in direct defiance of your orders, listening to our entire conversation." More tapping. "How convenient that she's standing near that particular bumper."

Zinnia cried out, "Vincent, don't!"

I backed away from the van, but not fast enough. A shock pulsed through me. My body seized. I had three thoughts, in rapid succession. *I should have gone into the house like Zinnia told me to.* And then, *I'm going to miss Chet's raid.* And finally, *this is a lot worse than the toaster.*

Everything went black. I felt nothing but pain. Saw nothing but darkness.

I smelled my aunt's perfume. She was talking. Her words were jumbled.

I felt pressure under my armpits. Zinnia's hands? I was moving, being dragged.

"Don't try to help," she said.

Was she talking to me or Vincent? I tried to ask, but my mouth didn't work. My jaw was clenched too tight.

"You're heavier than you look," she muttered. The pressure under my armpits released. I stopped moving. My eyes still wouldn't open. Everything hurt, and it was getting worse.

I heard her cast a spell. It was the same body-buoyancy spell she'd used on Frank. I felt a tingle that was... soothing.

I didn't need to hurt anymore. I could float up, free of the agony. I could float up, up and away.

My aunt's voice was far behind me, far away. I was free. Free as a blue jay, winging on the breeze.

Free from what? I couldn't remember. I didn't have a care in the world as I floated away.

CHAPTER 33

Big eyes.

The world was a swirling, confusing jumble, but I could see big eyes, the color of jade, framed by wispy hair so black it was nearly blue.

Corvin.

I was staring into the pale, round face of my ten-year-old neighbor.

How did I get there? The last thing I remembered was...

Pain. Blackness. A shock from Vincent's van. Zinnia moving my body. Telling me to relax. Zinnia casting a spell? Then I'd been free, floating above everything, and now I was here.

Corvin's lips were moving. He was talking to me.

What? Corvin, I didn't catch that.

He asked, "Are you dead?"

Very funny. Of course I'm not dead. Hey, how did I get here?

Where was here? I saw concrete counters. An enormous sink, big enough to use for dismantling bodies. Farmhouse Chic. I was inside the Moore house, at their kitchen table, with no memory of how I'd gotten there.

The windows were dark. The time on the microwave read 2:15 AM.

"Talk slower," Corvin said. "I think I can hear you if you talk slower."

What am I doing here? I asked the question with only my mind. I had no voice. Because I had no vocal chords. I had no body at all.

"I don't know what you're doing here," Corvin said. "I'm getting a glass of milk."

Is that all you were doing when I showed up here in your kitchen?

"Uh-huh. I had a bad dream." He went to the fridge and got a carton of milk. It was a brand new container. He clumsily ripped open the top to form the spout. I reached out to help him, but my hands kept passing through. I watched helplessly as he spilled milk everywhere.

Corvin, where is your father?

"Work. They picked him up in the big van. Grampa Don is supposed to be looking after me, but he fell asleep watching TV." He took a drink, giving himself a wide milk mustache. "I brushed my teeth by myself."

Good to hear. Apparently I'm a ghost now, and my daughter is an orphan, but at least we've won the battle against tooth decay for one more night.

Corvin gave me a confused look. "You're not a ghost," he said. "You're a witch."

You think this is a spell? Maybe it is. That means I'm not dead. Phew! If I had a forehead, I'd be wiping it right now.

"Where's your body?" He poked a finger through my translucent hand. "Did you put it on ice cubes? At school, they told us about a kid on a farm who got his hands cut off. Both of his hands. He picked them up with his teeth and he put them on ice. And then the doctors sewed them back on."

Did the doctors use black scarabyce blood? I hear it can be used for all sorts of things, like flying monkeys.

Corvin's eyes widened. "You're funny." He held up his fist and wiggled his thumb up and down. "You still owe me one."

For what?

"You took the clicky pen, and I'm the one who got in trouble. I know you took it, because I found it in your house, in the drawer next to your bed."

He was talking about Chet's multi-pulse click generator, the one he'd used to dissipate my sound bubble spell at the restaurant. In all the commotion, I'd forgotten about it.

Corvin, were you sneaking around in my house?

"You started it," he said. "You're the one who stole it, and stealing is worse than being somewhere you're not supposed to be."

Well, that's debatable. But you stole something, too. You stole the clicky pen back from me.

"I'm the one who got in trouble." His smooth forehead dimpled with the beginning of a worry line. "But I didn't tattle on you. I'm not a tattle tale."

Thank you. I guess I do owe you one. Hey, have you seen Zoey tonight?

"She's sleeping. I can see into her room from my room."

That was a relief. My kid was safe. I was missing out on the raid with Chet, but I wasn't too bothered by that. It was probably for the best I stayed clear of it. Now all I needed to do was reverse the spell I was under. Or go home and sleep it off.

Corvin played with the front of his hair, pulling the fringe down to cover his eyebrows. "Is Zoey your real daughter? You look exactly like her, but old."

Some people say she's the one who looks like me, since I came along first.

"Zoey is my friend."

I'm glad you two are getting along.

I looked around Chet's impeccably stylish, renovated kitchen, and then back at Corvin.

Am I imagining things, or is this the longest and most normal conversation you and I have ever had?

Corvin yawned. "I'm going to bed."

Want me to come upstairs and tuck you in?

He stared at me with his big jade eyes. Then he suddenly turned on his heel and ran out of the kitchen, shouting, "Witch! There's a witch in the kitchen!"

I heard the squeak of a reclining chair righting itself.

Corvin cried, "Grampy, there's a witch in the house!"

Grampa Don replied, "What the wing dang doodle! What time is it, boy? You should be in bed." He groaned, and the chair squeaked again as he got up. "Let's get you settled back down. Wipe that milk mustache off your face."

I listened to their footsteps as they went upstairs.

Time passed, and I heard Grampa Don singing to Corvin. The song sounded more like a funeral dirge than a lullaby. Things were different here in the Moore house.

I looked at the nearly-full carton of milk that Corvin forgot to put back into the fridge. *Kids.* It was going to spoil, and Chet would come home to sour milk after a long night of work. How could I get the milk back into the fridge without a body?

I was pondering this dilemma when Grampa Don entered the kitchen. He wore only a T-shirt and tightie-whitie underwear. He scratched himself as he lumbered around, completely unaware of me.

Hello? I waved my translucent hand.

He reached for the carton of milk and paused. He stared right through me.

Grampa Don, can you see me? Or hear me?

He grabbed the milk and put it away, muttering, "Dang old houses and their dang ghosts everywhere."

I'm not a ghost!

He scratched himself again and lumbered out of the kitchen, flicking off the light along the way.

I remained in the darkness. I wanted to leave, but I didn't know how.

The time on the microwave read 3:01 AM.

Nearly an hour had passed since the last time I checked. Yet I'd only spoken to Corvin for a few minutes.

The time read 3:25 AM. Time was fleeting.

I remembered something from Beatrizz Riddle's FAQ:

Spyryts... experience memory loss and confusion. Without the concrete structure of their bodies, even time loses its linear nature. While their knowledge seems to stay intact, their short-term memory is as slippery as a handful of tadpoles.

The time read 3:40 AM.

I certainly was confused. Time was slipping away on me. Was I a ghost now? Had I died? Corvin had assured me I wasn't dead, but the kid could barely open a carton of milk.

I stared at the Moore family's fancy stainless steel refrigerator. I remembered how I'd left my purse in my fridge. An image of my purse came to mind. Pink. Leather. Brass buckle on the strap.

That was it. My purse was with my body. If I found my purse, I'd find my body. Would I be in cold storage, laid out on a bed of ice cubes?

I thought back to my conversation with Chet about a spirit walker he was looking for. He said it wasn't Mr. Finance Wizard, but that I'd know when I found it. Was it me? Was I doing astral projection? He'd apologized to me in advance for a reason. Did he do this to me?

First things first, I had to find my body.

With the image of my purse in mind, I uttered the incantation in Witch Tongue. Would the spell work without vocal chords or hands? I focused my mind as powerfully as I'd ever focused on anything in my life. (Or in my death.)

Nothing happened. Where was that purse?
I tried again.
Still nothing.
But you know what they say. *The third time is always the charm.*

CHAPTER 34

THE WORLD WAS once again a topsy turvy, twirling jumble, but I could see something pink, with a brass buckle.

My purse!

Right before my ghostly eyes was my beloved pink leather purse, sitting next to the sink in a familiar-looking kitchen. Huge bunches of drying herbs hung from the ceiling. Zinnia's kitchen. The time on the microwave read 3:45 AM. I had transported from Chet's kitchen to Zinnia's kitchen in five minutes or less.

Now that I'd found my purse, where was my body? Nobody else was in the kitchen. The house was quiet. I wished I could float up to her room and check her bed.

As soon as I'd wished it, I was upstairs, in Zinnia's bedroom. Her bed was empty.

Where are you, Aunt Zinnia?

I performed the object-locating spell, this time with my aunt in mind. She'd warned me it didn't work on people, but I tried it anyway. Nothing.

What next? Did I dare check her bathtub for a redhead on ice? I didn't know, and I felt discombobulated. So discombobulated, I feared I might float away, lost forever.

Keep it together, Zara. Now think. Before you had magic, what did you do when you lost track of something? Where was the last place you saw your aunt?

The last time I'd seen Zinnia, she'd been holding Frank's feet and loading him into a Department of Sanitation van with Vincent Wick.

Frank! I'd completely forgotten about poor Frank.

I wished I could check on him. I wished it with all my heart.

Once again, something tugged at me, and off I went.

The world tilted, went cold, then hot, and I was inside a cool-blue room, looking at my coworker.

Frank lay on his back like a corpse, with his hands folded across his chest. His chest was moving, rising and falling. The bookwyrm ink had receded. He was inky only from his mouth to his eyebrows.

"You dummies should wait for backup," said a man's voice.

I wasn't alone. And the room wasn't cool-blue after all. The walls were concrete. They appeared blue because they were bathed in the light of several computer screens.

In the middle of what appeared to be a control or command center, was a man. He was lit in silhouette, but I recognized his sharp, hawk-like nose immediately.

It was Vincent Wick.

He'd been the last person to take Frank, so I shouldn't have been so surprised, but I was.

"Don't go in there," Vincent said. Was he talking to me? No. He had the tone of voice of a man talking to himself.

"Do *not* go in there," Vincent said, more emphatically.

Who's going in where?

Vincent didn't react to my question. Unlike Corvin, he couldn't hear ghosts or spirit walkers. He smacked his forehead. "Of course you're going in unprepared. Bunch of macho idiots."

Macho idiots? I knew of at least one person who was working late that night, out on supernatural business. Was Chet a macho idiot? He could be macho, and an idiot, so yes.

Vincent's big head was blocking the central monitor, where it seemed the action was going down.

I tried to get a closer look. My legs didn't move, probably because I didn't have legs. How was I supposed to ambulate?

I leaned forward, thinking of old-fashioned arcade joysticks.

No movement.

Probably because I couldn't technically be leaning if I didn't have a body.

I watched as Vincent tapped on a keyboard. The screen in front of him zoomed in on a high-resolution satellite street view. But I still couldn't see through his big head.

I looked around for ideas. The bunker didn't have any windows. It did have cots, a kitchenette, and a door leading to a bathroom. Beyond the bathroom door was a set of metal stairs, leading up to an upper floor. From where I was, I couldn't see what was on the upper level, but I wished I could.

Suddenly I was on the upper level, at the top of the stairs. I was getting the hang of this astral projection business.

And now I knew the location of Vincent Wick's secret headquarters. The bunker was directly below his shack of an office. Now I knew why he had all those filing cabinets lining the walls. They were fake. Hollow. They had folded away to allow access to the metal stairs leading down.

I wished myself back downstairs. I was right back where I'd started, next to where Frank was sleeping on his cot.

I still couldn't do small movements. Getting around in spirit form was like playing the world's most buggy video game.

I tried for several minutes, and only succeeded in getting annoyed. Without a body, my rage just grew and grew. I became so angry, I wanted to smash everything in the bunker. Especially the stupid mug sitting next to Vincent on his desk. The thing said WORLD'S BEST BOSS. How could that be true?

Suddenly, the mug flew off the desk and smashed on the concrete floor.

Vincent jerked with surprise. He looked at the smashed mug on the floor, and then rubbed his elbow. He swung his arm, testing the reach of his elbow. It passed through the space where the mug had been sitting. He shrugged and returned his attention to the monitor before him.

I tested my telekinetic powers on the smashed ceramic on the concrete floor. A large shard slid over an inch, as though I'd nudged it with my toe.

Either Zinnia's chocolate-flavored curse on my powers had lifted, or I was only grounded when I had my body.

I was back in business! Now all I had to do was figure out *how* to use my powers. My telekinesis was limited to things I could do manually. I couldn't pick up a car, for example, or throw a ball bearing at bullet speed.

But I could easily push Vincent out of the way. His chair had wheels. But then he'd know I was there. And he had more than computers and monitors in his concrete lair. The walls were lined with all sorts of scientific-looking equipment. He was liable to spray the air with ghost-revealing powder and then suck me up with a vacuum cleaner.

I glared at the back of his head. *Is this what kind of wizard you are, Wick? A technology wizard who spies on everyone and everything from your creepy underground lair?*

He couldn't answer, but I knew I was right. Zinnia's cleaner friend was a technology wizard. Of all the wizards a person could be, Wick was the least magical kind.

And his big head was still blocking my view. Rather than move him and call attention to myself, I had to move myself. I tentatively pushed down on the concrete floor.

The entire planet Earth shifted down about six inches. It worked? I was the most powerful witch in the world! Able to move entire planets with my mind! My jubilation knew no bounds.

My emotions in this ghostly state were wildly powerful.

I pushed again, until I was floating with my ghost-head at the bunker's concrete ceiling. I visualized rolling the world like a bowling ball beneath me. I overshot Vincent's command station, but then I got the knack of the roll and positioned myself just behind Vincent's shoulder.

He shivered and pulled on a jacket that had been draped over the back of his chair.

Finally, I could see the view on his central screen.

A large cargo van with tinted windows was parked in front of a house. The house was a plain box with a gravel front lawn. The Pressman residence. Three men in dark clothing were approaching the front door. The resolution was clear enough that I recognized the silhouette of one man's face. It was Chet.

Vincent Wick said, "Don't do it." He fidgeted, yet he wasn't doing anything to stop what was happening on the screen. His warning was as effective as that of a movie-goer talking to the film.

Chet and the other two men had reached the front door. The largest of the trio did something to the door handle. The door opened.

They entered the house.

I leaned forward, putting my ghost-nose up to the screen. If only I could get audio.

There was yelling. Men's voices, and a woman.

I was getting audio!

Something inside the house flashed bright, along with a bang. Two more flashes and bangs. And then the house was quiet.

A shadow appeared in the doorway. A petite woman. Josephine Pressman.

She turned her head and looked right at me. Even without a body, I felt the chill in her gaze.

How could she see me? I was a ghost, plus I was far away, in an underground bunker.

Except I wasn't in the bunker.

I was in front of the Pressman house.

I must have teleported when I'd leaned in close to the monitor. That explained why I'd heard the audio so clearly.

Josephine Pressman looked at me, and then through me. She was looking at the van parked on the street.

She took a step back and closed the door.

The house was quiet.

An orange glow flickered in the window on the top floor.

Chet was in there, and something was wrong. Vincent Wick wasn't helping. Nobody else was around. If backup was coming, they were taking their time. It was up to me.

It wasn't difficult for me to teleport myself into the house, and up to the attic.

But as soon as I saw what was inside the Pressmans' attic, I very nearly wished myself somewhere else. Somewhere far, far away.

CHAPTER 35

WHEN I SAW what horror resided in the Pressman attic, I nearly wished myself away but didn't.

I was thankful at least to be there in spirit form, to not have a mouth, nor a stomach to empty through that mouth.

The attic was lit by a sickly orange light. The walls were pulsing—no, crawling, like the surface of an anthill. There was sound, too. The chorus of a million bug feet shifting. And liquid dripping. And the wheezing sound of fluid being sucked or blown through pipes or tubes or even—horror of all horrors—arteries. The walls were alive. The house was alive.

On the back wall, the texture was different. It was lumpy, the texture more like the inside of peeled skin. A dozen fist-sized creatures emerged from a hole and skittered in a circular pattern over the lumpy wall, coating it with a film.

In that moment, I struggled to relate what I was seeing, and I struggle now to describe it to you.

Imagine opening an infrequently used cupboard in a dark basement, only to discover a bubbling pile of goo, where you forgot a bag of potatoes months earlier. It's summer, and the flies have laid eggs within the mess, but you don't realize it's crawling with maggots until you have your hands in the slippery slime, and then you see the eyeballs of a rat who died eating the rotting mess, only the rat isn't dead after all, and it's scurrying up your arm, and your arm is turning into blackened goo, wriggling with maggots, and then your own hand is rising up, your fingers tentacles now, reaching for your face.

Seeing the walls of the attic was shocking like that, and then it got worse.

The monstrosity wasn't just bugs and goo in need of an exterminator and cleaning products.

Within the mass of organic horror, there were gears. Clockwork gears turning. And a sound like the hiss of air from a punctured lung.

But wait. It gets worse.

One of the lumpy shapes embedded in the wall had Chet's face.

I went to him, pushing the floor to propel myself. I was getting the hang of movement in spirit form, but I felt no joy from my mastery.

Chet's eyes were closed. His nostrils moved with the rhythm of breathing. There were two other lumps in the wall, two other two men who were embedded along with him. They were in a similar condition.

A tentacle emerged from the wall and wriggled toward Chet's slack mouth. I used my magic to grasp the tip of a tentacle. The tentacle fought me, so I yanked it from the wall and threw it on the floor. It lay still for only seconds before wriggling away like a snake. It wormed back into the wall of fleshy black goo.

More tentacles emerged from the wall. I yanked them away from Chet's face. His eyelashes fluttered.

"Zara," he said, his voice barely a croak.

Can you see me? Hear me? I'm in spirit form, but I can move things, as long as they aren't too heavy.

His eyelashes fluttered again and his eyes opened.

He croaked, "Why are you here?"

I'm here to get you and the other macho idiots out of this mess!

His eyes focused, but he was looking through me.

I followed his gaze, across the attic, to a person standing in the doorway. This person had my face. And my body. All mine, right down to the boots, which were technically Zinnia's, but it was me.

Zara Riddle stood in the doorway, breathing heavily.

On the plus side, at least I wasn't lying in a bathtub full of ice somewhere. On the minus side, whoever had snatched my body had brought it here, to whatever this was.

Chet groaned. The tentacles that held his body to the wall were evidently causing him pain.

"This is incredible," said the impostor in my body. "I knew Perry Pressman was a gifted man, but I had no idea he was working on such a large scale."

"Go," Chet managed to say. "Get out of here now, Zara. Leave me here. I'll stay until backup comes."

The impostor replied, "Backup? How long?"

I screamed my thoughts at Chet. *Don't tell her! Chet, that isn't me. It's an impostor!*

Chet croaked out, "I don't know how long. Get out of here. I'll be fine."

No, you're not fine. You're plant food.

He groaned again. "I'm not plant food. Give me a minute to just... catch my breath."

You can hear me!

He mumbled incoherently. His eyes closed.

The impostor walked toward Chet. My body's boots clomped clumsily and the walk was both stiff and snakelike at the same time.

The impostor gave Chet a cursory glance and then reached out and ran her fingers over the wall's fleshy arteries. She mused, "Perry, you've done a fine job, even if you didn't know what you were building."

If only I could climb inside my head and see who was in there.

Who are you?

Her hand jerked away from the wall. "Zara? Is that you, wondering who's got your body?"

You can hear me? Yes. I demand to know who you are. It's only fair.

The impostor shrugged. "Demand all you want. I'm not ready to reveal myself yet. I'd rather wait and chat after I'm in a new body. Maybe we can have one of those meet-cute things you girls love in the movies."

I turned my attention back to Chet, who was wheezing. I tried to tug him from the wall. The wall didn't like that. It hissed and lashed out with more tentacles, clutching him tighter.

"Don't struggle," said the impostor to Chet. "What is meant to be will be."

Chet's eyes opened and he squinted through the goo at the impostor. "Zara?"

"Don't worry. Your death won't be meaningless," the impostor said. "We're on the verge of an incredible breakthrough. Magic and science, together at last. Demons will walk the earth. We will slay all who oppose us."

Chet spat out, "Never."

The impostor stroked Chet's forehead. "You're so strong and powerful, with your wolf energy. If only I could break off a piece of you for myself"

Chet growled, but it was with his human mouth. He couldn't shift if he was injured.

"Sleep now," said the impostor.

Chet's pupils dilated. "Zara?" He was whispering now. "I'll stop struggling if you tell me to. I trust you."

"Good," she said.

"But first, kiss me?"

The impostor who wore my face hesitated.

Chet, don't trust her! She's not me! She's trying to kill you!

I yanked more tentacles away from Chet's body, but for every one I removed, two more sprung up in its place.

"One kiss," he said weakly. "I can't sleep until I get one kiss."

"What the hell." The impostor leaned forward, lips pursed.

Suddenly, Chet's eyes flashed open. He jerked his arm free of the tentacles, and punched her under the jaw. Her head shot back from the force, her eyes rolled up, and she fell backward.

He howled in agony as he pulled the rest of his body free of the wall. He stumbled forward to catch my body before it hit the floor but he was too slow. My body fell hard, my skull hitting the floor with an ugly crack.

"I'm so sorry, Zara," he said.

You should be. If I wasn't dead before, I probably am now.

He leaned over my prone body and pushed up one eyelid and then the other. "Are you in there somewhere? I swear I can hear you. It's like you're buzzing around inside my head."

I'm right beside you.

He looked around, swooning a bit. Dark smoke swirled around him and rushed up his nose.

"What," he gasped. "What did you do?"

I don't know. Tell me what to do next, and I'll try to help.

"I need to..." He staggered around. He had gray holes on his bare chest. Now the wall was reaching for him again, its slimy tentacles groping up his legs.

Could I use my powers to heal him? I'd done it once before, but I'd been inside my body. Now my body was crumpled in a heap.

I tried putting my spirit hands on Chet's injured chest, but they right through.

Chet touched his chest. "I feel you."

You can feel me?

Something in the wall let out a wail. No, not something, someone. A man was struggling to pull himself free.

Chet ran to the wall.

"Rob," he said. "I'll get you out of this."

Chet got to work, his muscles bulging under his ripped clothing. I helped, pulling away the tentacles and fibrous cords holding.

Chet kept working with one hand while he used his other to call in a report. "This is Agent Moore. We need that backup you promised. Are you receiving my visual broadcast?"

A tinny voice replied through the hand-held device, "Your visual is coming in clear. What is that thing?"

"I don't know, but send the fire crew."

"The fire crew is on its way."

Another voice, a female one, cut in, "Maybe we should nuke it from space, just to be sure."

Chet cracked the smallest of grins, despite his injuries. "Charlize, you always have such a way with words."

Chet was making progress getting the guy he called Rob free of the wall. I switched over to helping the other guy, who was much larger. He fell forward, toward the floor, with a thud that shook the whole house.

This man had huge muscles, the build of a competitive body builder. He had to be close to seven feet tall. I tried to send healing powers at his wounds, but it only made me dizzy. I couldn't heal in spirit form. Not these men, anyway.

I teleported over to where my body was taking a nap. I looked so peaceful, and also much smaller. Was I really that small? My hands were downright tiny.

I willed myself back into my body. Nothing happened. I tried lying down on top of myself and sinking down. My vision, but I didn't stick.

Wake up! Zara, wake up and get your body out of here before the fire crew comes. Something tells me they're the sort of crew who sets fires rather than extinguishing them. Snap out of it!

My body remained lifeless, which made some sense, since I wasn't inside it.

I heard more groaning. The three men were having some problems standing up, let alone fighting the living house.

The noises coming from the walls were getting louder.

The guys huddled in discussion, and then the big one came over to my body. He scooped my body in his arms, and then everyone headed toward the door.

Something went bang, like a firecracker going off. The three men stopped in their tracks.

Someone new was in the attic. Standing in the doorway was a petite female figure. It was Josephine Pressman, holding a gun.

"Freeze," she said, pointing the gun at Chet's head.

The big guy tossed my body over his shoulder like a gym towel, and lunged at her.

Bang! She shot him in the leg. No hesitation. He went down, along with my body, in a heap.

"Easy now, Ms. Pressman," Chet said. "Nobody needs to get hurt today."

Judging by the blood spurting from the big guy's leg, it was a bit late for a nonviolent confrontation.

I had to get the gun away from the girl. I used my magic to whip it away. But the gun didn't budge. I pulled harder, focusing as intently as I could.

Josphine Pressman let out a low laugh. "That tickles," she said. "Is that one of the meddlesome Riddle witches?"

Chet said, "Zara is here, and you're in big trouble. Now let us go, or things are going to get much worse for you."

"I don't think so." She shifted the barrel so it was pointing at my head on the floor. "Zara Riddle, you're not welcome in this town. I rescind my welcome."

She was going to shoot me. She would have done so already if she wasn't enjoying the idea and relishing it. Why did Josephine hate me so much?

More importantly, what could I do to stop her from shooting me?

I couldn't move the gun, and I couldn't touch her. It was so frustrating. I wanted to smash everything. And then I had a plan. I shattered the glass in the window behind her, gathered the shards in the air, whipped them up to the peak of the attic roof, and showered them down on her.

"You witch!" Something flashed, and the glass whipped away from her, spraying the walls of the attic.

The walls began making a new sound, a chorus of unearthly banshee wails.

Josephine was still armed, but I'd thrown her off. Unfortunately, a few of the shards had found their way into Rob. He dropped to his knees, large pieces embedded in his chest.

The attic was a mess. Chunks of the wall were sprayed everywhere, along with human blood, and a whole bunch of stuff I couldn't identify. What a mess.

I thought of my microwave at home, and the plastic thingie my aunt wanted us to use over our food.

That was it! I needed a shield to protect Chet, his men, and my body. But what? There were chairs in the attic, and loose chunks of what appeared to be meat, but nothing bullet-proof.

"I can feel you, witch," the girl spat.

What is this monstrosity? You're pure evil, Josephine Pressman. Your mother would be so ashamed.

Her face cracked into a grin. "I'm not Josephine anymore," she said. "Didn't you notice my new hairdo?"

Her hair was split into two braids, in the style of Dorothy from the *Wizard of Oz*.

Dorothy? You're the spirit walker? You stole my body and now you're stealing the Pressman girl's?

"Oh, that old thing?" She pointed to my limp body, tangled up with the big guy's and getting soaked in his blood. "That wasn't me in your body. That was somebody you do *not* want to mess with. You didn't think I was working alone this whole time, did you?"

I didn't know what to think.

All I knew was that I had to get out of there. Between the banshee screaming of the living walls and the spirit of Dorothy Tibbits taking over bodies, things were only going to get worse. I had to get us out of there. Preferably without any more bullet holes.

CHAPTER 36

WHILE I'D BEEN having my unwanted reunion with Dorothy Tibbits, the world's worst Realtor, Chet had disobeyed her command to freeze. He was fastening a tourniquet around the big guy's bloody leg when Josephine—no, Dorothy—wheeled around to point her gun at his temple.

"Easy there, Mr. Moore. Hands behind your head, please and thank you."

Chet slowly raised his hands behind his head.

"Are you really Dorothy Tibbits?"

"I guess the cat's out of the bag now."

"What do you want, Dorothy? Give me your demands, and I'll see what I can do."

She licked her lips. "Look at you, with all your hunky muscles hanging out of your ripped clothes. Why are you still single? I know you miss that blonde you were dating, but she's gone. You've got to move on."

He growled.

"One day you'll wish—ack!" Her face contorted, her body twitched, and she howled, "Get out of here! Go back to sleep, stupid girl!"

Chet watched her but didn't make a move.

She shook and cried out, "Help me! I'm Josephine Pressman! You've got to help me and my father!"

"Drop the gun," Chet said evenly.

The woman shook her head and recomposed herself. The gun took better aim at Chet's head.

Calmly, in Dorothy's scratchy voice, the woman said, "Pay no attention to Little Jo. She'll be fully erased, soon enough, and then I'll have this body all to myself."

"Erased?" Chet glanced at the machinery on the walls. "Is that what you're doing with this abomination? You're going to erase people so you can take over their bodies?"

"That's why we call it an Erasure Machine, dummy. It's for erasing things, once we get all the bugs worked out." She cackled cruelly. "Get it? The bugs?"

"This machine has been causing the magic surges around town."

"Maybe, maybe not."

"Dorothy, you don't have to do this. You can still put the gun down and walk away. Nobody else needs to get hurt today." In a softer tone, he said, "Please don't erase Josephine. She's innocent."

"Oh, don't look so horrified," Dorothy said. "You would do the same thing, if you could. You could raise that weird kid of yours to eighteen, keep his body strong, then simply wipe his memory back to a blank slate at the first sign of him disappointing you, which is exactly what he'll do."

The muscles in Chet's jaw rippled as he bit back his words.

"Children are always a disappointment to their parents," Dorothy said. She patted her body with her free hand. "Do you know why this one's living here with her father? No, I suppose you didn't bother to ask when you and your goons barged in here tonight. Well, let me tell you about Little Jo Pressman."

Her face contorted again, and she coughed, choking on her words. "Let me go," the girl trapped inside her own body cried. "Let me and my father go."

The woman whipped her gun hand up and cracked herself across the face with the butt of the pistol. The blow split her lip. She spat blood onto the floor.

"Tell me about Josephine," Chet said. "Tell me what she did that makes her deserving of erasure."

The dark-haired woman wiped at the blood on her chin but succeeded only in smearing it. "Josephine Pressman thought she was special. She thought she deserved better than Wisteria. She packed her designer suitcase and headed to New York City. She went to pursue her dreams, but then she fell for a musician and ended up working dead-end jobs to support *his* dreams. As of two months ago, all she had to show for it was a pair of dishpan hands. So, back she came to mooch off her spineless father. Old Perry had to finish the machine he'd been dabbling with for years." She grinned. "He finally found the courage to hook it up."

Chet nodded at the wall of pulsating goo and gears behind him. "This thing? What exactly did he hook it up to?"

"Himself," she said plainly. "It runs on meat."

"And it erases things?"

"It erases anything. Would you like a demonstration?"

He shook his head. "Who's your boss? Who are you working for?"

Dorothy mimed zipping her lips with her free hand.

"Is your boss Perry Pressman?"

She laughed. "You tell me. Come out here, Perry."

Something the size and shape of a man stepped out from the shadows of one of the walls. He was coated in dark, ashy goo. It was Perry, or what was left of him.

He moved slowly and jerkily, like a marionette. His front looked solid enough, but his back was all hollowed out, nothing but gears and glistening tubes. The back of his head was a mass of tentacles. That must have been what he was hiding with his hat the night before, when Zinnia talked to him.

Perry Pressman seemed to look right at me. "Kill me," he croaked. "Ki-i-i-ll me-e-e."

"As you wish," Dorothy said. She lifted her gun, and what was left of Perry Pressman was obliterated by a bullet to the skull. He fell to the floor like a bag of shredded meat.

A wisp of smoke swirled up from Perry's body and swirled through the room. Was anyone else seeing that smoke?

The big guy had his eyes closed, apparently passed out from pain or blood loss. The smaller guy, Rob, was on his back, facing the ceiling. His eyes were open, but he was breathing shallowly, focused simply on staying alive with the glass in his chest. Chet had his eyes locked on Dorothy, and Dorothy was staring back at him.

Dorothy waved her gun. "Now that Perry has been relieved of his duties, I really must ask you to get back into the machine."

Chet stood his ground. "Not gonna happen, Dorothy."

She aimed the gun at my limp head, on the floor. "Chet Moore, you have until the count of ten to return to your spot on the wall, or I'm going to play target practice with your girlfriend's freckles."

"Dorothy, you're better than this," Chet said. "You had a bright future once. You can have it again."

"Inside a jail cell, serving a life sentence for murder?" She shook her head. "Oh, Chet. You must think I'm a bigger idiot than your father. How's he doing, anyway? I hear you two spend an awful lot of time arguing over how many vegetables the man eats, which is ironic, don't you think?"

Chet growled.

The smoke continued to swirl around the room, as though looking for an exit.

Dorothy said, "Get yourself moving. Back to that wall, or I give this witch a makeover that involves a bunch of bullet holes. Count of ten. Ten. Nine. Eight."

Still growling, he began backing up.

"Seven. Six. Five."

Here goes nothing. I grabbed hold of the swirling smoke and sent it into my limp body on the floor. Straight up my left nostril.

"Four. Three."

My body didn't move. The wisp of smoke had to be Perry Pressman, my helpful wizard. He was supposed to animate my body and attack the woman who'd killed him. But he wasn't doing anything.

"Two," Dorothy said.

I delivered a magical slap to my body's face.

Chet was surrendering to the wall, merging with it slowly. "You promise you'll let Zara go?"

"I promise," she said.

He stepped backward into the wall. It made a slurping, chittering noise, and enveloped him.

"One," she said.

The room was silent. The monstrosity had stopped shrieking.

Something clicked.

"Oops," Dorothy said, shaking her gun over my body. "Out of bullets already."

She turned away to reload.

Beneath her, a pair of hazel eyes flashed open. The body of Zara Riddle was reanimated. Who was at the controls? Not me.

Whoever it was looked angry. My body shoved the big guy aside like he was made of popcorn, got up, and grabbed the gun from Dorothy, who hadn't been paying attention while reloading.

She may have had a spell that protected her from my telekinetic powers, but not an old-fashioned grab. She whirled around and faced the person animating my body.

My body spoke, voice wavering, "Josephine, I know you're in there. Honey, you've got to fight."

The woman answered sweetly, "Daddy?"

"Is that you? How do I know it's you?"

The woman sobbed, "I'm so sorry, Daddy. This is all my fault."

His arm shook. "You're not my daughter!"

She blinked. "Daddy? Why would you say that?"

"My Josephine was far from perfect, but I loved her anyway. Josephine would never apologize or blame herself for anything that went wrong in her life. It was always bad luck, or someone else's fault."

The woman smirked. "Children can be disappointing like that." She put her hands on her hips. "You got me. It's still me. Little Jo is taking a nap."

"I just want my daughter back."

The woman frowned. "That face. It looks so pretty when it's crying. I like the freckles. Maybe I want that body, not this one."

My body? Mine?

Dorothy Tibbits wanted to erase my mind and take over my body?

OH, HELL NO.

Desperate times call for desperate measures.

My gaze fell upon the lump in the pocket of my skirt. The bookwyrm. Using my magic, I yanked it up and out of the container.

Dorothy Tibbits was too busy scoping out my body and gloating to notice.

Her spell prevented my magical assaults, but she wasn't prepared for every possible attack.

I placed the bookwyrm in Perry's hand—my hand, powered by him.

Perry Pressman, you've always helped others, I thought at him. *We can still get your daughter back. All we need is one good shock, one powerful blow to her electrical system.*

Either Perry heard my thoughts or he did what came naturally to him once he felt the warm, vaguely damp bookwyrm in his hand. He wound his arm back like he was about to throw out the starting pitch for a ball game, and he tossed the wriggling bookwyrm right into the woman's mouth.

She convulsed and shook as the blackness spread out from her mouth, across her face. She collapsed on the ground, still shaking. With one final shudder, she violently spat out the bookwyrm. Squealing with what sounded a lot like glee, the bookwyrm flew across the attic and landed in the midst of the pulsating fleshy wall of machine.

The walls began shrieking again.

Chet, who was in the wall, struggled to break free.

Smoke filled the room.

And then there was pain.

I was gagging, choking on smoke.

I coughed and rolled onto my knees.

My lungs were filling with smoke.

Good news: I was back in my body.

Bad news: The bookwyrm had set off a chain reaction of explosions in the living walls, and we were all going to die.

Groaning from the effort of being back in my beat-up body, I made my way back to the wall to free Chet. I pried away two tentacles, and four took their places.

The house shook. It was Chet's backup, storming in at last. They wore gas masks and hazardous materials suits.

My head was reeling. The punch Chet had delivered turned out to be a real skull-rattler. I was concussed and losing consciousness.

"Chet," I croaked, hoarse from the smoke. "He's trapped in the wall."

A voice behind a mask replied, "Don't try to talk. Don't worry. Everything's going to be okay. The good guys are here."

"Chet," I croaked again.

I was being picked up, moved somewhere.

All around me, there was pandemonium. The person who'd been carrying me set me down, and not very carefully.

I got myself upright and looked around. So much for being rescued. This princess was going to have to get herself out of the castle.

I scanned for an exit. A familiar face appeared in the chaos of flashing lights and smoke.

"Aunt Zinnia," I croaked.

She came to my side and knelt over me. She had deep gashes down her cheek, and bruises around her eye. I lifted my hand up, trying to heal her, but no power came from my hands. She flinched from my touch and caught my wrist.

"Please be you," she said.

"I'm me." I tried to pull my wrist away but her grip was tight.

"How can I be sure?"

I tore my eyes off her beat-up face and looked at her clothing. It was hard to focus through the pain in my head, and hard to think straight with all the chaos and noise around us. An unbelievably ugly pattern swam before coming into focus. Her blouse had both paisley and flowers on it.

"Nice shirt," I said. "Is there a window at your house that's missing a curtain?"

"Zara!" She let out a cry of relief, released my wrist, and hugged me. "Let's get out of here," she said.

CHAPTER 37

WE GOT OUT of the house, and then into Vincent Wick's van.

He used a handheld device to determine I had a concussion.

"I got punched, right here." I touched my jaw, wincing as I felt the bruise."

Zinnia said, "She probably wouldn't be so bruised if not for the damage she already took today, thanks to your shocker."

He said, "I didn't know. I thought you witches could take a shock or two."

Zinnia said, "You ought to be ashamed of yourself. Get out of here and find us some water and blankets."

He left, and my aunt and I were alone in the back of his van. I looked around at the equipment lining the walls, trying to figure out what it all was, but I had some problems focusing my eyes.

"Vincent didn't kill you," she said. "I did."

"I know."

"You know?"

"It happened when you cast the body-buoyancy spell. Aunt Zinnia, I'm more than capable of putting two and two together. Plus there was that dream you had, where you said you were going to kill me. I guess it wasn't a metaphor dream after all, was it?"

She pressed her fingers to her mouth. "Oh, Zara, you have to believe me I didn't meant to hurt you. Spells are like prescription medicine, in a way. If you use two at once, they can have unexpected interactions."

"Like dying."

She looked down.

I patted her arm. "Don't worry. I won't tell Vincent Wick what really happened. We can let him think he's the one who killed me. I'm guessing he's the sort of guy you'd rather have owing you a favor than the other way around."

She gave me a weak smile. "You are very good at putting two and two together, even while concussed."

I pointed to her face. "Did I do that to you?" The bruise under her eye was a nasty purple.

"Of course not. It was the person who stole your body when I..." She looked away. "Never mind what I did. I know it wasn't you. Not right away, mind you. We got you into the house to recover, and you were behaving a little oddly, but we chalked it up to the shock from the van." She kept her gaze on the floor of the van. Her face looked so fragile and delicate, lit only by the blue devices inside the vehicle. "Honestly, I didn't know until I leaned in to examine your eyes, and you punched me."

I sucked in air between my teeth. "Sorry about that." Now it was extremely obvious that her bruise matched the width of my knuckles perfectly.

"Not your fault," she said. "It must have been Dorothy Tibbits." She met my eyes. "That is who was in your body, isn't it? That's what the men from the DWM said when I got here, but as you can see, it's pure bedlam in there."

"The DWM?"

She blinked. "You didn't hear it from me, but it's high time you had clearance to at least know what they're called. Chet Moore works for the Department of Water. They do look after the town's water supply, but they're also a cover for the larger organization, the DWM."

"DWM," I repeated. "Department of Water and Magic?"

She nodded. "But you didn't hear it from me. They're a bit funny about witches."

There were some banging sounds outside, and shouting. We listened while someone with a loudspeaker instructed people in the area to stay clear of the area, which was closed off due to a leak in the gas main.

Zinnia asked, "What happened in there?"

I got the sense she already knew, and was only asking to keep me talking and conscious. I told her what I'd witnessed, then asked, "Do you think Josephine will be okay? Her body took the bookwyrm pretty hard, right in the mouth."

"Her vitals were stable when I saw her. I, uh, cast a spell to help reverse the inking."

"I know about your spell. I know you lied to me after I inked myself. I heard you talking to your buddy Vincent right before he zapped me."

"Zara, you have to believe me, everything I do is for your own good."

"You're just killing me with kindness. I know."

She pressed her lips together. We listened to the chaos outside. They were evacuating houses all along the street.

"It wasn't Dorothy Tibbits in my body," I said. "It was someone else."

"If you say so. The woman is quite mad."

The back doors of the van burst open. It wasn't Vincent Wick returning with blankets and water. It was a trio of people in hazardous materials suits and masks.

"Zinnia Riddle, stay where you are and don't cast so much as a lightning bug," said one of the masked people in an electronic voice that was neither male nor female. "We are taking Zara Riddle in for decontamination."

I opened my mouth to say I didn't like the sound of decontamination one bit, not unless there was a lot of hot cocoa with tiny marshmallows involved, but I didn't get out a single word. Even with all my powers and the adrenaline in my system, I was no match for what they injected me with.

Fade to black.

CHAPTER 38

WHEN I OPENED my eyes, I was in a plain, gray room with a window looking out onto a tropical beach with white sands and palm trees.

A woman in a mint green nurse's uniform came in with a tray. She was pretty, for someone whose hair was made of snakes.

Was I dreaming? I blinked repeatedly. The snakes became ringlets of golden blonde hair.

"You're awake," the blonde nurse said brightly. "How do you feel?"

I pointed to my throat and croaked. She offered me water from her tray. It was the best water I'd ever had. So good, I choked.

"Easy does it," she said.

I coughed and took another sip.

"Better now?" she asked. "How do you feel?"

"I feel like toothpaste that's been crammed back into the tube."

"Sounds about right, considering what you've been through."

I looked out the window. Something about the sandy beach view wasn't right. The palm trees were moving on a fixed digital loop. It was just a television screen, set into the wall and made to look like a window.

She followed my gaze to the screen. "We can change that to any location you'd like. Would you like to visit Rome?" She walked over to a control panel and pressed a button. "Isn't it wonderful? I have this on the ceiling in my office."

"Nice."

"These rooms don't have windows, but it's not like our patients down here complain."

"Down here," I repeated. "Underground."

She gave me a curt nod. "Aren't you going to ask how long you were out?"

She seemed strangely excited for a nurse, and her outfit was off. The skirt was short, like a Halloween costume version of a nurse's uniform.

Sure, I'll bite. "How long was I out?" I asked.

She gave me a gentle smile. "Twenty-five years," she said. "We have flying cars now."

I touched my jaw, where I'd been bruised from Chet's punch. There was no tenderness.

A male voice said, "Charlize, that's not very nice."

Charlize? I knew that name. She was the person Chet had talked to about backup, when we were in the attic.

The man drew closer. The blonde nurse whipped her head. The snakes on her head whirled out from the movement. If it was a glamour, it wasn't just visual. I heard the snakes hissing. Dozens of them. And then, in the blink of an eye, the snakes were blonde curls again. Just ringlets.

"Charlize, don't be evil," the man said. "We're supposed to be the good guys."

"Doctor," she said sweetly. "I was just testing the patient's response to humor. She was going to laugh about the flying cars. Weren't you, Zara?"

"Sure," I said, even as my brain screamed. *Gorgon! Right in front of you!* "Flying cars. It's a fun thing to say to someone waking up in a secret underground hospital."

She laughed. "I know, right?"

The doctor made a tsk-tsk sound. "Go back to your office, agent."

"But I got all dressed up."

His voice boomed with authority. "Go."

She turned to me. "Farewell, Zara. Please send Chet a hug for me, and give that adorable little Corvin a pinch on the cheeks. He loves it when you do that."

"Corvin?" Now I laughed "I got away with it once, but I won't try again. I'd rather keep my fingers."

The doctor chuckled. "That boy is a handful."

His voice was coming from beside me. I hadn't heard him move there from the foot of my bed. I whipped my head to see what he was doing. He injected a clear fluid into an IV line, the same line that was snaking across my hospital sheets and into my arm.

"Nighty night," the gorgon said.

The doctor barked at her again to leave, and there was more, but I didn't hear it.

My consciousness drifted, mostly asleep. One bit of my mind remained aware, like a single tiny light bulb flickering in the darkness.

I felt a woman beside me, watching over me as I slept. She was blonde and pretty, like the gorgon dressed up as a nurse, and also like the gorgon named Chloe, who ran the bakery, but she wasn't either of them.

Her hands were cool like water on my forehead. She was watching over me, and she was happy I had come to help everyone. And, if I ever needed her, she would have my back. If it ever came to that.

* * *

When I gained consciousness, I was on a hospital gurney, in a hallway. A strong disinfectant odor made my eyes tear up. I heard someone coughing in a nearby room, and muffled voices coming from behind closed doors. It sounded and smelled exactly like a genuine hospital, unlike the last place I'd been.

I sat up slowly, expecting to see stars and chirping cartoon birds. To my surprise, my head felt fine. I could use an extra-large cup of coffee, for sure, but other than that, I felt reasonably good. *One of the perks of being a witch.*

A nurse walked down the hallway in my direction. She had a juice box in her hand. Orange juice.

I pointed to the juice box. "Is that for me?"

"Now it is," she said cheerfully, and handed it over.

I stabbed the straw through the silver foil. I flashed back to cutting through silvery gray flesh and machinery to free Chet.

I focused the orange juice. It was—no lie—the best orange juice I'd ever had in my life. And that's saying a lot, because it was lukewarm.

The nurse asked, "How are you feeling?"

"Not bad." I was especially glad to see she had normal short hair that wasn't snakes. "What day is it?"

"Saturday morning."

I did the math in my head. I'd been at the Pressman house on Thursday night. If it was Saturday, that meant...

"I missed FPF," I said.

The nurse gave me a patient smile. "What's that, hon?"

"Fresh Pastry Friday." I finished my juice box, and swung my legs over the side of the gurney. "I'll just have to make it Fresh Pastry Monday, assuming I still have my job. I hope someone made up a good cover story for me."

She put her hand on my chest to stop me from leaving. "There are organizations that can help."

"Oh?" Was she talking about the DWM? Or a coven? What did she know?

"Get yourself to a meeting and take the first step," she said. "The journey is worth it." She looked deeply into my eyes. "You're worth it."

I gave her a slow nod. "You mean..."

She handed me a flyer for Alcoholics Anonymous.

CHAPTER 39

I ARRIVED HOME to the sweet aroma of fresh waffles. I'd always been grateful to smell waffles, but after what I'd been through—and I do mean missing Fresh Pastry Friday—I was more grateful than ever.

I closed the door behind me and called out, "Have I died and gone to heaven?"

"Mom!" Zoey came running to greet me with a big hug. "You're back early. Auntie Z said you might be in the hospital for a week. I missed you so much. I need you, Mom."

I patted her hair and squeezed her tight to my chest.

Zinnia emerged from the kitchen with a tea towel in her left hand. Her right arm was in a sling. The scratches I'd seen along the side of her face were all but gone. Only a few pink lines remained on her cheek. The bruises around her eyes were barely visible.

Zoey said, "Corvin told me the funniest story. He said you came over to his house, but as a ghost, and you offered to tuck him into bed."

"That kid has quite the imagination."

"He said it was the scariest thing he's ever seen in his whole life."

I snorted.

"I'm just glad you're okay," she said. "You must have had quite the adventure. I squeezed a little bit of information out of Auntie Z, but I'm sure it was just the sanitized, PG version."

Behind her, Zinnia nodded.

"The good news is, Mr. Financial Wizard has moved on," I said. "He saved his daughter from a gruesome fate, and now he's at peace."

"Is it true he was the walking dead?" She looked excited. "With the back of his head missing, and all sorts of cool gears and stuff where his brain was supposed to be?"

I raised my eyebrows at Zinnia. That was her sanitized, PG version? She shrugged.

"Yes," I said to my daughter. "But there was nothing cool about it."

Zoey asked, "Did he give you any final money tips before he left? Any fun facts?"

"How about this one: Serve your guests diluted ginger ale instead of *Dom Perignon* and you'll save thousands of dollars annually because nobody will eat at your house."

Zoey laughed. "Good one. But if you ever see him again, be sure to thank him for everything he did for us."

"Remind me again, what did he do for us? Other than the half-price haircuts."

"We're rich!"

"No kidding! Did we quadruple our nest egg thanks to some savvy stock picks?"

"Don't get too excited," she said. "We're not actually rich, but while you were in the hospital, you got a call from the bank. I pretended to be you, since I know all the answers to your security questions."

"I don't know whether to praise you or punish you. Go on. What did the bank say?"

"That you were very smart for reviewing your loan agreement, and that you were right about the error. They corrected the percentage rate, and they paid back the retroactive difference with a lump sum, which they used to pay off all your credit cards, just like you asked them to. We're now free of debt! I mean, besides the mortgage, but that debt is offset by the asset value, which will hopefully appreciate."

I gave her a sideways look. "Who's the finance wizard now?"

She grinned. "It's fun to learn practical stuff sometimes."

Zinnia cleared her throat. "All's well that ends well, as Shakespeare wrote four hundred years ago."

I turned to my aunt and gave her a stunned look. "You knew Shakespeare?" I turned to my daughter. "She knew Shakespeare." I turned back to her. "Aunt Zinnia, what were the dinosaurs like?"

Zoey giggled.

Zinnia sighed. "I'm glad you're back." She swung the tea towel over her shoulder. "Let's get some breakfast in you. Would you like some waffles?"

"Would I like some waffles? Since the beginning of time, a more obvious question has never been asked."

We followed her into the kitchen.

There was a perky bouquet of orange and pink roses in a vase on the island counter.

"Those are for you," Zoey said. "Mr. Moore stopped by this morning to drop them off."

I played it cool, giving the arrangement only a cursory glance and a quick search for a note. There was no note, just a ribbon that read Get Well Soon.

Zoey was watching me.

I asked her, "Did he say anything?"

"He asked me how school was going, and he gave me this." She handed me a recipe card. It was for zucchini chocolate cake.

I shook my head. "Who puts zucchini into perfectly innocent cake?"

"Someone devious," Zoey said.

"That man is devious," I agreed.

Zinnia placed a stack of waffles on the kitchen island. She peered over my shoulder at the recipe card. "He is thoughtful, in his own way."

The three of us gathered around the kitchen island on our stools and enjoyed a luxurious Saturday morning brunch. As we were finishing our second round of waffles, I noticed my aunt and my daughter kept exchanging knowing glances.

"You two have been scheming," I said.

Zinnia got up and began clearing away the dishes.

Zoey pressed her hands together in a pleading gesture. "Mom, can we get a pet?"

"Sure," I said. "We can make another bookwyrm, and you can keep it in a terrarium."

Zinnia said over her shoulder, "Don't you dare!"

Zoey waved a hand. "I don't want anything weird. Just something I can pet and cuddle."

"I could probably make a furry bookwyrm. Just switch up a few ingredients to make a soft, fluffy version. You could comb its long, luxurious fur. Like a My Little Pony. Whatever you do, though, don't taste it. No matter how much it invites you to."

Zinnia stared at us, too horrified to even protest.

Zoey groaned. "Mom! I want a cat or a dog, like a normal kid."

"It's a lot of responsibility," I said. "And as for being a *normal kid*, don't you think it's a bit late for that?"

She rolled her eyes.

"Fine," I said. "A dog, or a cat, but not both. And only one."

She squealed and clapped her hands. "I'm going to go tell Corvin." She ran from the kitchen.

I looked over at Zinnia. "It's going to be a cat," I said.

"Oh? Are you getting some magical vision of the future?"

"We're a family of witches. It has to be a cat."

"Yes. I suppose some forces are bigger than all of us."

I looked at her cheek. The scratches were looking much better now.

"Thanks for looking after her while I was at the hospital."

"She's no trouble at all. She looked after me, actually." She adjusted the arm that was in the sling. "I was so full of adrenaline that night, I didn't realize how bad I was hurt."

We both looked over in unison to make sure the kitchen window was closed. Then we smiled at each other.

"I'm sorry I couldn't stop them from taking you," she said. "Do you remember any of it?"

"I remember waking up briefly in an underground medical lab. There was a blonde gorgon in a fake nurse's uniform who tried to convince me I'd been in a coma for twenty-five years."

She frowned. "They do things differently there."

"At the Department of Water and Magic."

We both looked at the bouquet.

"And how is Chet?" I asked. "Have you seen him?"

"Just for a few minutes this morning, when he came by to drop that off and check on us."

"But how is he? Did you check the back of his head to make sure it's not a swirly mess of tentacles?"

"He seems tired." She fluffed the bouquet. "It's good that you both have each other."

"Like how you have Vincent Wick?"

She pretended to gag. "Oh, please, Zara. I'd like to keep these waffles down."

We finished cleaning up from breakfast.

She asked, "How's your magic? Is everything working as it should?"

"I don't know. I haven't tested it yet."

"Well?"

I crossed my arms. "Maybe I don't want to be a witch. You know, nobody ever asked me if this was a gift I wanted."

She gave me a thoughtful look. "I thought this might happen. It's a common side effect when a novice witch gets her powers grounded. Life becomes simpler, and she starts to wonder about her other life, the one where she doesn't have magic."

"What happens if I don't use any magic? Will my powers go away?"

"No."

"Is there any way to get rid of them? Permanently?"

Her forehead wrinkled. "You wouldn't want to do that. There are... side effects."

"Like what? Not getting possessed by ghosts? Sounds like a pretty good side effect to me."

"You should get some rest."

"I've been asleep for the past thirty-six hours."

"It's different when you're in your own bed at home."

"If you say so." I leaned over and smelled the flowers. "I'm not ready to rest just yet. In fact, I'm going next door to check on a certain secret agent of the DWM." I winked at my aunt. "Someone's got to check the back of his head for tentacles."

CHAPTER 40

I WAS WALKING up the path to Chet's house when he emerged from the front door. He froze when he saw me.

"You're back," he said.

"In one piece, and working as advertised."

"What?"

"Just a joke. How's your body?"

"What?"

"Oh, no. Did they wipe your memory, or just the remainder of your sense of humor?"

He frowned and jogged down the steps toward me. "This is where we live," he said in a hushed tone.

I cast the sound bubble spell. It shimmered around me, brighter than I'd ever seen. So much for me not using magic. I'd made it all of five minutes after talking about giving it up.

"My sound bubble is up now," I said. "Sorry about blurting. I was just excited to see you not embedded in a wall or bleeding from chest wounds."

"Right."

"How are the other guys? One got shot and the other got all that glass in his chest."

"They're as good as new and back on duty. We have an excellent medical team."

"If you say so."

He looked at my jaw where he'd punched me. "You've recovered."

"Thanks to your crack medical team at the... D-W-M." I waggled my eyebrows.

"They told you. Well, good. It's probably better that you know. Plus I was getting tired of all your terrible X-Files jokes."

I snorted. "Like *that's* going to stop."

He leaned to the side as if to go around me. "Listen, I'm on my way somewhere. Can we pick this up another time?"

"Sure. But I think you're forgetting something. A little phrase that sounds like, 'Gosh, Zara. Thanks for helping me track down my fugitive spirit walker.' Something like that."

He blinked at me. "But you didn't."

"Okay, okay. So I didn't track her down quite so much as I bumbled onto the scene while she was killing you with her living machine thing, Project Erasure."

He frowned. "Zara, I wasn't looking for Dorothy Tibbits. We didn't even know she was involved with the Pressmans until she outed herself."

"Then you must still be looking for the other one. Her boss."

He shook his head. "There is no boss." He looked straight into my eyes. "Tibbits was working alone. She was quite crazy, but we don't have to worry about her anymore. She's been taken care of."

I stared at him, temporarily speechless. "Uh... if there is no boss, and you weren't looking for Tibbits, who were you looking for? And don't say Pressman, because you already told me it wasn't him."

He rubbed the stubble on his cheeks. Zinnia was right about him looking tired. He looked like he'd been awake all of the last thirty-six hours that I'd been sleeping.

"Forget it," he said. "Forget I said anything. I need to learn how to let go."

"Let go of what?"

He walked around me, and out of my sound bubble. He waved goodbye as he jumped into his vehicle.

A woman with her dog was walking by.

Chet gave the woman a breezy wave then called out to me, "See you around, neighbor!"

I waved back as he drove away.

Chet Moore was hiding something. But at least the back of his head was intact.

* * *

Monday morning, I visited the Gingerbread House of Baking to pay off my tab and pick up fresh pastries for the library.

There was one other customer inside. Detective Bentley. He was sitting on a stool at the counter along the window. He looked anything but surprised to see me there.

"Fancy meeting you here," he said.

"Detective Bentley, aren't there a dozen other bakeries within walking distance of the police station?"

"I like the scenery at this one."

I glanced down at his plate, which was empty except for a few multicolored sugar sprinkles. "And the rainbow sprinkle donuts, I see."

"How was your weekend, Ms. Riddle? Did you experience anything interesting or unusual?"

"That depends on what you consider unusual." I tossed my hair over my shoulder.

He narrowed his steel gray eyes at me. "Were you anywhere near that gas explosion that happened early Friday morning?"

"It's a small town, Detective. Unfortunately for us citizens, we were all uncomfortably near that shocking gas explosion."

"So, you were at home in bed?"

I batted my eyelashes. "I wasn't drinking hot cocoa with mini marshmallows and watching that old house burn down, if that's what you mean."

"No, I suppose you weren't. You don't strike me as a firebug type."

"Oh? What type do I strike you as?"

His eyes narrowed even tighter. "A whole new type."

"Thanks, I think." The scent of sweet vanilla wafted over from the display cases. "I should probably order my pastries. Good to see you, Detective. I'm glad to know you're keeping us all safe."

I strode up to the counter and showed the owner, Jordan Taub, a handful of money. He yawned as he pulled my tab from a drawer and ripped it up.

"What'll it be today?"

"A dozen of your rainbow sprinkle donuts, please."

Jordan wrinkled his nose. "Sorry, but we only make a dozen of each kind. I could give you eleven, plus one of something else?"

"That works." Louder, I said, "I guess if I want a *full dozen* of your finest rainbow sprinkle donuts, I'll have to get here a bit *earlier*."

"Sure."

"Then whoever doesn't get here before me will be out of luck, and he won't get a rainbow sprinkle donut of his own."

Jordan seemed confused, but shrugged and started filling a box with donuts.

I had my back to Detective Bentley, so I couldn't see his expression, but he did cough on whatever he'd been sipping.

Jordan finished boxing my donuts. I heard the door chime as the detective left. Now was my chance.

"Mr. Taub, is there any chance your wife is around with her baby?"

"You just missed them. I can tell her you stopped by."

"Oh, I wouldn't want to bother her. We've actually never met, but I believe we have some mutual friends."

He gave me a wary look. "In a town this small, that's not surprising."

"I think I met her sister the other day."

He said nothing.

I waved my hand around my head. "Same blonde ringlets. Exactly the same."

"I will let Chloe know you came by."

"Thanks, and good luck with the new baby. Those first few weeks can be a challenge."

"How old is yours?"

"Sixteen now. Barely."

"Sixteen?" His dark eyebrows lifted higher than most people's did when they learned my daughter's age. I took that as a compliment, and left the bakery feeling great.

CHAPTER 41

AT WORK, EVERYBODY was talking about the strange gas explosion that had taken place at a house in town.

"Probably an insurance fire," one library patron said to her friend. "The man who owned that house was a notorious penny pincher. He used to run that cheap little newspaper. Real eccentric guy. Used to cut his own hair, and it always looked terrible. I bet he burned it down himself for the cash."

"But he died in the fire," her friend said. "There's not much good in getting a big payout if you're not around to spend it."

"True. It must have been an accident, then. Maybe he set the fire but didn't give himself enough time to get out."

"That's probably it," the friend agreed. "Insurance fraud is not a good way to get rich."

"That's true. If we want to live it up, we'll have to get divorced from our current husbands, and marry rich! Maybe one of those billionaires that are so popular these days." She waved the romance paperback she had in her hand.

The friend laughed. "Great idea, but I like the husband I've got too much. He's broken in just how I like him."

"Same with my husband."

They both winked at me knowingly, finished checking out their books, and left.

Frank, who'd been helping them, gave me a bored look. Earlier that morning, I'd been so relieved to see him back at the library, with his face the regular color, that I'd hugged him. As far as he knew, he'd come down with stomach flu and a fever on Thursday, then slept it off at his apartment for a few days. He had no memory of being at Vincent Wick's underground bunker, or anything else.

Frank sighed. "That fire was only three days ago and I'm already sick to death of hearing about it. Don't get any older, Zara. You start to see the patterns in life, and you stop being surprised."

"Okay, Frank. I promise to not get old and jaded like you."

He had the bar code scanner in his hand, and proceeded to shoot it at me while making PEW PEW sounds.

I clutched my chest and pretended to die dramatically.

He applauded my performance and helped me to my feet again. "Zara, I'm so bored. Please tell me you did something exciting over the weekend. Anything. Tell me all the gory details about cleaning gutters or fluffing up dandelions or whatever it is you homeowners get up to over the weekend."

"I had a quiet weekend at home." It was half true. Zoey and I had enjoyed a pleasant Sunday at home, doing nothing but reading novels and snacking.

"Did you tackle that back yard of yours? I don't envy you that task." Frank lived in an apartment because he claimed to be allergic to home ownership and all the responsibilities attached to the "care and feeding of a house."

"Not yet," I said. "I was thinking about letting it go full jungle, and charging admission."

"Sorry that you caught my stomach bug and had to miss work Friday." He winked. "I'm sure you were very ill, and not spending a three-day weekend at some luxury resort with your beau."

I thought of the underground hospital. "My accommodations were anything but luxurious, I assure you."

Frank made a few more quips about my nonexistent love life then we got back to our work duties like good, responsible librarians.

We didn't joke around or prank each other again until eleven o'clock, when Frank jumped out at me from behind a bookshelf while wearing a *papier mache* bunny head from the children's storytime props closet.

"I'll get you back, Frank Wonder," I threatened.

At three o'clock, I finally did get him back.

I'd spent half of my lunch break working on my little surprise.

You know those spring-coil snakes you can plant inside a fake canister of peanuts? The cheap kind you buy at a novelty store? I'd found one such item in our Lost and Found box the week before. Frank had seen it, too, so I couldn't use the peanuts can that came with the snakes. Instead, I carefully loaded the snakes into Frank's plastic snack container—the one he used to store his midafternoon teddy-shaped graham wafer cookies.

I switched my afternoon coffee break time with one of the pages so I could be in the staff lounge at the same time as Frank, to witness my most glorious plan coming to fruition.

As he reached for his container of cookies, my heart started pounding. My forehead was hot. A trickle of sweat sprang from my armpits and streamed down my sides.

It was just a simple prank, but I was beyond excited to see if it worked.

Finally, after a very long diatribe from Frank about how his generation had contributed the most to modern fashion, he began prying open the container.

The spring-loaded snakes shot up as though being fired from a starter's pistol.

Frank let out a strangled shriek, and suddenly his pink hair was no longer hair.

His hair was feathers.

Frank was gone, and in his place stood an elegant, stunned-looking pink flamingo.

He'd turned into a big, pink bird.

Right there in the staff lounge.

I didn't know the spell for turning a person into a flamingo, and I certainly didn't know the spell for turning a flamingo back into a person.

"Easy now," I said soothingly. "Frank, everything's going to be okay."

The flamingo eyed me and made a noise that I took to mean *I doubt that very much.*

I circled around the flamingo slowly. Frank squawked and rotated to face me, his large beak between us.

I closed and locked the door to the staff lounge. Kathy was at the circulation desk, and she'd probably be knocking on the door any minute, but I couldn't risk her seeing this. With the room secure, I went to get something from my purse.

I pulled out the business card I'd found in my pocket when I was doing laundry on Sunday. Someone from the DWM must have slipped it in when I'd been under their care.

The card had only three lines of text: Wisteria Department of Water, Emergency contact line, and then the phone number.

I called the number.

Meanwhile, Frank-Flamingo strutted around the tall tables in the staff lounge, his long neck flexing left and right gracefully.

I held the phone to my ear. It rang twice then clicked.

"Hello?" I asked tentatively. "Is this the receptionist? Do I need to ask for a specific department?"

A female voice came through. "Go ahead, Zara."

"I need to report an emergency, but it's not water related."

"What is your location?"

"I'm at the Wisteria Public Library."

"The nature of your emergency?"

"It's my coworker, Frank Wonder."

"Is he asking questions?"

"Not really." There was no delicate way to put it. "He's turned into a pink flamingo."

"How did it happen?"

"By accident, I think. I scared him with some snakes."

"What? Snakes, too?"

"Those springy snakes you put in a fake can of peanuts. It was just a prank. I stuffed them in his cookie container."

The woman on the other end chortled. "Good one." She cleared her throat. "You might have triggered a natural response through his adrenal system, or this could be... something else."

"Yeah, it's the *something else* that's why I called you. He's not acting like someone who knows how to shift back and forth between forms."

"Frank Wonder is not registered with us, no."

"That's good information. So, what do I do now?"

"Is he flying?"

"No. We're inside the staff lounge."

"Keep the doors and windows closed. Someone will be there shortly," she said.

"Are you... is this Charlize?"

The line went dead.

For a full list of books in this
series and other titles by
Angela Pepper, visit

www.angelapepper.com